LAST RITE

TOR BOOKS BY LISA DESROCHERS

Personal Demons
Original Sin
Last Rite

Lisa Desrochers

LAST
RITE

TOR®
TEEN

A TOM DOHERTY ASSOCIATES BOOK

NEW YORK

LAST RITE

Copyright © 2012 by Lisa Desrochers

A Tor Teen Book
Published by Tom Doherty Associates, LLC
175 Fifth Avenue
New York, NY 10010

www.tor-forge.com

Tor® is a registered trademark of Tom Doherty Associates, LLC.

Library of Congress Cataloging-in-Publication Data

Desrochers, Lisa.
    The last rite / Lisa Desrochers.—1st ed.
        p. cm.
    "A Tom Doherty Associates Book."
    ISBN 978-0-7653-2810-6 (trade paperback)
    ISBN 978-1-4299-6713-6 (e-book)
    1. Demonology—Fiction. 2. Angels—Fiction. 3. Supernatural—
Fiction. 4. Love—Fiction. I. Title.
    PZ7.D4545Las 2012
    [Fic]—dc23

                                                    2011042474

First Edition: May 2012

Printed in the United States of America

0 9 8 7 6 5 4 3 2 1

To Suzie,
for believing

Here, one must leave behind all hesitation; here, every cowardice must meet its death.

—Dante Alighieri, *Purgatorio*

LAST RITE

1

☦

Run Like Hell

FRANNIE

This isn't the first time I've seen myself dead, but this time it's different.

The pain in my head starts to soften as the image becomes clearer. *White clouds, blue sky.* My stomach lurches. *Lightning in my veins.* I don't have time for one of my stupid visions right now. *Consuming me.* I breathe back the nausea . . . *burning alive . . .* and force the image out of my head.

I glance sideways at Gabe, whose eyes flit between the narrow dirt road in front of us and the rearview mirror. I thought I drove fast, but I can't even make myself look at the speedometer as he weaves through the pitch-black woods to God only knows where.

The headlights of Rhen's silver Lincoln and Marc's hearse light up the inside of Gabe's Charger. They've followed us, first on the highway and now through the woods, for the last hour, since we left Haden.

When I turn to look over my shoulder at our demonic tail, I see Luc, in the backseat. It takes him a second to realize I'm looking. When he does, he presses his hand to the bloody bandage over his left forearm and lowers his eyes.

My stomach knots and I wonder again what happened in the park with Lilith. He went after her. Did he kill her? No. He couldn't have. She would have transferred her soul into his body and taken control if he had.

I look at him more closely. His eyes are tortured, but they're clear. I know in my gut that this is Luc. No Lilith.

But he's not *my* Luc.

Not anymore.

In my room, when I asked him if he was coming with us—told him I wanted him to—he said no. But Gabe made him come. He said it was too much of a risk to leave Luc behind. When Luc still refused, Gabe lifted a hand, white lightning cracking over his skin. For a second I really thought Luc was going to let Gabe kill him. But, finally, he moved away from the window and pushed past both Gabe and me without ever looking at either of us.

Just like he won't look at me now.

I realize I'm still staring when a flaming streak of red Hellfire takes out the back window of the Charger. Gabe speeds up, fishtailing on the dirt road. Luc reflexively levels his fist out the back window before remembering that isn't gonna get him anywhere. He ducks behind the seat and his eyes lock on mine for a heartbeat, flickering with something that I can't read, before he lowers them again.

I close my eyes and breathe away the knot of panic in my chest. My heart leaps into my throat as my eyes snap open to a flash of red, and I jerk them toward the road in time to see a blast of Hellfire streaking toward us. I duck and throw my arms over my head as the windshield explodes in a shower of glass. Gabe floors it as I lift my head, but the demon in the road vanishes just as we rev through the spot where he was standing. Marc.

At the sight of him I feel suddenly cold.

Taylor.

At the memory of what he did to her my stomach lurches. I bite my lip and wrap my arms around myself, pushing the image away.

Gabe shoots a look in the rearview mirror at Luc. "It appears Marchosias has figured out we're leaving." The Charger spins in a 180 when he slams on the brakes and we skid to a stop. He and Luc bound from the car.

In front of us, a microscopic jet sits on a long, narrow runway next to an old wooden barn. Luc rips my door open and I see he has my duffel bag in one hand. He yanks me from the car with the other as Gabe repeatedly launches bolts of white-hot lightning toward some unseen target in the dark of the trees lining the tarmac.

As Luc herds me toward the plane, I notice lightning shooting from that direction into the woods as well. He's careful to keep himself positioned between the trees and me as we move, but the thirty feet between the jet and us might as well be a mile. Blasts of red Hellfire erupt all around us, leaving shallow craters in the pavement. The air crackles as a red streak scorches past my head, and the smell of singed hair and brimstone is suddenly heavy in the damp night air. I swat at the small flame that erupts in my hair as something thuds heavily behind me. I turn to see Luc on his hands and knees. My duffel bag is singed on the ground and there's a smoldering hole in the right side of Luc's T-shirt.

"Luc!" My stomach twists into a painful knot as I run to his side and kneel. Adrenaline hammers through my ears, louder than the boom of exploding Hellfire all around, but all I care about is Luc.

A grimace pinches his face, but what I see in his dark eyes isn't pain or panic. It's fear—for me.

I pull him from the ground. "Go!"

Gabe covers us with booming white eruptions from his palms, faster than machine-gun fire, and the red blasts stop for a moment.

Luc starts to reach for my bag, but I push him toward the plane.

"Go!" I yell again, shoving him and scooping the bag into my arms. We bolt for the plane and I push him up the stairs in front of me. He lands hard in the backseat with a wince, and I throw myself into the seat next to him.

"Let me see," I say, reaching for his shirt.

"I'm fine," he responds, brushing my hand away. They're the first words he's spoken since we left my room, and I barely hear them over my hammering heart and the echo of the war being waged outside.

Gabe appears in the seat in front of us. He pulls the door shut and settles in at the controls.

"So . . . who's flying this thing?" I ask when I realize there's only one more seat—and it's empty.

He turns and raises his eyebrows at me, almost apologetically.

Red and white light flashes outside, illuminating the night sky in bursts, like Fourth of July fireworks. I look out the window at a glowing form in the dark: a girl with thick copper curls and iridescent white skin. She stands next to the plane, launching bolts into the woods. Trees on the edge of the airstrip detonate in a shower of sparks as her white lightning strikes, and the returning red streaks are sporadic and poorly placed.

"Who is that?" I ask Gabe breathlessly over the roar of the engine.

"Celine," Gabe responds, but then we're rolling away from the girl, down the narrow runway, and I decide I probably shouldn't distract him for more details. As I watch, the girl spreads her wings and takes flight, moving with us along the airstrip. Marc chases us out onto the runway, throwing red flashes after us. Rhen stands in the smoke and shadows at the edge of the trees, arms crossed, watching as we rocket away.

And that's when I remember he doesn't want us dead . . . or even in Hell. He wants me to make him mortal. He thinks it will help somehow with his uprising against Lucifer.

It feels like the earth belches us straight up into the air, leaving my stomach behind. The ground falls away at an alarming rate.

"Are there any airsick bags on this thing?" I ask, just as a red blast—Marc's last-ditch effort—hits the plane.

Red electricity skitters over every metal surface, and our tiny bird lurches sharply before everything goes dark.

I'm thrown forward, then slammed back as we suddenly change direction from what felt like straight up to what I'm sure is straight down. The sensation of falling is sickening, like the initial drop of a roller coaster, leaving my stalled heart stuck firmly in my mouth.

In the dark, I see Gabe begin to glow and realize his hands are no longer on the controls. He's holding them up and, just over the roar of the straining engine, I hear him say something that I can't make out.

The force of the fall has me plastered to the seat, but I feel Luc's fingers lace into mine. I turn my head and my heart lurches again when our eyes connect. There's a sudden overwhelming rush of emotion as I realize he could die, right now, because of me. I turned my beautiful demon mortal with my Sway, and, once again, I've put him in danger. Staring into his eyes, what flashes before mine isn't my life. It's his—his very short life and all the pain I've caused him in that brief time.

Gabe's glow lights up the tiny cabin and, suddenly, the whine of the engine stops. I glance forward and see he has one hand back on the controls. With the other, he reaches forward and flicks a switch.

The plane lurches to the side, throwing me against Luc. I look back at him and his gaze doesn't waver. I want to reach up and touch him, stroke his face and tell him I love him, but my hands are plastered to my sides, heavy as anvils. Desperation sucks at my aching chest. It can't be long. Any second we're going to become a crater in the ground. Any second, I'll have killed him.

My heart strains against the force of the fall—against the force of the memories. A tear slips from the corner of my eye and drips sideways, landing on Luc's arm. Only then does he close his eyes, his face pinching in a pained grimace. When he opens them again, they're moist, and deep, and beautiful.

All of this lasts only a heartbeat, but lost in Luc's eyes, it feels like forever.

A growl rips from Gabe, and I'm sure this is it. This isn't the image I saw after the lightning in my head—*white clouds, blue sky*—but it's close enough.

But, at that instant, there's a screech of twisting metal and the engine roars to life. The falling sensation stops, and I glance forward to see Gabe pulling up on the controls. His glow fades and the control panel lights flicker then illuminate as power returns. Once we start climbing again, Gabe flashes an anxious glance over his shoulder. "Sorry. It's going to be bumpy."

Luc drops my hand and pulls his eyes away from mine, and whatever it was that just happened between us is over.

"No shit," I mutter.

We climb in silence, me grasping the edge of the seat cushion so hard I rip the seam. Finally, we level out and I chance a sideways glance at Luc, pressed against my side in the backseat. He's doing his best to ignore me while I'm doing my best not to throw up on him.

"Let me look at that," I say again, pointing at his side.

His jaw clenches and he stares straight ahead. "It's nothing."

From here, through the hole in his shirt, I can see reddened flesh with white patches that are sure to become blisters soon.

"Please," I say, catching his eyes.

He holds my gaze for an instant, then gives in, raising his arm so I can get a closer look. The singed edges of his T-shirt are already starting to stick to the wound. I carefully peel the fabric back and lift it to expose the burned area, and my breath catches when I notice the souvenirs of his latest trip to Hell. Smooth pinkish scars still cover most of his chest and back.

Tears sting my eyes, knowing this was all 'cause I let him down. They never could have taken him if I'd loved him enough. He was human and tagged for Heaven. If I'd believed in him, he never would have turned demon again, and Rhenorian couldn't have taken him back to Hell.

I breathe the tears away. They're not gonna help.

I run my finger gently around the periphery of the red patch on his side and he shivers as goose bumps pebble the flesh under my finger. His skin is hot, and the center of the burn is dark red and already starting to ooze clear fluid.

"This is bad."

"It's just a burn. It'll be fine," he answers, his expression stoic as he tugs his T-shirt down.

My heart crumbles as I push back into my seat, staring out the window, and I find myself fighting tears again. I can't blame him for hating me. After all the ways I hurt him, I don't deserve anything else.

It's dark and, in the distance, I see lightning flicker. But other than that, it's a charcoal gray blanket of clouds as far as the eye can see.

We're all alone up here.

It's eerie, but despite the fact that we're rocketing through space in a tiny tin can, it also feels oddly safe. I glance at Gabe, then lean my forehead on the window and let myself zone out. I feel all the adrenaline that had been fueling me during the escape run out into a puddle on the floor, leaving me empty and exhausted. But I'm too scared to close my eyes . . . because the dreams . . .

I nearly jump out of my skin when the plane lurches and realize my eyes had slipped shut. I grasp the back of Gabe's seat and pull myself forward. "Why couldn't we just take a regular plane?"

"A small group in a small plane is easier to Shield. And, unless you're willing to use your Sway to persuade the crew of a commercial jet to change course mid-flight, all Marc would have to do is phase to our arrival airport and wait for us."

I don't want to use my Sway at all, let alone to hijack a plane. "Good plan," I say. The plane is tossed again and my stomach protests. "How much longer?"

"Another five hours." He throws an assessing glance over his shoulder at me. "How you holding out?"

"Okay," I lie. "Where are we going?"

He leans forward and rifles through what looks like a glove compartment in the console, then pulls out a white envelope and hands it over the back of his seat. I take it from him and pull it open.

Luc's ID is on top and I hand it to him. It says he's Damon Black. I look at mine. My face smiles out at me from the shiny surface of the Florida state driver's license. The smile is fake, just like the name. It says I'm Colby Black. I'm not. It also says my eighteenth birthday was on April 12. It wasn't. It was on August 22, somewhere in the haze following Taylor's funeral.

Taylor's dead. My best friend. And it's my fault.

The weeks since Lilith killed her are just a jumble of random memories—nothing but a blur—ending with Gabe whisking Luc and me to the airport.

I lean against the window again and concentrate on breathing. The ride smooths out a little and I tip my head back into the seat and close my eyes, knowing I won't sleep but needing to settle my stomach. But it won't settle. It churns with the thoughts whirring through my brain.

Luc's hand brushes against mine and I look up. "Are you okay?" he asks softly, just audible over the hum of the engine.

Something stirs inside me at the concern in his voice. I nod, even though it's a lie. I'm so far from okay, there's not even a word. I went to Luc's apartment tonight to tell him I loved him. But Rhen showed up. He told Luc he and some others wanted to start a rebellion against Lucifer . . . asked for our help. Then there was Lilith in the park, and everything went to Hell. Literally.

I never said it. I never told him how I feel.

And now I can't. He doesn't want to be here . . . with me. He said it. I don't blame him. If I didn't have to be with me, I wouldn't.

I breathe deep and try to slow my throbbing heart and racing mind, but there's not a single thought I can conjure to calm me down. Every memory leads me back to this place and how we got here—my endless list of bad choices.

I pull my iPod out of my bag and press in the earbuds, then do the best I can to relax as Alicia Keys tells me "everything's gonna be all right."

But I know better.

Lightning in my veins. Consuming me.

I'm not going to survive this.

I've learned to trust my visions. Matt, Grandma, Taylor . . . even Luc. Each time, I saw them dead before they died. There's only once my vision hasn't come true. The first time I saw myself dead, Luc and Gabe were able to save me. But this was more than a vision. More concrete. I didn't just see myself dead—I actually *felt* myself dead. I felt myself floating, like air, without physical form. Nothing but light.

I won't take Luc or Gabe with me. No one else is gonna die 'cause of me.

I turn off the music and listen to the hum of the engine, white noise, as I stare out the window. Out of the corner of my eye, I catch movement—a black shape moving over the gray blanket of clouds below. I stare for a moment, startled, but then realize it's just the shadow of our plane cast by the moonlight on the clouds. I close my eyes and focus on slowing the beat of my heart.

LUC

Frannie's breathing becomes slower and deeper as she sinks into me, causing mine to become more erratic. I hesitate before laying my arm over her shoulders, sure that, if I let her this close, I won't be able to let her go again. But I've made my decision. As a mortal, I'm useless. I need my demonic powers. As a demon, not only can I protect Frannie, but I can blow things up.

21

Like Gabriel.

When he shoved his lightning hand into my face tonight and told me I was coming with him and Frannie, I would have loved nothing more than to blast him into oblivion.

I glare at the back of his head as Frannie leans into my side, pressing into the burn on my ribs. But the sting of her pressure there is nothing compared to the sting of my heart. Her whole life has just exploded into chaos, and it's my fault—me and my infernal brethren.

Before we left, she asked me what happened tonight with Lilith in the park, and I couldn't answer. It's just one more of the many ways I've failed her. Killing Lilith would have been a small gesture, but a significant one—a way I could have helped instead of bringing Frannie constant pain. I'd had the knife to her throat. I was going to do it. But then I realized, if I followed through on my plan I wouldn't kill Lilith, only her host body. Angelique would be dead and my tag would reverse. I'd be a murderer—tagged for Hell. I couldn't have turned the knife on myself fast enough to keep her essence from entering me.

Being human is working to my distinct disadvantage.

Worse, I didn't take Rhenorian as seriously as I should have. If I could have figured out a way to be useful to his uprising—lobbied Gabriel harder, or found a way to go over his head, which I would have enjoyed immensly—maybe Frannie'd be safe right now.

But she's not, and I'm having a hard time imagining that she ever will be.

I know what she is, and I'm going to have her.

Black dread snakes through my insides at the echo of King Lucifer's words in my head, as perplexing now as they were when He said them.

I know what she is.

What does He think she is?

Gabriel said she could change the shape of Heaven and Hell, but I don't think I ever really believed it until now. My heart thrums, aching with my fear for her—my need for her—as I gaze down at her, so soft in my arms. But I know she's anything but soft. She has strength of spirit seldom seen in a mortal, especially one this young. There's something about her beyond her Sway, and the king of Hell wants it. He's going after her with more determination than I've seen in Him since my creation.

I know what she is.

She moans and stirs against me and I quickly move to unwrap myself from her, sure she's woken. But she hasn't. Her breathing is irregular, coming in fits and bursts as she fights the demons in her dreams. I fold her more tightly into my arms and pull her as close as I can without waking her, needing to make this okay for her. Picking up a lock of her singed blond hair, I rub it between my fingers and bring it to my nose, taking in the faint scent of currant and clove that's so uniquely Frannie. I kiss the top of her head and try to ward off her demons the only way I can now—by sending her all my strength.

Gabriel shoots a glance over the seat at us. "She sleeping?"

I nod. "Finally." Frannie jumps in my arms and I shift in my seat, pulling her deeper into me, then look back at Gabriel. "How is this going to work? Marc and Rhen were both at the airstrip. They'll know where we've gone."

"Our Shields will continue to hide us, and they'll have no idea where we land. The only way they'd be able to track us is to physically follow us, and last I looked, neither Rhenorian or Marchosias had wings."

My gut twists. Marc and Rhen may not have wings, but others do. "And if you're wrong?"

"Then we're all screwed."

I hear Gabriel's frustration and it sparks my own. I look down at Frannie, twitching in my arms. "Please, for the love of all things holy, tell me you have a plan."

Gabriel is silent for a long moment. "I'm working on it."

My heart sinks. No plan. This is worse than I thought. "Why did you drag me along on this field trip? You know I'm no help in a fight." I hold up my hand. "No spark in the plugs."

He glances over the seat at me, then his eyes glide to Frannie and something mournful darkens his face. "You two are connected in a way I can't explain. The only way I can keep Frannie safe is to keep you close. You're the only demon who's ever been able to see past her Shield. You know Lucifer will use you to find her if He gets His hands on you."

I do, which is why I couldn't let Lilith take me. But, if he'd left me—if Frannie gave up on me—I could have hidden out until I turned demon again, then gone vigilante on Lilith, Marc . . . all of them.

I settle deeper into Frannie, propping my cheek on the top of her head. I know it's dangerous to let myself go around her, but for just a minute, while she's sleeping, I can pretend things are how they were before I killed any chance we had at happiness. I close my eyes and remember.

FRANNIE

The plane is tossed, startling me awake. There's a warm body wrapped around me and hot breath in my hair. And cinnamon.

Luc.

For an instant, I think it all must have been a horrible dream and my heavy heart lifts. I'm in Luc's bed, wrapped in his arms. Just where I belong.

But the plane tosses again, scaring the snot out of me, and I grip Luc harder as panic and despair start to choke me. It's not a dream. It's real. All of it. Lilith. Luc. Matt.

Taylor.

My heart goes dead in my chest for a second, then slams back into rhythm with a jolt that jerks my entire body.

No. I'm not going there right now. I can't.

Luc's breathing is slow and deep, and I realize he's asleep. *God, I miss this.* I breathe him in and try to lose myself in the feeling of being in his arms again. The gaping hole in my chest fills a little as I let myself remember what it was like to open up and let someone in. I'd never let anyone touch my heart before Luc, and he'd filled it completely. So, even though I know I've ruined what we had, I lie here in his arms and pretend he still loves me. But I don't let myself fall back asleep. I don't want to miss a minute of this.

As I lay here, drawing on Luc's strength and feeling safer than I know we are, my mind drifts to my family and a thread of panic tickles deep inside my chest. I've left them behind. Will they be okay? Can Dad protect them?

Dad.

I picture him and Mom as they watched us pull out of the driveway. They knew something wasn't right, but they also knew better than to ask. I wonder if Dad knows I'm not in L.A. Guilt eats me alive at the lie.

How was nothing in my life what I thought it was? Luc, Gabe, Lilith, Dad, *me*? I'm a Nephilim, the product of a mortal mother and a fallen angel. I don't even know what that means, except it's probably why I have Sway.

And the whole reason we're rocketing through space in a tin can—running from everything I've ever known into God only knows what.

And the reason Taylor is dead and Matt is gone.

I sigh and sink into Luc, trying to force the knot in my chest to loosen. If anything happens to him or to my family before this is over, I don't know what I'll do. But I'm not gonna think about that now. Luc is here, holding me. I want to stay here forever and just forget the world. I nestle my face into him, my ear against his chest, and listen to the beat of his heart.

2

✝

Personal Demons

FRANNIE

"We'll be down in ten." Gabe's voice jars me from my temporary bliss.

I open my eyes and look up into Luc's. They're open, and in the instant before he knows I'm looking, I can see how haunted he is. His face is pulled tight with worry, making me hate myself even more for putting him through this.

Still lost in my fantasy, I start to reach for his stubbled chin. But his expression hardens and he pulls away from me, straightening in his seat and reminding me that it was just that—a fantasy. My heart, which had been pounding out its love for him, contracts into a hard ball as I remember he hates me.

He looks so unbelievably tired, dark circles rimming sunken obsidian eyes, his clothes rumpled and burned, and his black mop of hair every which way. The bandage on his arm is coming loose. The bleeding has stopped, but the skin under the gauze looks purplish white and swollen around the knife wound. I lift my eyes to his and he holds my gaze for just a second. I want to ask him about what happened in the park with Lilith, but before I can find the right words, he looks away. I take a deep breath and peer out the window at the rising sun, a gold orb low in the brightening sky. We circle under the clouds, over terrain that is very flat and very sandy. I can see the glare of the sun off patches of water here and there in the distance and not much else.

Gabe puts the plane down on a narrow runway in the middle of nowhere, and we taxi to a stop near what looks like a large metal shed. He opens the hatch and I'm slapped in the face with hot, humid air. I tread down the stairs into a puddle and can almost see steam rising off the wet pavement at my feet. Gabe pulls my bag from the floor and we jog across the narrow runway to a black Jeep Wrangler parked there. He throws my bag in back and I notice there's another duffel and a few Target bags in the back already. A set of keys dangles from the ignition. We climb in, Gabe driving, Luc in the passenger seat, and me in back.

"What's all this stuff?" I ask, peering over the back of my seat.

"Luc needs some clothes, since we left without his things. The rest are just provisions."

"Any bandaging stuff in those provisions?"

Luc shoots me a glance over his shoulder as Gabe answers. "Afraid not."

"Can we stop for some?" I say, looking around at our surroundings as we pull away.

Gabe glances over his shoulder at me, and I know from the look on his face that the answer is no.

There's not much to see. No people, no buildings, no cars. Nothing. I start to get a little nervous about what kind of "provisions" we need and why. "What is this place?"

"The safest place I could think of," Gabe answers without turning to look at me.

We bounce over sandy potholes on our way to a poorly maintained road.

I look back at him, starting to panic a little. "Please tell me there are flush toilets wherever we're going."

He must hear it in my voice, 'cause he smiles at me in the rearview mirror. "There are all the creature comforts."

We drive for what feels like forever and everything looks the same. Finally, I start to see signs for Miami, and little by little, we start passing more cars and eventually reach civilization.

When we stop for gas, I see an old pay phone on the corner.

"Can I call home?" I ask as Gabe steps out of the Jeep.

"Not until I know it's safe."

I see the apology in his eyes, but it doesn't help. I want to talk to Mom—tell her I'm okay.

And Riley.

Cold emptiness folds itself around me as I think of her. Taylor called Riley our accidental friend. Accused me of taking in strays. But Riley was the best friend anyone could have ever asked for. I wish I could have seen her before we left . . . to explain. But what would I have said? I hadn't seen her or Trevor since Taylor's funeral. Couldn't. It hurt too much knowing what I did to them. I took away Riley's best friend and Trevor's sister when I got Taylor killed.

My throat tightens and I slump deeper into my seat. 'Cause I know that pain too well. I lost Matt. Twice.

We pull out of the gas station back onto the road and a big guy on a Harley follows us. Gabe spends more time looking into the rearview mirror than out the windshield until Harley Guy turns off on a side road. When he does, Gabe visibly relaxes and flips a U-turn. We start heading in the other direction like a bat out of hell.

We drive silently for another hour over bridges and flat, sandy islands, and I sneak peeks at Luc when he's not looking, wondering what he's thinking.

It's late afternoon when we finally leave the highway. We weave our way past dark houses toward the water and finally pull up to a cottage on the beach. Gabe parks the Jeep next to the tiny gray-shingled house, and we walk around to the ocean side of the cottage, which, apparently, is the front. We climb the three stairs to the front porch, and Gabe unlocks the door and throws it open. I stand on the porch for a minute watching the gentle waves crest and roll lazily onto the golden sand. Gabe steps through the door and, as I follow him into my new home, it hits me.

This is real.

I can't go back.

Marc and Rhen are out there, looking for us. And so is Lilith.

At the thought of Lilith, overwhelming sadness bubbles up, and I dart a look at Luc where he stands in the window, staring out at the lapping waves. 'Cause it still hurts.

I know what Lilith is. A succubus. *Queen* of the succubi, apparently. I also know what she's capable of. I've felt it firsthand. So, technically, what happened wasn't his fault. She seduced him to get to me. If I'm honest with myself, that makes it *my* fault. But I can't stop thinking the whole series of events that lead to Taylor dying in my arms started when Luc slept with Lilith. As much as I know it's not rational—or fair—I can't help wondering if part of him knew what was going on. And wanted it.

Instantly, I'm buried in guilt. Was I any better? When Luc betrayed me, I turned to Gabe. I wanted to lose myself in him—to forget everything and just live in his peace. And I almost took it too far. If he hadn't found the strength to make me stop, I would have taken everything he had, including his wings.

At the memory of Gabe's body against mine, my face twists into an involuntary cringe. I've let everyone down: my friends, my family . . .

I feel my legs start to shake dangerously as I think of Matt, and lower myself into a heavy wooden kitchen chair. I let him down most of all.

He fell 'cause of me. How was I so stupid to think he could have a life? Instead of a life, he got eternity in Hell.

My stomach knots and I prop my spinning head in my hand. I lay my ID on the mismatched table next to Luc's and read the

31

names again, then look up at him as he stands in the window, raking his hand through his tousled black mop of hair.

I close my eyes and drop my face into my hands, focusing on the rhythmic waves breaking on the shore outside the window.

"So, are you going to be okay here?" Gabe says from the couch.

I open my eyes and really look around for the first time. The cottage is small: basically an open, airy living room–kitchen area with two bedrooms along the left side and a bathroom in between. The walls and curtains are done in shades of blue, to make you think of the ocean I guess, and the floor is well-worn hardwood. Scattered around the room are prints of sailboats and serene stretches of beach, and under them are a navy blue couch and armchair. It's cheerful, which, at the moment, makes me feel worse.

I smile, but it feels as bogus as my new ID. "We'll be okay, Gabe. It's perfect. Thanks."

Gabe doesn't buy it. He pulls himself off the couch and his eyes search mine. The golden light of the waning sun glints off his platinum waves, making him look like the angel he is. Something inside me stirs, tugs at my core, and makes me want to go to him, to feel his arms around me. I look away so he won't see it in my eyes.

There's a long minute of silence before Gabe says, "I'll run out and get you something to eat." He sounds weary, and I know everything that's led up to us coming here has worn him down.

I lift my eyes back to his and hope he can see the apology in them. "'Kay."

When the door closes behind Gabe, Luc finally turns from the window and stares me down, his eyes hard obsidian.

I want to go to him—to tell him everything's going to be all right. But I'm done lying—to myself—to him. I love him. I know that by the way my heart breaks every time I look at him. The real proof, though, is in his transformation. He's human again. I'm the only one who could do that to him—make him mortal just by wanting him, by loving him.

After everything, I'm not sure love is enough.

He turns back to the window, bracing his hand on the frame, his forehead against the glass. I sit in silence with my head in my hands, fingers twisted into my wild hair, and stare at the floor between my feet.

My heart feels like a trapped bird, flapping wildly against the cage of my ribs, and I can totally relate. All of a sudden, I feel claustrophobic. I need to get out of here.

I bolt off the chair and out the door. I know Luc is watching me, maybe even following me, as I leap off the porch and run full speed down the beach, but I don't turn around. I hit the edge of the water at a sprint and the surf splashes up all around me as I careen down the beach. I'm soaked by the time I stop running and flop into the warm sand, sucking wind.

"Feel better?"

I expect Luc's voice. Or maybe even Gabe's. But the voice is female. I pull my head out of my hands and look up.

Then do a double take.

'Cause the girl standing on the beach in front of me looks so much like my friend Riley—tall with fair skin and long brown hair pulled into a ponytail, with floppy bangs that hang down one side of her pretty face. And curvy in her pink bikini top and cutoffs in that way that turns boys' heads.

The girl's chocolate-brown eyes gaze down at me, concerned. "You okay?"

I nod and pull myself to my feet, not even bothering to try to brush the sand from my soaking self. "Yeah . . ." Glancing back toward the cottage, I see Luc silhouetted in the window, watching.

The girl tugs on the leash in her hand as her dog, a big, wet golden retriever, strains to get closer to me. "I'm Faith," she says. "And this is Jasper," she adds with another tug of the leash. "We live right there." She points to the cottage next door, about thirty feet up the beach from ours.

"I'm Fr—um . . ." I hesitate, trying to remember what that stupid license said. "I'm Colby," I finish and nod toward our cottage. "We're neighbors."

Jasper finally gives up on getting to me and starts to pull Faith back toward home. I follow and we make our way up the beach.

She shoots a look toward our cottage and her mouth drops open, literally. "Whoa."

I look back to where Gabe is now standing on the porch, grocery bags in hand, tight white T-shirt over faded jeans, bare feet and windblown locks of platinum hair in his tanned face. A beach god.

"That's Gabe," I say, then instantly realize I don't know if he's supposed to have an alias too.

Her eyebrows raise hopefully. "Is he like . . . your boyfriend or something?"

I smile despite myself. "No."

She tucks a stray strand of escaped hair behind her ear for a better view. "Brother?"

"Friend," I say. "He's kind of living with us for now, I guess."

She turns her eyes to me. "Us?"

"Yeah," I say just as Luc steps through the door onto the porch, as dark as Gabe is light. "Us," I say, nodding toward the cottage.

She glances back toward the house and her eyes bulge. "You must have been a very good girl to deserve all that hotness." She looks at me in awe, but there's a lascivious gleam in her eye that instantly reminds me of Taylor. I think for a second how strange it is that this girl is like my two best friends rolled into one—Taylor inside Riley's body—and it makes my heart ache to think of everything I left behind.

I pick up my pace before I can go too far down the tracks of that train of thought. Jasper yanks his leash, nearly toppling Faith. She gives the leash a tug, adjusting the strap of her bikini with her free hand.

"Cut the crap, Jasper. Don't embarrass me in front of the hot boys," she mutters. "Or . . . *men*? How old is Gabe?"

Loaded question. "Um . . . we're all eighteen," I say, after thinking about the dates on Luc's and my driver's licenses.

She nods, satisfied.

Luc and Gabe watch us intently as Faith, Jasper, and I pad through the sand up the gradual rise away from the water. Faith slows as we near the porch, holding Jasper back, and Gabe is already on the beach, heading toward us.

"So, Gabe," I say when he reaches us, "this is Faith. She lives next door."

"Hi Faith. It's been a while." He crouches to rub Jasper's ears. "And, who's this?"

"Jasper," Faith says, more breathless than she should be from just the walk over.

But I'm still trying to figure out what Gabe just said.

Luc strides down the stairs.

"Um . . ." I say, still frowning at Gabe. "This is . . ."

"Damon," he finishes. "It's a pleasure." He holds out his hand.

Gabe stands as Faith shakes Luc's hand, and, in the awkward silence, I'd almost swear I see him check Faith out. Which makes me think of Matt with Lilith.

Cold suspicion stabs through me like an icicle. My heart pounds in my throat, making it hard to breathe. I climb the stairs onto the porch and knock half a beach out of my hair and off my clothes. "So, I guess I'll see you later," I say, sorry now that I brought this girl over.

"Oh. Yeah . . . sure. Okay," Faith says with a glance at Gabe.

"Come on, Gabe," I say, my hand on the doorknob.

He flashes a glance in my direction before turning back to Faith. "I'm right behind you," he replies, clearly waving us off.

I give Luc a wary look, then head into the house. He follows and closes the door behind us. I pull him into the kitchen by his arm, forgetting for the moment that he hates me. "Could that be Lilith?"

His eyes fly wide and his head snaps around to the door. "Why would you think that?"

36

I shake my head. "I don't know . . . just the way Gabe looked at her, I guess. It reminded me of Matt."

"How did Gabriel look at her?" He sounds less concerned now and more measured.

"He kind of, you know . . . checked her out."

Luc relaxes back into the counter. "She's not Lilith."

"How can you be so sure? I've never seen Gabe look at anyone like that."

A thread of jealousy, the first I've heard from Luc in a while, is clear in his voice as he answers. "He looks at *you* like that all the time."

The argument dies in my throat as I glance at the door. Is that all this is? Jealousy? I shake my head. "How can you be sure it's not her?"

"She's Grigori," Luc says, reaching into the cupboard for a glass. "You want some water?"

I spin on him. "Grigori? Like Dad?"

He nods.

"How was I the only one who didn't know?"

Luc sets the glass on the counter and holds up his hands. "There's no conspiracy. I just figured it out."

"How?" I say, incredulous.

He shrugs. "Deductive reasoning. One: Gabriel is going to want extra eyes. Two: She's not an angel. She cast a sharp shadow on the beach. Compare it to Gabriel's and it's easy to tell. Three: Grigori are the Watchers—the protectors. I figured there'd be a few nearby. And four: Gabriel knows her, which was really the dead giveaway." He says this like any idiot should have been able to figure it out.

The front door swings open and Gabe steps through.

The door's not even closed before I rip into him, not caring if Faith hears. "You could have told me!"

He shoots a look at Luc then moves to the kitchen. "I didn't really have the opportunity," he says, setting his bags on the counter. "But it did give me a chance to see how you interact with strangers."

"Did I pass your stupid test?" I spit.

There's an amused sparkle in his eye, but I can see he's being careful not to smile. "You did."

"Why didn't she just tell me what she was?"

He quirks a perfect platinum eyebrow. "Because I asked her not to."

"Jerk," I mutter. I move to the window and look down the beach. "So, how many others spies are there?"

Gabe shoots me a hard look before answering. "Faith is not a spy."

"You could have fooled me."

He pulls our dinner out of the bags—a rotisserie chicken and fries. "There are no others. Too many Grigori in one spot would risk drawing Hell's attention."

Luc settles into a kitchen chair and serves himself. "Especially because I'm sure they're looking for it," he agrees.

I cut off a hunk of chicken and dump some fries on my plate then drop into the chair opposite Luc.

Gabe sits between us but doesn't take any food. "We ended up here because of Faith. She knows most of the people on the beach, so she'd notice anything . . . unusual." He turns to me. "And she's going to help you train."

"Train?"

"Faith does martial arts. She'll help you stay sharp." He cracks a smile. "She gets your body and I get your mind."

Luc dips a French fry in ketchup and lifts an eyebrow at Gabe. "Guess I know who got the short straw."

Gabe smirks at Luc. "You got *no* straw."

Luc shoves the fry in his mouth and chews with narrowed eyes. "Fine by me."

"So, what do you mean? What is this training?" I ask as I pick at the chicken on my plate.

Gabe looks at me out from under thick white lashes. "You need to sharpen your mind—refine your Sway."

"Great," I say, remembering how abysmally things went last time Gabe and I worked on my Sway.

No one has much else to say, and when everyone is done not really eating, I get up and clear the table. Luc and I do the dishes without ever looking at each other.

When we're done, I grab my duffel off the floor near the front door. "Does it matter which room I take?"

"That one," Gabe says, pointing to the door on the right, toward the back of the house.

"'Kay," I say, feeling suddenly exhausted. "I'm gonna take a shower and crash, then, if that's okay."

Gabe nods, but there's a look in his eyes—something sad and a little ominous that makes me want to climb right into his arms and stay there.

I breathe deep and push the bathroom door closed behind me.

LUC

Frannie takes her bag into the bathroom and I wait until the water is running before I turn back to Gabriel. "So, cherub, admit it. You've got nothing."

"I have a plan," he says, his eyes rolling from the bathroom door back to me.

I wait, but that appears to be all the information he's volunteering. "Have you thought any more about Rhenorian's uprising?"

"No," he says, dropping into the couch.

"Why not?"

"Because it's Rhenorian's uprising."

I lean into the table. "If you're the best and brightest Heaven has to offer, no wonder Hell is kicking your ass. How could an uprising in Hell be a bad thing? It can only work to our advantage."

"Or bite us in the butt."

"Think about this, Gabriel. If anything's going to change in Hell, I think it's going to have to start there. If you could rally some celestial support, Rhen and his crew might be able to make a difference."

He shakes his head slowly. "They're too unpredictable. They'd take our help as long as it suited their purpose, but you know better than anyone that a demon's word isn't worth the breath it takes him to utter it."

"So, you have something better?"

He hesitates. "More definitive."

I breathe back my angry frustration at his nonanswers and

work to keep my voice even so Frannie doesn't hear. "What, exactly, is this plan?"

"I'm still working some things out."

"You already said that. I'm interested in details. Give me what you got."

"Let me sort it out first," he says.

My muscles coil tight and I want nothing more than to punch something. "Perfect. You dragged us off to God only knows where without a plan."

He glares up at me. "You need to get your ears checked. Somewhere in the transition from demon to mortal they must have gone on the fritz, because you're not hearing me."

"I'm hearing you say absolutely nothing just fine," I say through gritted teeth.

He bounds off the couch. "And you're the expert on protecting Frannie? On your watch she was attacked by Rhenorian, stalked by Andrus, Chax, and Marchosias, and her soul was nearly stolen by Lilith." He ticks these things off on his fingers while glaring back at me. Lightning crackles over his skin and I'm sure he's about to start foaming at the mouth. "Maybe you should leave it to the professionals from here on out."

He's right, of course. I don't have a leg to stand on. Technically, it was on Matt's watch, but that doesn't change the fact that all those things *did* happen and I was powerless to stop them. But even though I'm painfully aware that Gabriel's devotion to Frannie goes beyond his sworn duty to protect her, I'm still having more than a little trouble standing by and leaving her safety in his hands.

I cross the room and get in his face, unable to help myself.

"Considering that not only Frannie's safety, but the fate of all humanity rides on keeping her out of Lucifer's grasp, I was hopeful you might actually have a clue what you were doing. Didn't think that was asking too much."

At the mention of Lucifer's name his eyes flare and his posture stiffens. The next second, he has a handful of my T-shirt. "I know what I'm doing," he snarls. "I have a plan."

I stare into his face and suddenly have no doubt that he has a plan. It's the fact that it's tearing him apart that has me worried. Frustration roils inside me, the pressure building like lava itching to explode from a volcano. "Fill. Me. In," I growl.

He pushes me back, releasing my shirt. "She needs to master her Sway. Quickly. We don't have much time."

"Until what?"

He stares at me, debating how much to say, before spinning for the door. "There's no way to do this without her."

I'm back in his face in a heartbeat. "Do *what?*"

"She's going to be part of this . . . part of the fight. It's the only way."

My stomach drops to my knees. "You're insane." The words are mostly air as they leave my throat.

"It's the only way," he repeats, as if trying to convince himself.

I just stare at him, unable to find words to explain just how crazy this is. She needs to be as far from the fight as possible. Now I know beyond a doubt I was right. I need my demonic power if I'm going to be any use to her. She needs me now more than ever. I shove him off. "How long do we have here?"

"That's up to your boss," he sneers. "A few weeks, maybe."

A few weeks may be long enough. She's changed me that fast before. I need my power back now, and the only way to get it is to make Frannie hate me.

FRANNIE

As I twist the shower knobs I'm surprised to find my hands shaking. I slide off my tank top and step into the water, letting it run over my aching body. I brace my hands against the cool tile and breathe in the billowing steam, imagining it burning away all the guilt that coats every surface of my insides like thick sludge.

I go through the motions on autopilot, and when I step out of the shower, I feel a little better. The bubble gum in my brain making all my thoughts stick together is almost gone.

I'm twisting my hair into a towel when I step out of the bathroom in my Hendrix T-shirt, ready for bed. My heart sinks when I see Gabe and Luc, standing in the middle of the room glaring death at each other. The air is so thick with tension that I can barely breath it. They're fighting again. And from the glance they both throw my direction, I'm sure it's about me.

"What's going on?" I ask, afraid of the answer.

"Nothing," Gabe says, his voice tight. His eyes lift to mine and he tries to pretend he and Luc weren't about to rip each other to shreds. "So, I guess I'll take off—let you guys get settled in and all that."

I step into the room. "Where are you going?"

Gabe shrugs. "Out."

"Out," I repeat. "Listen, I know you don't need to sleep or anything, but it's stupid for you to go 'out' when I know that means right there." I point to the front porch. "You should just stay here."

I think about why I said that. Was it for Gabe, or was it for me? I haven't spent a night without him in weeks.

Gabe, who doesn't miss much, seeing as he can read minds and all, slouches onto the couch. "I'll just crash here."

Luc glares at him and slides into the chair under the window. "You've been in her bed for weeks." His lip curls in disgust and his eyes harden as they flick to me. "Why resign yourself to the couch now?"

The room feels suddenly cold as Luc picks up the remote and starts channel surfing. His expression is indifferent, as if he didn't just stab me in the heart. I slide onto the couch next to Gabe.

"My only goal is to protect her, Lucifer," Gabe's voice is hard. "Don't make this into something it isn't."

Luc's face pulls into a sneer. "Honestly, I really don't care what it is," he says with a dismissive flick of his wrist toward me. "I took what I wanted. Whatever's left is yours."

I swallow hard and glance between them, trying to follow what's happening. I'm pretty sure Luc is saying he's done with me . . . that he was just using me. My eyes scour his face, trying to read him, but he won't meet my gaze.

I swallow again. "So, what's the general plan?" I ask no one in particular, ripping my eyes away.

A distressed look passes over Gabe's face but clears as his eyes meet mine. "For now, we stay put. We need to figure out your Sway, Frannie. That's priority one. It's not only your best defense, but also our best offense."

"*Our* best offense?" Luc repeats, his voice measured.

Gabe ignores him. "We need to figure out what you're capable of. You need to learn to control your power—to use it."

My face screws into a grimace and I feel a little sick. "So you want me to work on my Sway again? Remember how well that turned out before?"

His expression becomes sympathetic but not soft. "There's no choice. Either you're going to master this thing now, with my help, or you're going to master it for Lucifer."

My chest tightens at Lucifer's name and I can almost feel His leathery arms around me again. "How am I supposed to do that? I have no idea how it works."

"You'll practice until you know how to control it."

I don't like the sound of that. "On who?"

"Us, for now," Gabe says, shooting a glance at Luc. "I also think it's important you learn how to keep others out of your head."

I raise my eyebrows at him. "Like you?"

"Yes, me, since I'm handy and I can give you feedback. But I'm not the only one who's capable of messing with your head. I can hear your thoughts, but others can cloud them, which is much more dangerous."

I shudder, 'cause I know by others, he means Lucifer. My heart turns to lead in my chest remembering how I was when I was near Him—the things He made me want.

I shoot a glance at Luc, who's running his palms over his knees. "So, you're going to train Frannie to use her Sway. To what purpose? What's the end game?"

Gabe's jaw tightens and he can't hold Luc's gaze. "Let's just worry about one thing at a time," he evades. "You'll stay here, where it's safe. I'll go out for whatever you need."

I feel myself bristle at the thought of being held prisoner here. "Gabe, I can't live in a cage."

"And besides, that's not a plan." Luc's voice is low as he stares Gabe down, calling him on the evasion.

Gabe shifts on the couch and won't look at either of us. "I'm working on something, but in the meantime, we need to lay low."

The itch under my skin tells me I'm not gonna last very long. I just stare at him.

He blows out a sigh and pushes deeper into the cushions, some of the tension finally leaving his body. "Frannie, I know this is hard, but my priority right now is keeping you safe."

"Is that even possible?" I ask.

"No," he answers, 'cause he can't lie. "But I have to try." He finally raises his eyes to mine, and in them I see his resolve. I also see there's something he's not telling me.

I'm so tired. Too tired to think about this. I slump onto the couch and try to watch the show, but my eyes keep drifting to Luc.

His finger mindlessly rubs over a seam in the arm of the chair, and goose bumps crawl over my skin at the memory of that finger tracing patterns on my face. He looks over and my eyes flick back to the TV, but in that brief instant, I'd swear I saw loathing in his gaze. Directed at me.

My chest aches as I pull myself out of the couch and head to my room.

3

✢

Guiding Light

GABE

I can't believe I'm thinking this.

How can I consider putting her in danger—directly into His path? This isn't a plan. It's insanity.

But it's all I've got.

I pull myself to my feet and watch Frannie disappear behind her door. I don't know how long we have. A few months, or maybe just weeks. Whatever it is, it's not long enough. I won't be able to hide her forever, so something needs to change.

Luc is staring at me, waiting for me to come clean. He's not going to let this drop. And he shouldn't.

I should tell them. I know that. Eventually, I'll have to.

Ha. Eventually.

Who am I kidding? Eventually is now. Because time's up.

But I keep praying for something different; a safer plan for

Frannie. So far my prayers have gone unanswered—and I'm afraid I know why.

I head for the door and Luc cuts me a parting glare. Once on the porch I look out over the predictable tides. They've ebbed and flowed for eons, just as good and evil have ebbed and flowed. But the balance is shifting. Lucifer has decided the Rules don't apply anymore. And Frannie is our best weapon to shift it back.

I've always known Frannie was special, but I'm starting to think it's bigger than her Sway. There's a subtle power that radiates off her. I sensed it in the beginning, and, despite her insecurity and doubt, it gets stronger every day. I can't identify it—it's nothing I've ever felt before—and I'm afraid of what it means for her. But despite my feelings for her, she's a soldier and this is a battleground.

I walk out onto the beach and settle into the sand. Its warmth radiates through me as I lie back, closing my eyes. I let the tension run out of me and wash myself in peace, then give myself up to the last crimson rays of Light. There's a painful tug in my gut as I move with them, nothing more than light myself, and, when I open my eyes, I find myself standing in the Collective. All around me is a whole lot of nothing. White energy. Except, floating in the center of all that nothing is the Board.

The Board is really a misnomer. It's not a board at all. It's a sphere. The Earth. It's ethereal, like a floating cloud, and, at the moment, relatively small—about four feet in diameter. I glance up at the mass of twinkling blue lights dancing over the surface of the Board like fireflies. Humanity. The white lights of the celestial move among them, but it's the red ones I'm interested in. I step back and ask the Board to size up for better detail.

Instantly, it's easily a half mile across.

"Gabriel," a voice says.

Without turning, I spin the Board and take several minutes to peruse it, stopping at the Florida Keys. No red lights within at least a mile of the bungalow. I'm sure the infernal are looking, but they haven't found her yet. Frannie's safe for now.

"Thanks for your help at the airstrip," I finally say.

Celine paces to my side as I reach forward and touch the blue light that represents Frannie.

"You're welcome," she says with a crisp nod, her copper curls bouncing with the gesture. "You wanted to know when Marchosias had been located."

My eyes slide from the Board to Celine. She folds her wings behind her slender frame and points a long finger at a flashing red light just north of Boston.

I rotate the Board and scan the area for white lights. "Who do we have on Frannie's family?"

She cringes. "You didn't leave orders . . ."

Because I was hoping that our leaving would draw them away. "Who's available?"

Celine sweeps her hand over the Board and a series of white lights flicker, each representing a guardian available to take on a new charge. "Not many. Lucifer's crews are marauding and there's more instances of coercion." Her expression is a mix of sadness and rage as she turns her eyes on me. "He's cheating, Gabriel, sending them into synagogues, churches, and mosques. He's actively seeking out innocents and the faithful, influencing them to sin." She runs a finger over the Board. "We're bringing new guardians on line every day, accelerating the training program to try and cover the growing need, but we don't have enough guardians to protect all of humanity."

The sense of dread that's been growing steadily in my gut settles deeper and takes root.

It's starting.

The Almighty has overlooked Lucifer's contravening of boundaries for too long and now things are starting to spiral out of control.

Frannie.

I can't help thinking this escalation has something to do with her. Her power is growing, and so is Lucifer's brazenness—and His disregard for the Rules.

I look back at my options on the Board. "We'll send Aaron to Haden. Let him get a feel for the situation."

Celine's brows lift in surprise. "Aaron?" she says cautiously. "You're sure?"

As much as I understand her apprehension, he's the obvious choice. His last charge—a nun bound for sainthood—just died of natural causes at the ripe age of 104, despite Lucifer's early and numerous attempts to corrupt her. "He's my oldest and most experienced," I say, wincing at the memory of what happened when I sent someone younger and greener.

Celine's head jerks in a sharp nod. "Done."

I spin away from the Board as Aaron fades in next to me. He leans his broad frame nonchalantly into a rail that solidifies next to him and quirks a cocky half smile, which brings out his deep dimple on that side. "You rang?" he says with a lift of one platinum brow.

"I need you for a job." My eyes shift between him and Celine and I wonder, briefly, if I'm making the right call. "Do you think you can stay out of trouble?"

"O ye of little faith," he says, picking at his perfect teeth with a perfect fingernail.

I sit back into a white executive chair that materializes under me. "This is serious, Aaron. I need you on your best behavior."

He stops picking at his teeth and cuts me a look. "If you don't think I can handle it, why did you call me?"

I hold his gaze. "Because I need someone with your experience."

His mouth twitches into a sardonic smile. "I guess you'll just have to trust me, then, oh mighty one." He bows with a flourish.

I pinch my forehead against the sudden sharp pain there.

A headache? What next?

"Don't make this personal," I say through gritted teeth.

His expression twists into something hard. "You're the one who made this personal when you—"

Celine steps between us, a hand on Aaron's chest. "He'll be fine," she says, her voice low but potent.

Aaron bites back his comment and turns to the Board. "What's the assignment?"

I haul myself out of the chair, which disappears the instant I push away from it, lift my hand and tap my finger on the Board over Haden. "Help Daniel with whatever he needs."

He glares at the Board for a moment. "*Daniel?* You're not serious," he sneers. "I'm supposed to take orders from a Grigori? He's fallen, Gabriel," he adds, folding his arms defiantly across his chest.

Again, I second-guess myself. I'm within a hair's breadth of telling him to forget the whole thing when Celine speaks. "That's *her* family, Aaron. What's wrong? Too big of a job?"

Aaron spins and cuts a glare at me before turning to the Board. "So what is it that I'm supposed to do, exactly?"

"What you do best," I reply.

He puffs out his chest. "I am the best, though no one around here seems to remember that little factoid."

It's useless to point out that being older does not automatically make him better. It's been a bone of contention since my creation. But the fact is, his real beef is with the archangel Gabriel—not me.

After the War in Heaven, Lucifer fell and started creating His army. Gabriel determined he could no longer serve as the sole protector of all humanity and asked the Almighty for an army of guardians. Aaron was one of the first trained and one of Gabriel's favorites. Shortly after, when it was decided that Gabriel would delegate control of the guardians to another, Aaron believed he was the obvious choice. So when Gabriel asked the Almighty to create a Dominion to serve as his Left Hand—one more powerful than the guardians who could watch over them—Aaron was furious.

And still is.

He resents me for being what he couldn't, but he's smart enough not to take out his frustration on Gabriel. He believes he was slighted, and for the six thousand years since my creation, he's never let me forget it.

As Aaron smirks and fades out, and his white light pops onto the Board near Frannie's house, I have to remind myself that he is, in fact, one of the very best.

I follow the Light back to the beach, where I sit and stare out over the waves, red in the glow of the setting sun. I pull myself out of the sand, praying I'm making the right call. If there was a way I could just hide Frannie away forever, I would. But they're going to find us. With all of Hell looking, it's just a matter of time.

LUC

Gabriel has gone insane. It's all I can come up with. Too many eons of breathing ozone has eroded his judgment. And it was questionable to start with.

How he thinks he can put Frannie in the middle of this and have her—and therefore humanity—come out intact is beyond me. The thought sends a chill up my spine.

When I'd resolved to stay behind in Haden . . . away from Frannie . . . it was because I thought she was better off with Gabriel—he'd keep her safe. It's only now, as I walk past him lying on the dark beach, that I realize how wrong I was.

How could he gamble with her life like this? Knowing what she is—what's at stake—how could he risk it?

I'm so unaccustomed to this role—the helpless bystander. But if Gabriel isn't going to protect her, it falls on me. There's no choice. And no going back. The wheels have been set in motion.

I couldn't even look at Frannie as I said those things— implied I didn't care about her, had only been using her.

And worse.

I know my words hit the mark because I could hear the pain in her voice when she answered. The certainty that my words couldn't have possibly hurt her any worse than they hurt me does little to assuage the guilt. My words cut through my insides like a dull knife. Even the echo of them stings.

I walk slowly through the gentle lap of the surf. Water spreads out in front of me, a velvet black carpet as far as the eye can see. The ocean is nearly still, the crescent moon reflected in the vast blackness.

The calm before the storm.

I drop into the sand and stare out over the water, praying that I have the strength to follow through with this. We need to fight Hellfire with Hellfire, and the only way for that to happen is if I'm demon again. Which means Frannie needs to stop wanting me. I need to let go of any lingering hope that she and I can have a life together at the end of all this. The few months I had with her were a beautiful dream.

But I'm awake now.

The dream is dead, and my harsh reality is that Frannie will be too if I can't keep up the charade. She can't know how I feel about her. She needs to hate me.

I prop my aching head in my hands, my elbows on my knees, and try to convince myself this is how it should be. I was never meant to be human, and as a human I'm weak. If Frannie is going to stand a chance, I need to stop being selfish.

I need to give her up. For good.

"I've never seen Gabriel this stressed."

I start at the voice behind me. When I pull my head out of my hands, I find Faith standing barefoot in the sand, Jasper's leash in her hand. He's tugging against it in my direction. Faith smiles and lets up on the leash. Jasper gives my ear a sniff and plunks himself in the sand next to me, tongue lolling. Faith lowers herself to the sand on the other side of Jasper, legs crossed in front of her.

I look back out over the ocean. "There's a lot at stake."

"So it's true that Frannie has Sway."

I nod.

She throws another glance down the beach at Gabriel, where he's still sprawled in the sand. "I was surprised when Gabriel showed up with *two* mortals. Figured it would be just Frannie. Two of you are harder to Shield."

I think about telling her everything, but end up just saying, "It's complicated."

"You're . . . together? You and Frannie? That's why?"

"Not anymore." I almost sound like I don't care.

The moonlight gleams in her eyes as she scrutinizes me, and I know I didn't quite pull it off. I wait for her to say something—to push it—but, finally, she turns her gaze toward the water. "I love the beach at night. It's so peaceful."

"Mmm," I agree, feeling anything but.

My mind is racing, plotting. There have to be a hundred ways I can hurt Frannie—a hundred ways I can destroy her, and myself in the process.

We sit here for a long time, the only sound the gentle lap of the surf and Jasper's panting. And the storm brewing in my head.

"How well do you know Gabriel?" Faith finally asks, pulling me from my thoughts.

I shrug. "Better than I want to."

She hesitates. "Does he . . ." She trails off and her eyes flick toward him. Her gaze dips to the sand in front of her. "Has he ever said anything . . . about me?"

I look at her then, surprised by what I'm hearing in her voice. "Sorry. No."

She chews her lip but doesn't respond.

"How much has he told you about Frannie?" I ask.

"Just that I should keep my eye out. He said she had Sway and the infernals would be coming for her."

Hearing it out loud is almost more than I can bear. My insides clamp at the thought of Marchosias or Lilith getting anywhere near her. "I want you to tell me if you see anyone . . . suspicious hanging around."

Her eyes lift to my face and she cracks a smile. "You're mortal. What are you going to do about it?"

I hold her gaze and her smile fades. "Just tell me. Please."

She looks at me suspiciously for a moment, then nods as her eyes shift over my shoulder. "Well, good night," she says, pulling herself out of the sand.

I look up and see Gabriel is now standing, staring out over the water.

"Good night," I say as Jasper pulls her past me, toward him.

When she reaches him, he loops an arm over her shoulder.

I haul myself up and head back to the house. I start for my room, but stop. My resolve is set. No time like the present to finish this. I cross slowly to Frannie's door, but then hesitate as I picture her in her bed. My body reacts—a ripple of heat through my insides—and I breathe deep, steeling myself for what comes next. When I have my hormones mostly in check, I push open her door.

I open my mouth to tell her I'm leaving but then see that she's asleep. The sheets are tangled around her as she thrashes in her bed. I glide closer and gaze down at her for a long time. Finally, I sit on the edge of the bed and gently sweep her tousled hair off her face.

"Tay!" she gasps, but doesn't wake.

I breathe against the crushing pressure in my chest. She'll be forever haunted by what happened to her best friend.

And I'll be forever haunted by the fact that it never would have happened—none of it—if I hadn't found her.

She was Shielded by Gabriel. No other demon had been able to locate her.

But I did. It wasn't even hard.

Gabriel says we're connected. He doesn't understand how, but he says our connection is strong.

And I know he's right. Everything I am is tied to her.

She tosses again and I lay my hand on her shoulder. But as much as I want to take all her pain away, I can't do for her what Gabriel does. Her face pinches and she groans. I lean in to kiss her forehead, then stand.

I have to get out of here before I do something I'll regret. Because what I want more than anything is to curl myself around her, feel her close.

The memories flood my senses—Frannie under me, over me. The scent of currant and clove surrounding me.

I back away from her, my heart dying a little more with every step. I back through the door and close it. I lean my forehead into the door and try to hold it together. When I feel like I can breathe again, I lift my head from the door and turn for my room.

And find Gabriel standing in the front door, staring.

FRANNIE

I toss and turn in the sticky sheets, trying to let the rhythm of the rolling waves outside my window calm me. I see things in the shadows dancing over my ceiling. Taylor. Angelique. And blood.

Always blood.

It's nearly impossible to turn my revving mind off. No matter where I shift my thoughts, they always come back to that night—Taylor shoving the knife into her own stomach.

Taylor dying in my arms.

"Sheep," I whisper to myself. I close my eyes and picture puffy white sheep in a field. I start counting, focusing on their fluffy white wool, the grass, the sky. I'm up to 274 when I notice that the sheep is bleeding. I look around.

All the sheep are bleeding.

Blood is pouring from their bellies onto the ground. And Taylor is standing in the middle of the field with a knife in her stomach, adding her own blood to the growing river.

I sit up with a gasp, realizing I'd drifted off. The room comes into slow focus, and, in the moonlight I can just make out a face, drifting in the darkness.

Matt.

My heart screeches to a stop and I gasp again, choking on it. I stare harder at the spot, struggling for air. The silver light flickers off the ocean and wavers across my wall, and, where I was sure Matt was standing a second ago, all I see now is the face of a white clock telling me it's two in the morning.

I'm going crazy.

I swallow hard against the acid rising in my throat. On the night table next to my bed are a pill bottle and glass of water. Part of those "provisions" in the Jeep was a bottle of Unisom.

Gabe knows better than anyone that I haven't really slept since Taylor, 'cause he's the one who's been there every night when I wake up screaming. Tonight is the first night that he hasn't stayed with me in weeks. I pick up the bottle and spin it in trembling fingers. I open it and shake one out, then swallow it before I have time to think better of it.

I push the tangled sheets aside and sit on the edge of the bed. The feel of the cool hardwood floor helps to ground me, and my shaking slows a little. My gaze gravitates to the door, knowing who's on the other side of it. I find myself on my feet and walking toward it without even realizing it. But, just as my fingers brush the doorknob, I stop. I can't keep relying on Gabe. I have to figure this out on my own.

Forcing myself away from the door, I turn to my open window and lean my palms against the sill. The sound of the breaking waves is soothing, and my heart starts to slow to a normal pace. I sit on the sill and lean back on the frame. For a long time, I focus on breathing in the fresh air, clearing out the darkness inside me. Closing my eyes, I sync my breathing with the rolling surf.

When I finally feel calmer, I glance over my shoulder at the door, then slip my legs over the sill and drop into the soft sand under my window. It feels warm as I curl my toes into it, and I feel lighter just being outside the house—my prison. I wander to the water and the surf laps lazily at my ankles. I look up and down the beach and find I'm totally alone. It's a deep crimson sunrise and the air is heavy with the scents of the ocean—that combination of salt, fish, and something sweet but rank. I walk deeper into the warm water and it's soothing, washing away all my pain, fear, guilt.

I let the waves lift me and I float on my back, staring up at the swirling scarlets and grays of the oncoming day. The swell of the waves lifts and lowers me gently, cradling and rocking me like a baby. I close my eyes and drift, finally at peace.

But, slowly, I realize that the salty smell has taken on a metallic tinge, coppery and sharp. When another swell lifts me and I move my arms to steady myself, the water feels thick. I open my eyes and look up at the bloodred sky. Panic tickles at my insides when I try to stand and I find I've drifted so far out that I can't touch the bottom.

I tread water and look wildly for the shore, but it's nowhere. I'm surrounded by nothing but red ocean and red sky, blending together and making it impossible to find the horizon. Panic kicks harder in my chest as I become disoriented. A wave of dizziness sweeps over me, threatening to take me under, and I gasp for breath. My limbs begin to feel heavy and tired. I know I can't stay afloat much longer, but I don't know which way to swim. What if I choose wrong?

Something bumps into me from behind, startling me, and I spin in the water.

A scream freezes in my throat. For an endless second, all I can do is stare in horror.

Taylor is floating in the bloody waves, a fountain of red pouring from a gash in her stomach. Her breath comes in sputtering rasps, and more blood flows from her mouth with each gasp.

"Oh God." I grab her arm and pull her to me, trying to keep her above the waves. And that's when I realize that the water isn't just tinged with blood. It *is* blood—thick, sticky, and coppery. Taylor and I are floating in an ocean of blood. Taylor's blood. Taylor's blood is on my hands, and there's no way I can save her.

I open my mouth to scream, but before I can, something pulls me down. Under the bloody waves, all I can hear is the hammer of my wild pulse in my ears. A dark shape takes form in my consciousness—red eyes in a black face. I fight against it—fight for Taylor. But when I taste salt in my mouth, I know this is what I deserve. I'm drowning in Taylor's blood.

I give in and let the thick liquid seep down my throat. But just before I black out, whatever was holding me is suddenly gone and I'm rocketing toward the surface. I feel Gabe's peace and love, his summer snow.

Then . . . there's nothing.

4

✣

Morning Star

FRANNIE

My eyes open to pitch black.

Absolute darkness.

A tiny point of white light forms above me, and I focus on it as I cough and struggle to breath. It grows increasingly larger and brighter.

A star.

One singular star in the black velvet sky.

As it illuminates my surroundings, I realize I'm still on the beach. I feel the powdery sand sift between my toes as I jerk and cough, smell the briny air. Then I'm drowning again, but this time in Gabe's peace. He holds me and rocks me, humming a soft melody under his breath. It's a tune I know, but I can't place it. As his summer snow washes over me, my jagged nerves start to soften. His gentle hand smooths over my cheek and runs through my hair. I lift my head to look at him—and cough violently when my body attempts to gasp.

Because it's not Gabe.

The boy holding me is gazing up at the brightening star. When he turns his face to look at me, the light of the star is shining in his astonishing green eyes, and I realize he *is* the star.

Ethereal. Like a whisper.

The soft white light is coming from him. I feel myself instantly relax as a smile spreads across his beautiful face.

Just as I'm about to ask him who he is, he sweeps a finger lightly across my forehead and everything inside me explodes in a burst of pure white energy.

I wake with a choked gasp, as if I'd been drowning, and roll onto my side, sure I'm gonna be sick. The nausea passes slowly, and I lay back on the bed, staring at the eerie moonlit shadows dancing across my ceiling. I listen through my gasping breath and hammering heart for anyone moving in the cottage. Everything is still and silent except for the waves breaking on the sand outside my open window. I lay motionless and listen until my breathing and pulse slow.

As the pound of blood hammering through my ears fades, a haunting melody swirls through my thoughts, comforting.

Something from my dream?

Maybe. But it feels deeper. Older. Rooted in my subconscious somehow. I can't really remember the dream, except for Taylor.

I remember she was in the waves. And then there was. . . . A face tickles the edges of the memory, and I remember I felt safe. And the song. But that's all.

I close my eyes again, but acid rises in my throat as I see Taylor, floating dead on a sea of blood. I open my eyes and stare at the ceiling . . . and see Taylor.

I glance to the night table, where the open bottle of Unisom sits. It did exactly what I knew it would. Trapped me in a never-ending nightmare. I pick it up and throw it in the trash before getting up and walking to my door, knowing there's only one thing that can truly calm me. Just being around him always does. I promised him I'd try not to *want* him.

But that doesn't mean there aren't times that I *need* him.

I shrug my green terry robe over my baggy T-shirt and under-wear and pull the door open with a trembling hand.

Gabe is slouched into the couch cushions, one leg hanging over the arm, with an open copy of *The Great Gatsby* in one hand and a pair of glasses perched on his nose.

Despite my heavy heart, I crack a smile. I can't help it. "Glasses? You're joking, right?"

He straightens up, pulls the glasses off, and quirks half a smile. "You're surprised?"

"It's just so unexpected—" I wave my hand in a circle at him "—a flaw in all that perfection."

His smile widens. "I'm not as young as I used to be."

He straightens up and I slide into the couch next to him and pull the book from his hands, glancing at the page he's on. "Poor, tragic Gatsby. Deception, forbidden love, and ruined lives. Sound familiar?"

He sighs and loops his arm around my shoulders, nestling his face into my hair.

"I was hoping I could make it the whole night without you," I say, burrowing into his side.

A purr rumbles up from his chest as he pulls me close and kisses my forehead. "I told you I'd always be here for you, and I meant it. Whatever you need."

I press into him, feeling calmer already. "Is this okay?"

"My self-control is never what it should be when I'm with you." I feel his lips curve into a smile against my forehead. "Are you sure you trust me?"

I settle into him, knowing it's really me he should be concerned with trusting.

"I think we should have left Luc in Haden," I blurt, not really sure where it came from.

"Why?"

I hesitate, not sure how to answer. "He's mortal. If they come after me . . ."

"He knows the risks, Frannie," he says, his voice hard.

I pull away and look up at him. I want to tell him about my vision as we were racing away from Haden—that I know I'm gonna die. Soon. I want to tell him it's okay as long as everyone else is safe. But all that comes out when I open my mouth is, "I don't want him here."

There's sadness in his gaze. "Whether you—or I, for that matter—like it or not, you and Luc are connected. He can't leave you without putting you in danger. I'm not going to let that happen."

"What if they find us here?" I ask.

"We'll go someplace else."

The tune from my dream floats through my consciousness, and I have a sudden flashing memory of a beautiful face with green eyes. "Do you think Heaven might have sent another guardian angel?" I breathe against my closing throat at the thought of Matt.

He pulls back and an amused smile plays at his full lips. "Why? Are you requesting a replacement?"

"No." I smile and lean into him, twisting my finger into his platinum waves. "I've got the boss. Who could be better?" One last nagging thought pushes its way through his summer snow. "You'll look after everyone, right? Riley? My sisters?"

"Of course."

"I can't let anything happen to anyone else 'cause of me."

"I'll do my best, Frannie, but right now my focus is you. We need to keep you out of Hell's reach until you're ready. I was wrong to think they'd give up after you were tagged for Heaven. Lucifer isn't going to give up—ever."

"Until I'm ready?"

I feel him stiffen under me. "We won't be able to run forever . . ."

"So I'll have to fight eventually," I finish.

"Eventually," he sighs.

I start shaking again, thinking of King Lucifer, of how I was when He was near—how completely I lost myself and how much I lusted for Him. I'm no match for Him.

And He has Matt and Taylor.

I start to shake harder. "What if I can't? What if my Sway is really nothing?"

Gabe's hand strokes my hair. "It's not nothing. You'll learn how to use it. That's why I'm here, Frannie. To help you." His soft lips move against my forehead as he speaks, his warm breath tickling my skin, and I fight the urge to climb right into him—to live in his peace, where it's safe.

Instead, I stand and pad toward the bathroom, feeling more than a little sick. I sit on the toilet for a few minutes, my fingers woven into my wild hair, and wait for my stomach to settle.

There's a soft knock, then Gabe's voice floats through the door. "Frannie? Are you all right?"

"I'm fine," I lie. "I'll be out in a minute."

When I stand and stare into the mirror, I hardly recognize myself—drawn features and purple hollows circling my sunken, haunted eyes. A month of being scared to close your eyes will do that to a person, I guess. I gag myself on my toothbrush before heading back to the living room.

Gabe has turned off the light, and, in the pale moonlight slanting through the open window, I see him stretched out on his back on the couch. He holds an arm out to me.

I move across the room to him, and he grasps my hand and squeezes gently. "You okay?" The concern in his voice pulls at my heart.

"I will be." I drop my robe on the floor and crawl over him, curling up between the back of the couch and his body. I wrap my arm around his chest and let his peace wash over me. He's really turned it on, for my benefit, I'm sure, 'cause in only a few minutes I feel calm and start to drift off.

GABE

If there's Heaven on Earth, this is it. I kiss the top of Frannie's head, where she lays curled against me on the sofa. Her scent fills my nose: Ivory soap, the vanilla of her shampoo, and something spicy that's uniquely Frannie. I can't help shooting a glance at the used-to-be demon's door as a shudder works through me. A smile pulls at my mouth knowing this is the one thing she'll always come to me for. The one thing he'll never be able to give her.

Her breathing is shallow and irregular as she twitches in my arms. Reliving some horrific part of her recent past in her dreams, no doubt.

A past that I should have been able to protect her from.

The thought cuts like a blade. Her whole world has been turned upside down. I want to blame Luc—everything was fine until he showed up in Haden—but, deep down, I know it's all on me.

I told her I'd always be here for her. I wasn't. I wasn't strong enough to watch while she and Luc grew closer. So I took the easy road.

I abandoned her.

I made up all kinds of lame excuses to make myself feel okay about leaving, but at the end of the day, Taylor's death, Luc's betrayal, Matt's fall—I could have stopped all of it if I'd been there and paying attention.

My heart pounds in my chest. I feel it crash against my ribs, wrenching my entire body with each unrelenting beat. And I savor it.

Because I've never had a heart before.

I force myself to loosen my grip on Frannie before I wake her and twist a strand of sandy-blond hair in my fingers. Moonlight streams through the window and lights Frannie's pale face. I stare at that small, vulnerable face for an eternity. How any Earthly creature can be so beautiful is beyond me.

I lie back on the sofa, concentrating on the feel of the rhythmic beat of my heart, and imagine what it would be like to let the process continue—to let Frannie change me completely.

I'm a Seraph. A Dominion. One of the Second Sphere. I was never of the Earth, so if I were to lose my wings, I've always known I couldn't return to it. I'd belong to Lucifer—to Hell.

My new heart throbs as I think back on the night I almost lost my wings. I didn't realize until after, as I was standing in her hall struggling for breath that I'd never needed before, that I was changing. I know now that it had started long before that. And with the physical changes came others. Things I'd never experienced before.

Like Earthly desire.

I've always loved, but I've never *needed*. Feelings of yearning, craving . . . *desire* are uniquely human—something I didn't even have the framework to begin to understand before. Needing something so much you'd die for it . . . I never would have thought it possible until I felt it for myself.

But I would have.

That night I let myself go and nearly gave in to my desire. A huge part of me wanted that more than anything—to trade everything for one night with her. But it would have been just that. One night. After I'd lost my wings, I'd be useless to her.

She needs a protector, not a lover.

I'm going to have to stop this—sooner rather than later. She has to stop wanting me.

I stare into the darkness and try to think of what to say. I can't lie and tell her I don't want her, but I *can* say something that would embarrass her . . . or hurt her.

We'd all be better off if she hated me.

I realize I'm squeezing Frannie too tightly again when a wounded moan rolls up from her core and she jerks in my arms. I loosen my grip and drown her in peace. I want to take away all her pain. The only way I know to do that is by softening it some, so the edges don't cut so deep.

Her eyes flutter open and when she lifts her head and looks up at me, they're tortured. "It's never gonna end." It's not a question. Her voice is tired, defeated.

I inhale, slow and deep. Also something new for me. "It *is* going to end, and you need to be ready."

A shadow passes over her face and she nods. Her gaze shifts to Luc's door then back. "What if Luc turns back into a demon?"

The pain in her expression is unmistakable. She knows the only way that will happen is if she doesn't want him. But she'll always want him. Deep in my new heart, I know this to be true. Frannie will always love Luc. And he will always love her. At the thought, some deep, aching physical need works its way through me. I can't deny thinking about what might have happened between us if Luc was never in the picture. But the cold, hard truth is that Luc's leaving is impossible. He and Frannie are bound together in ways that I can't begin to comprehend. If Hell gets their hands on him, he'll be able to lead them to her.

We need to keep him close. Which means Frannie needs to keep him mortal.

Which also means I need to stay out of the way.

"He'd be a risk. My Shield would still protect him as long as he didn't draw on his infernal power. But that might be a challenge for him."

"So, if he starts turning back . . . ?" She levels her devastating gaze at me, and I almost can't answer.

"He'd be a liability. They'd most likely be able to find him . . . us."

She throws a concerned glance at his door.

I draw a deep breath to firm up my resolve. She can never be mine. I've accepted that. But she needs someone in her life who can support her, who understands what she is—what's at stake. No mortal boy could ever fill that roll. "You and Luc belong together, Frannie. You need each other."

She sighs and settles deeper into the sofa, resting her hand on my chest. My heart hammers out its need for her, like an SOS, and I know she can feel it. A cold sweat breaks across my forehead and my palms—one more new and not so pleasant sensation.

What the Hell is wrong with me? I laughed at Luc when he complained about teenage hormones. Guess the last laugh is on me.

I need a cold shower.

Forcing my thoughts from my body's reaction to having her next to me, I give myself a mental swift kick. "Go back to sleep, Frannie. You need to get some rest." I stroke my index and middle fingers over her eyelids and they close, but a smile teases the edges of her mouth, and I have the sudden overwhelming need to kiss her.

"Am I allowed to dream about you?"

The part of that sentence she leaves unspoken is, "instead of Taylor," but I groan internally, wishing she meant something else. "As long as you keep it PG."

Her eyes open and she laughs. It's the first time I've heard that sound in weeks. My heart lifts. "Sleep."

She closes her eyes again and settles into my arms, and I flood her with peace as she dozes off, hoping to keep the dreams at bay.

For hours, I watch her breathe, praying for a better plan— one that guarantees her safety. But still nothing.

She stirs in my arms. My lips brush her cheek and I chastise myself. I have to stop this. She can never be mine.

Ever.

But still, as much as this is my own personal Hell . . . it's also Heaven.

I lie perfectly still and listen to her breathe. Dawn breaks over the ocean and I roll onto my side to shade Frannie's eyes from the light of a new day streaking through the windows, hoping to give her a few more minutes' peace. She nestles her face into my neck, and I'm so lost in her that I jump when I realize the sound I just heard wasn't a seagull, but the creaking of door hinges.

5

✠

Penance

FRANNIE

I jerk awake from the first real sleep I've had in weeks. I open my eyes and find myself lying on the couch wrapped around Gabe, my head on his shoulder—drooling on his shirt, actually—my legs entwined in his and my arms in a death grip around his neck. My robe is on the floor and my T-shirt is hiked up around my waist. I tug it down over my underwear, and when I look up I find a grin on Gabe's face, directed at Luc.

"I couldn't sleep," I say, unwinding my limbs from Gabe's and sitting up. Which, considering the puddle of drool on Gabe's shirt, must sound like a total lie.

Luc stands in his bedroom door wearing black cotton boxer briefs and nothing else. There are pillow creases on his cheek and his black hair is sticking up every which way. He rubs his eyes with a thumb and forefinger, as if he thinks he'll see something different when he stops.

A knife carves its way through my heart. After yesterday, I don't even know what to say. He as much as told Gabe he was done with me.

Whatever's left is yours.

"Chill. She's just using me for my body." Gabe's face explodes into a grin and the glare blinds me.

I smack him again, this time on the thigh as he swings around and sits next to me on the edge of the couch, still in his T-shirt and jeans. "I *am* using you."

"And I'm totally cool with that."

Luc stares at us in silence as I shrug into my bathrobe, then turns and walks back into his room, closing the door behind him.

I drop to the couch, my aching head in my hands. I'm so confused.

Once again, my thoughts have given me away. "Sorry," Gabe says, leaning his shoulder into mine. "I can't resist busting his chops."

I tug at my hair and stare at my toes. "I just wish I knew what I was supposed to do. Why does everything have to be so complicated?"

He sighs deeply, then his hand is on my back, over my heart. "Because your situation is complicated."

My heart feels as heavy as lead in my chest as I stand and drag myself to my room. Just as I reach my door, Luc steps back out into the family room, now in a black T-shirt and faded jeans, and points to the kitchen. "I'm cooking. Anyone else want an omelet?" he says, his tone totally neutral, as if everything was business as usual.

I just stand there for a second, working on breathing, 'cause what wants to burst out of my mouth has nothing to do with omelets. When I finally think I can speak without saying something desperate, I say, "Yeah . . .'kay. I'll be out in a sec."

I slip through the door, closing it behind me, and just stand at the mirror, staring.

What am I doing?

I squeeze my eyes closed and breathe. I have to figure this out. I want Luc close, but I want him safe, and the two just don't go together.

Finally, I grab whatever's on top in my dresser and throw it on. It turns out to be a green cami top and cutoff shorts.

When I step through my door, there's already an omelet on a plate, sitting on the table.

"Eat," Luc says, gesturing to the table with his elbow as he flips another omelet in the skillet.

I slide into the seat and Gabe slips a steaming mug of black coffee onto the table in front of me. I lift it to my face and inhale. "Mmm . . ." I look up at him as he sits in the chair next to me. "A godsend."

He arches a platinum brow and quirks an amused smile. "I am."

I smirk at him. "I was talking about the coffee."

A minute later, Luc is at the table with another plate. But just as he sits, there's a knock at the door.

Gabe slides out of his chair and moves to the door. When he

pulls it open, Faith is standing there. She's traded her cutoff shorts and bikini top from yesterday for black shorts and blue sports bra, but she's still barefoot.

"I was heading out for a run," she says, tucking a loose strand of hair behind her ear. "But I wanted to bring this by first." She holds up a shoebox with a blue ribbon around it. "A housewarming gift."

"Entrez," Gabe says, stepping aside to let her pass.

Faith steps through the door and walks over to us at the table, still holding the box. I take it from her. "Thanks. You didn't need to get us anything."

She shrugs. "It's just something I made No big deal."

I untie the ribbon, pull the lid off the box, and gingerly lift out a small sculpture of driftwood, shells, and sea glass. An angel, complete with halo and wings. "This is . . . beautiful." My gaze slides past Faith to Gabe.

"Thanks. I do sea art. I make a ton selling this stuff to the tourists."

Gabe pulls out a chair for Faith and she settles into it.

I admire the piece, turning it gently from side to side. "I'm sure." I lift it to show the guys, then push my chair back and stand, looking around the room for someplace to put it. I finally settle on an end table near the window and place it next to the lamp there. Immediately, tiny flecks of light refracting through the sea glass color the room like a rainbow.

"That's the perfect spot," Faith says with a smile.

I nod and head back to the kitchen, where Luc is already pouring beaten eggs into the skillet. I pull a plate out of the cupboard. "Have some breakfast. You'll love Luc's omelets."

"Only if you have extra," Faith answers with a glance at Luc.

He holds up the cutting board with chopped tomatoes and peppers. "Extra," he says. He smiles at her and my heart pinches. "It'll just take a second."

Gabe pulls a mug out of the cupboard. "Coffee?" he asks Faith, holding it up.

"Yeah, thanks," she says. "Cream, no sugar." Then she turns to me with raised eyebrows and an impish grin. "They cook too?"

"Good thing," I answer. "If it was up to me, we'd starve."

"Or just survive on eye candy. One or the other . . ." Faith mutters under her breath with a glance at the boys.

My face feels warm, and I'm sure I'm blushing as my eyes flick to Luc.

"So, Gabriel says I'm supposed to help you train," she says loud enough for the boys to hear.

I shrug, pulling my eyes back to Faith. "I guess. Do you do judo?"

She nods. "There's a martial arts studio on Key Largo . . . or, really, more of a mixed martial arts gym. I work out there." She turns to Gabe. "I'll take her up tomorrow?"

"You've checked this place out?" he asks Faith.

"I've been going there for years. She'll be fine."

He lowers himself into his chair, sliding Faith's mug toward her, and drums his fingers on the table, contemplating. I catch myself hoping he'll say yes. I've missed the outlet of judo. At just the thought of being on the mat, slamming someone to the ground, something heavy lifts off my shoulders.

"You said she needs to train, Gabriel," Faith interjects.

His chair creaks as he pushes into the back of it, staring hard at Faith.

"Just let them go," Luc says from the stove, sliding Faith's omelet from the pan onto a plate.

Gabe leans onto the table and folds his arms, eyeing Faith. "You're sure it's safe."

"Yes," she says, rolling her eyes, but then smiles at Luc as he places the plate in front of her and slides into his seat.

Please, I think, crossing my fingers.

It's only when Gabe's face softens that I realize how hard I'm pushing the thought. Why does my Sway only seem to work when I don't mean to use it?

"Once," Gabe says, his eyes shifting between us. "We'll try it once. But any sign of trouble—"

"There won't be trouble," Faith interrupts through a mouthful of eggs. "This is really good," she adds with a glance at Luc, pointing to her plate with her fork.

I try to ignore the stone that forms in my heart at the way Luc smiles back.

"Fine," Gabe concedes.

Faith flashes me a victorious grin and high-fives me across the table. "I'll pick you up tomorrow at ten." She stands and lifts her empty plate from the table.

Luc looks up from his plate. "If you're really going for a run, I was going out after breakfast. You mind company?"

She smiles at him and I suddenly wish I'd taken up running as a tendril of jealousy slips out of my black pit. "That'd be great. There are some good footpaths that cross to the other side of the island. It's really quiet over there. I could show you those, if you want."

"Sounds good," he says with a raise of his eyebrow, and I see Faith's cheeks turn pink.

The rest of us stand from the table, bringing our dishes to the sink, and I start to fill it. But then I realize Luc is standing next to me, ready to dry. I look up at him. "Go. I got it this time." He holds my gaze for a moment, and I feel my insides flip at the intensity of his.

"We need to talk when I get back," he says.

It's not a request. It's a demand. And it makes my insides ache. "Okay."

His lips press into a hard line as he nods then pushes away from the counter. I breathe in his cinnamon as he brushes past me. He pauses as he passes Faith. "I'll be right out," he says, heading to his room.

When they're gone, and I've finished with the dishes, I turn to find Gabe near the door. "I'll check back later," he says, tugging the door open and stepping through. But before he closes it, his gaze finds mine, and in that brief second, he can't hide the pain—or longing—in his eyes. Then he's gone.

I trudge to my room, stick my iPod on the speakers, and drop into the soft brown armchair in the corner, curling into a ball as Breaking Benjamin sings for someone to show me a sign. I feel so nervous. I'm not sure what Luc means to say to me. Is he leaving? Staying? I don't really know which I'm hoping for.

Breathe.

I close my eyes and my heart stings as my mind shows me what Luc and I had. I see us at the quarry, kissing under the stars; Luc, grease smeared across his face, under the Mustang; Luc and me in his bed. Here behind my closed door, I mourn our loss and let the tears fall.

It's over an hour later when the front door clicks open. I listen as Luc's bare feet pad across the family room on the way to his room. He's breathing hard from the workout and I imagine the sweat trickling down his chest, between his shoulder blades, over his lips. I close my eyes and push the image out of my head. The bathroom door clicks shut and I hear the shower start.

A reprieve.

I have a few more minutes to pretend that this might not be the end of everything.

I stand and yank a brush through my wild hair, tying it back in a knot, and then just stare at myself in the mirror over the dresser.

Could you stay together . . . get married and have kids and all that?

Grandpa's question rolls around in my head, and I remember the hopeful look Luc wore when he answered. Luc was the first person I dared let in—the only boy I've ever really loved. My heart pounds with the memory of what it felt like to be that close to another person. I wanted a life with him more than anything. But what I know without a doubt is that a normal life with a normal family isn't in my future.

If there was some way I could give Luc that life, I would. I want him to have that, even though it can't be with me. I saw how he looked at Faith. Could I keep loving him—keep him mortal—so he could love someone else?

When I hear the shower shut off, I take one last look at myself then head to the family room and settle into the couch. The bathroom door opens a few minutes later, and Luc steps through with a towel wrapped around his hips. The black serpent tattoo around his upper arm stands out more sharply against skin a few shades paler than I remember, and he's a little thinner. But what really draws my eyes are the pinkish-white scars crisscrossing his chest and arms. I have the sudden urge to kiss the angry burn on his ribs and make it all better.

I want to make everything better for him.

"I'll just . . ." He gestures awkwardly toward his room. "Let me get dressed."

"'Kay."

He hesitates and his lips part to say something else, but then he looks away and strides across the room, disappearing behind his door.

I can't stop thinking about what he wants to say—what I'm gonna say.

Figure out what you want, Frannie.

I want things to be how they were before Lilith.

I push the image of Lilith in Luc's bed out of my head as I walk to the window and peer past Faith's, down the beach.

At first, my mind is elsewhere and I don't notice them. But then I realize Faith is out there, at her front porch. And she's not alone.

Gabe is sitting with her.

They look deep in conversation, and, as I watch, she leans her shoulder into his and I see him nod and turn his head in my direction.

I tuck behind the window frame just as Luc's door swings open.

Luc stands there in his T-shirt and jeans, curling his bare toes into the wooden floor and staring at me, looking more tentative than I've ever seen him. He's usually so sure of himself. A true Creature of Pride.

LUC

I stand in the doorway, staring at Frannie and trying to remember how to breathe. I spent my entire run on the beach with Faith totally ignoring her and working up the courage to do this . . . thinking of just the right words. Frannie thinking I'm interested in Faith can't hurt, but I can still screw this up in so many ways.

I pull a deep breath, set my jaw, and walk to the couch. I sit on the edge, elbows on knees. She follows and lowers herself cautiously onto the other side.

"I wanted you to know I'm only here because I have to be." I work to keep my gaze hard and not let her see it as all my insides collapse on themselves.

She continues to stare at me, her expression blank, not sure what to make of what I just said.

"This is bigger than just you, Frannie. Everything is at stake. I've thought about just bringing you to Him and getting it over with, but, unfortunately, I seem to have grown a conscience, and the blood of all humanity on my hands is a little more than I'm willing to deal with at the moment. So, my only alternative is to stay here." I push back into the cushions, struggling to keep my voice even. "Against my will."

For a long minute her only response is a distinct pallor as the blood drains from her face. I don't even see her chest rise and fall, making me wonder if she's having some kind of a seizure. I hold my breath, waiting for some reaction.

Finally, she exhales, long and slow, and her eyes shift to her fingers, where they pick at the fringe of her shorts. "Maybe Gabe can do something . . . find somewhere you could go." Her voice is flat and her eyes look hollow—empty.

"A prison is a prison," I say, my voice hard. "Though somewhere away from you might be preferable." And more likely to achieve the desired results. Out of sight, out of mind.

For the briefest of instants, she seems to deflate, like someone pricked her with a pin. But then she shifts on the couch and looks me straight in the eye. "I'll talk to him."

I stand from the couch, my gut twisting so hard that I almost can't get upright. "Please do," I say, relief clear in my voice knowing that it's done. I only need to hold it together for another minute.

She pulls herself to her feet, where she sways dangerously for a second before catching her balance. She nods without looking at me, then turns for the front door and slips through.

I close my eyes and sink back to the cushions, my head in my hands, fighting back the despair threatening to take me under. I've just murdered the only thing that made my existence tolerable. The only thing that ever truly meant anything to me. But this is how it has to be if I'm going to help her.

FRANNIE

I feel totally dead inside, as dry as the sand under my feet as I stumble out onto the beach. I can't believe I let Luc blindside me with this. I knew he would probably leave eventually, but I guess, deep down, I believed that, despite everything, he still loved me. I thought I saw something in his eyes when he looked at me.

I was wrong.

And it's good. He'll be safe if he's away from me.

I glance up the beach and see Faith is still sitting on her porch, staring out over the ocean, but she's alone now. I look past Faith's, farther up the beach, and see Gabe lying on his back in the sand at the edge of the surf, knees bent and his forearm over his face.

I start to go to him—to tell him that Luc wants out. But my feet slow before I get too far. I have to stop running to Gabe every time I'm upset. It's not fair to him. I don't feel so bad going to him when it's the fate of mankind stuff, but I need to learn to deal with my *own* stuff on my own. With one more glance in his direction, I turn and walk the other way.

I can't totally stop the tears, but I'm able to keep them mostly at bay by thinking about what comes next. Gabe says I'm gonna have to fight, and I know he's right. He wants me to work on my Sway, so I do.

I walk out onto a rocky breakwater and lower myself onto a slippery boulder. A family is parked on the beach just up from where I am. They've got their red and white umbrella spread wide, but the only thing under it is a radio. From it, the pounding rhythm of the Rolling Stones' "Sympathy for the Devil" wafts to where I sit.

Grandpa's anthem.

A wet, aching lump forms in the back of my throat, and I close my eyes, remembering Sundays in his garage under whatever Mustang we were restoring.

I miss him so much.

I miss our talks and the comfortable silence in between. I miss the smell of exhaust and the feel of grease on my hands. But most of all I miss knowing that, no matter what kind of trouble I got myself into, I could always go to him.

I need him now.

I scrub away the tears leaking over my lashes and focus on Beach Family. Mom and Dad are working on their tans, sprawled on a double beach towel, as a little towheaded boy kicks his sister's sand castle over. She shoves him away and turns another bucket of packed sand onto the mound—which the boy promptly kicks over.

The boy reminds me of Matt, all blond curls and dimples. I think of him and my sisters, of how much I miss them, and focus on the little boy, telling him he loves his sister, just like I love mine.

She flips another bucket, and he steps forward, as if to kick it, but then he sinks to his knees and starts to fill the bucket instead. As I watch, the two of them turn the four corners of the castle and start to build walls between them. By the time I stand and move down the beach toward the cottage an hour later, it's a masterpiece. And even though I didn't build it myself, it still feels like an accomplishment.

I check in with myself as I meander up the beach toward the cottage and find I'm surprisingly okay. I'm even feeling a little proud of myself. My heart aches, 'cause it always does, but, for the first time in a long time, I also feel the tiniest ray of hope. I'm dying to tell Gabe that I've been practicing my Sway . . . and it might have even worked.

6

✟

Trial by Fire

GABE

As I sit in the sand, looking out over the ocean, I see bloodred waves crest and roll onto shore. The vision was too strong, too tied to Frannie's terror, for me to fully block it. Her nightmares are getting worse—more real.

Those are demons I can't protect her from, as much as I might want to.

I lie back in the sand and close my eyes, giving myself up to the Light. The deep throbbing ache in my chest as I slide between planes is worse this time, and I stiffen and hold my breath. I've let it go too far. Human flesh was never meant to be ripped through planes. If I continue to let Frannie change me, soon I won't be able to shift at all. At the thought, the ache in my chest intensifies. Because, as much as I need to, I don't want to give this up—this concrete proof that Frannie wants me.

"Gabriel? Are you okay?"

I stand in the Collective with my eyes closed for a second longer as the pain recedes, then heave a sigh and turn to Celine. "I'm fine. Any word on Lilith?"

She glides forward, shaking her head. "She doesn't appear to be on the coil—" she says, waving a hand toward the Board, "—as best as we can tell, anyway. She's tricky to get a fix on."

I step back from the Board so I can get a broader sense of where my guardians are and sit as my chair materializes under me. I lean back and kick my feet up onto the footrest that solidifies just as I need it. I scan the Board, noting that there are the typical masses of red, mostly around cities and prisons, and white interspersed fairly evenly with the blue—business as usual.

"Gabriel?"

I pull my gaze away from the Board and look at Celine. She shuffles nervously next to my chair. "There's something else." She hesitates and I wait for her to continue. "We got a report that He's trying to use a Mage and the Other to find her."

"The Other?"

Her gaze drops to the floor. "Matthew."

I grimace, because the pain is almost physical.

Matt.

He had so much promise and I threw him to the wolves before he was ready. He was Frannie's twin, and I thought he'd flourish as her guardian. But he wasn't prepared to withstand the likes of Lilith and lost his wings because of it. And worse, he chose Lucifer over life on Earth as a Grigori. He's lost to Heaven forever.

So, He'll use Matt and the Mage to find her . . . "In her dreams," I mutter to myself as I pinch my forehead. That would explain the intensity of them. My gaze slides back to Celine. "How connected is the Mage?"

She waves her arm in the air and looks over the grid that appears there. "I don't have specifics on that." She touches the grid, enlarging a portion. "He found her in young Lucifer's mind. That's all I have. I suppose it depends on how strong *his* connection to her is."

My gut rolls—more evidence that I've let this transformation go too far. "It's only a matter of time," I say under my breath, fighting back the urge to strangle Luc. I knew our time was short, but now . . . they may have already found her.

She closes her hand over the grid, as if crumpling a sheet of paper, and it's gone. "Can you Shield her from the Mage?"

"No." I lean back farther in the chair, closing my eyes. I have to think. How am I going to pull this off?

"Gabriel."

Luc's voice coupled with a sharp kick to my ribs pull me from the Collective and I follow the Light back to the corporeal world. I open my eyes and sit up in the sand, and I can't stop the groan as every muscle in my body clenches against the pain of the shift.

He looks at me curiously for a moment, then his mouth pulls into a tight line. He crouches down, getting into my face. "I need to know how much time we have."

The pain recedes slowly and I take a deep breath, expanding my lungs. "I don't know. Why don't you tell me?" I growl, pushing him back.

"How would I know that? This is your plan, cherub," he sneers, shoving me. "How long?"

I shove him back, feeling rage bubble inside me. "Not as much time as we need, thanks to you. Why didn't you tell me about the Mage?"

He drops back onto his butt in the sand as his face pulls into a mask of shock. "Unholy Hell."

Over his shoulder, I see Frannie crossing the beach toward us. I glare at Luc as she reaches us, trying to contain my fury.

LUC

"What's going on?" Frannie's voice startles me, and I lift my forehead from my hand. "What's a Mage?"

"Tell her," Gabriel spits, darting me a look that could kill.

I sigh deeply. How did I not remember the Mage? When I realized I was demon again—that Frannie didn't want me anymore—I'd willingly gone back to Hell with Rhen, hoping Lucifer would throw me into the Fiery Pit and be done with me. But instead, He decided to make an example of me. He tortured me for days, then sent the Mage into my head looking for Frannie. And I was weak. I couldn't stop myself from thinking of her—giving it what it needed to find her. At just the memory I can almost feel it tearing through my mind, looking for her. And I can see Lucifer's satisfied sneer when He knew the Mage had found her.

"Mages are creatures of the Abyss." I stare out over the water because I can't make myself look at Frannie. "Like me," I add, and feel my face twist into a grimace. "But they live in the Shadowlands—the space between planes."

"What does that have to do with us?" Frannie asks impatiently.

My eyes flick to her. "One of Lucifer's Mages found you in my head when Rhen brought me back."

She just stares blankly at me. "What does that even mean?"

My jaw grinds tight as self-loathing eats at my gut. "It means I've put you in danger."

She looks at Gabriel. "So, what's new?"

He reaches up for her hand and holds it as he says, "This is serious, Frannie. Mages can invade a mortal's dreams. So I need you to be honest with me. Have you had strange dreams?"

"How would I know if there was a Mage? In my dreams, I mean?" she evades, sinking to her knees in the sand next to Gabriel.

He heaves a sigh of frustration, but I speak before he can press her further.

"Mages are the demonic equivalent of a nightmare. They work their way into mortals' heads, which is easier when your conscious thought slows—just as you fall asleep. They may or may not show themselves in the dream, but either way, they'll show you things—what they want you to see—through other people's eyes in your dreams."

"If it showed itself, what would it look like?" She sifts sand through her fingers as she asks, avoiding eye contact with either of us.

"It would appear as it is, I suppose. Black, shadowy, insubstantial." I try to read her face as I say it, but it's intentionally blank.

She drags in a heavy breath and holds it for a moment, thinking, then blows it out, seeming relieved. She straightens and looks at Gabriel. "I haven't . . ." but she goes pale as her eyes widen. "Wait."

Gabriel leans toward her, and I can see the concentration on his face.

"You've seen it," he says.

"Get out of my head, Gabe!" she shouts, pulling her hand away from his.

"Make me," he says, shifting onto his knees, closer to her. "Push me out."

Frannie's face sets, determined, but after just a minute she crumples, defeated. "I'm never gonna be able to do this."

"So, answer my question," Gabriel says, softer.

She stares hard at him, but then her face softens and she nods. "I had a . . . Taylor was floating, dead, and I was drowning. There was a black face with red eyes . . . just for a second. It pulled me under the waves," she says, looking haunted.

I have the distinct feeling there's more she's not saying, but, for now, it's enough to know the Mage has found her.

Alarm flits behind her gaze as she looks at Gabriel. "How do we get away from it? Do we have to leave?"

He shakes his head. "This is one demon we can't lose so easily."

Panic cuts through me like a cold dagger. I need to distance myself from her—to gain my infernal power back. But if the Mage has already found her, there's no time.

I hold her gaze, trying to keep my head straight and not get lost in her eyes. Steeling myself, I take a deep breath. "In the dream where you saw the Mage . . . did you see anyone else?"

She shrugs. "Taylor . . . like I said."

"No one else?" I press, my voice hard.

"This thing is just in my dreams, right? If it's only in my imagination, what's the big deal?" she asks, her jaw set and her eyes narrow.

"It's much more than your imagination, Frannie," Gabriel interjects. "Don't make the mistake of underestimating it just because it's not part of our physical world. In reality, that makes it even more dangerous."

"Okay, fine," she says, her glare swinging back to me. "So, you're the expert on stuff from Hell. What's the danger?"

My chest clamps tight and I'm having trouble finding air. "It'll show up in your dreams for one of three reasons. First, to show you something it wants you to see; second, to try to decipher where you are, or third . . ." I hold Gabriel's gaze, ". . . to allow Lucifer to follow it in."

Gabriel's eyes narrow and Frannie's widen. "Lucifer?" she says and shudders despite the sticky heat. "What do you mean, follow it in? To my *head*?"

"Mages are splinters of His essence. Once one is in your head, if its connection is strong enough, it's like a part of Lucifer is there, and the rest can follow."

Panic spreads across Frannie's face. "You mean, for real? He could show up here?"

"Not in corporeal form, but His essence, which is no less dangerous."

She pushes herself to a stand, staring down at me. "I need to think." She turns toward the water.

I watch as she staggers down the beach and drops into the sand on the other side of the bungalow.

"What are the chances that Lucifer has already found her?" Gabriel asks, his voice tight with barely contained fury.

I shake my head. "Hard to say." My eyes shift to him, where he still sits in the sand. "You'd have a better handle on that than I would."

Quicker than lightning—literally—he's on me. Before my human eyes can even register that he's moved, my T-shirt is wadded in his fist, and his face is an inch from mine. He grits his teeth and spits, "I had one shot at this. Now there's no way she'll be ready in time."

I plant a hand on his chest and shove him back. "What the Hell are you talking about?"

"You've killed her."

7

✝

Soul Kiss

FRANNIE

I lie back in the sand and stare up at the haze of the cloudless sky. I've never felt so trapped in my life. Caged. Even in my dreams, I'm not free.

Staring out over the cresting waves, I work on letting them calm me, slowing my racing mind. My mini victory over my Sway seems pretty insignificant now.

Lucifer—in my dreams.

I close my eyes and the memory is so sharp it cuts—the feel of His black bats wings pressing me to Him, the burn of His cold heat, and how much I lusted for Him.

My breathing comes in short pants. I feel sick.

I force the thought of Lucifer away and think of nothing but the rolling waves. With the waves comes a rhythm. And with the rhythm comes a tune—a familiar tune that I can't quite place. I hum along softly as it loops through my head, feeling more relaxed, and see the flashing image of a beautiful green-eyed boy.

I open my eyes, trying to remember. I know the boy. I've seen him before. *But where?*

When I glance up the beach, I catch sight of the guys, and at first I can't figure out what I'm seeing. They're moving across the sand, just at the edge of the surf, close and then apart.

Are they dancing?

I squint at them and, despite everything, feel a smile pull at my mouth.

But the next second, Gabe lunges forward, grabbing Luc, and they go down hard on the sand. Gabe's fists fly, and, at first, Luc only seems to be trying to push him off, but then he cocks his fist and pounds it into Gabe's face. Gabe's head snaps back, and he rolls to the side. But then he's back on top of Luc, his hands around Luc's throat.

I sprint up the beach as Luc twists Gabe into a leg lock and throws him off. Luc hauls himself out of the sand and stands over Gabe.

"Stop!" I yell as I reach them, standing between them with my arms out. "What the hell are you doing?" I realize I'm shaking when I hear it in my voice.

"Tell her!" Luc demands, wiping away a trickle of blood from his split lower lip with the back of his hand. "You're putting her life in danger. The least you can do is have the decency to tell her."

Gabe pulls himself to his feet. He leans toward Luc, and I hold him back with a hand to his chest. *"I'm* putting her life in danger? You've done nothing but endanger her from the moment you set foot in Haden. We wouldn't be here right now if it wasn't for you."

A shadow passes over Luc's face and his gaze drops to the sand.

"What's going on?" I ask, feeling the shake work its way into my legs, which suddenly feel like Jell-O.

Gabe's eyes connect with mine, and there's something in them, a combination of shame and fear, that I've never seen there before. He grasps my arm, not so gently, and starts walking. "Inside" is all he says, but his expression is deadly serious.

Gabe all but throws me onto the couch when we get inside, but I have the distinct feeling it's not me he's mad at. And I don't know what to think about Luc. He sits in the chair glaring at Gabe as he lowers himself onto the couch. For someone who just got done telling me he didn't care what happened to me, he seems pretty concerned.

I look between the two of them. "So?"

Luc glares death at Gabe. "Enlighten her."

Gabe sighs deeply and hangs his head. "This isn't how I was hoping it would go," he says.

"How is it going?" I ask.

He lifts his head and glares at Luc. "Too fast."

I touch his arm, drawing his eyes. "Tell me."

He blows out another sigh, but he doesn't divert his gaze. "We were supposed to have time. I was going to work with you—train you to protect your mind and use your Sway."

I nod. "You said that. I've been working on it," I say encouragingly, thinking of the boy on the beach.

"But we're out of time, and you're not ready."

"You're worried about the Mage," I say.

"Tell her," Luc interjects, and when I glance at him, his face is hard, his lips pressed into a tight line.

"It's not just that." Gabe drops his gaze. "The rest of the plan was to use you to lure Him here."

"Him?" I ask, afraid I know the answer.

His eyes flick to my face then away. "Lucifer."

I feel light-headed as all the blood drains from my face. "G . . . Gabe . . ." I stammer, but that's all I can manage through my shock.

"You're insane," Luc finishes for me, glaring out from under his hand, where it pinches his forehead.

"Maybe, but He's coming anyway, thanks to you," Gabe spits. "And now there's nowhere we can run."

"So, you're just going to let Him come here?" I ask. "Take me?"

Gabe's expression is caught somewhere between panic and resolve. "No. He won't take you."

My heart beats out of control. "Who's going to stop Him?"

He locks his gaze with mine. "Me."

LUC

Frannie just stares at Gabriel as he sits with his face in his hand, then lifts his head and looks at me.

"Can anyone but Lucifer travel with the Mage?" he asks.

"No."

He thinks for a moment more. "So, this might work to our advantage."

I narrow my eyes at him, not liking where this is going. "How so?"

"I intended to have Frannie lure Him here and use her Sway to find His vulnerability—something I could use to destroy Him. But if He comes through her dream . . ." His eyes lift to mine, and I see something resembling hope or madness, which often resemble each other. ". . . He's got to be less of a threat to Frannie in that form and also more vulnerable."

"This is pure insanity." Rage churns my insides into a raw, bleeding mass, and it's everything I can do to stay planted in this chair. I'm going to kill him. I don't care that he's a Dominion. I don't care that my power is gone. I'm going to find a way to kill him for this. "Even if Frannie could find His weakness, do you truly think you—one angel—could defeat Him?" My voice is tight as I fight not to snarl at him.

"This could work . . ." he muses. "Time . . . that's our only problem."

That's all I can take. The last straw.

I bound from the chair and grab him by the shirt, flinging him around and slamming him into the wall, where I clamp my hand around his throat. All this time, I've believed that he had Frannie's best interests at heart. That he would protect her. But instead, his plan was to use Frannie as bait in some misguided attempt to play the hero. Mage or no Mage, this never would have worked. I was a fool to trust anyone but myself.

"You have truly lost your mind," I spit in his face. "Time is not our problem. The Underworld is our problem. The legions of *Hell*!" I add with a punctuating slam of his back into the wall. "They will all be at our doorstep in a matter of seconds once He finds her."

Frannie's on her feet, pulling me off Gabriel. "What do you care? You're leaving anyway."

I turn and look into her eyes, hoping I'll find hatred, fury, disgust. But what I see instead as she gazes at me isn't even fear. It's sadness and despair.

I let go of Gabriel and, for the thousandth time, I second-guess myself. If the Mage has already found Frannie, is there time? Gabriel's right. We may be down to days. Hours, even.

It's only been a few days, but I can't help trying it out—testing to see if I can change. I focus on sloughing off my human form—letting my inner demon out . . . and nothing happens. I don't even sprout a horn.

Damn.

I need my infernal power if I'm going to be any use protecting her, but the change takes time. Even if it started today—now—it wouldn't happen fast enough.

Gabriel's eyes slide to me and narrow. "He's not going anywhere."

Frannie turns to him. "It might be better, Gabe. Is there somewhere else he could just hide out? Faith's, maybe?" she says with a glance toward me. "He'll be safer."

And, with those words, my gut flips. I thought I'd said enough to stop her from caring. Obviously, I was mistaken. This is my chance. It's not too late to undo what I've done and tell her how I really feel.

My mind reels, trying to decide what the right thing is.

The Mage has found her. There's not enough time for the change.

It's too late.

Gabriel shoves me away and steps to the door. "I'll talk to Faith," he says and disappears into the night as the door slams closed behind him.

Frannie sits back on the couch, her fingers woven through her tangled hair, staring at the floor.

"Frannie . . ." I start, but then I can't find words to undo what I've said.

Her eyes connect with mine, distant and empty. "He's gonna find me, maybe sooner than we'd thought. No matter where we go, He'll find me. I just want it over, one way or the other."

The resignation and exhaustion are clear in her voice. She's not going to be able to live like this for long—running, always looking over her shoulder. And seeing her like this, defeated, I know what I have to do.

FRANNIE

Luc sits next to me and keeps his eyes trained on his laced fingers. I don't like the look on his face—drawn and tormented. My insides ache just looking at him. After everything that's happened today, I can't do this with him.

I push myself to my feet and head toward my room before he can remind me how badly I've screwed everything up.

"Frannie . . . wait."

I can't read Luc's voice. It's hard, but not cruel the way it was earlier. There's an undercurrent of warmth. It's enough to make me turn around.

He's standing, but he hasn't moved from the couch. "Gabriel is going to get you killed. You can't seriously think his plan is going to work."

Fear kicks in my gut, but fades nearly as fast. I'm so tired of being scared. "Everybody dies."

His face twists and a soft groan escapes his throat. "No. I'm not going to let that happen."

Something snags my heart. "Luc . . . there's nothing you can do."

From the look on his face, you'd think I slapped him. He drops his chin to his shoulder and screws his face into a grimace, his hands balled at his sides, and I jump when a frustrated roar rips from his lungs. He spins and paces toward the front door, and I'm sure he's gonna leave . . . until he spins back and storms to where I'm standing. He wraps his arms around me and lifts me off my feet, pressing me hard against his body. His face is buried in the crook of my shoulder, and I feel his hot, uneven breath on my neck, sending a shiver skittering over my skin.

I loop my arms over his shoulders and stroke his hair, and we just stand here, Luc crushing me in a hug and me trying not to cry, for a very long time. Finally, he lowers me to the ground, his arms still tight around me, and gazes down into my eyes.

"I don't know how to do this," he finally says, his words clipped with frustration. "I'm totally useless. There's nothing I can do to help you."

I just look at him, not sure what to say. I don't want him

anywhere near this. If he believes he can't help, will he stay out of the fight?

Tension rolls through his body in a wave, his muscles tightening under my arms. "I can't stand by and watch while Gabriel gets you killed," he growls through clenched teeth.

"Then go. Please." I fight for control, but the hitch in my voice betrays me.

He sighs and dips his face into my hair. "I can't," he says, his voice as shaky as the sigh that preceded it. He pulls away and smooths the backs of his fingers slowly over my cheek, down my neck to my shoulder, where he rests his hand. "As a mortal—as this person," he says, bringing his other fist to his heart, "all I've ever been is part of you. As wrong as I know it is, I don't think I can live without you."

I open my mouth, but nothing comes out past the throbbing lump in my throat. He's going to have to live without me, but how can I tell him that? Despair blankets my heart and squeezes. Tears roll over my lashes onto my cheeks and Luc pulls me tighter. His uneven breath in my hair tells me he's fighting tears too. I squeeze my eyes hard to stop mine and pull back. "Luc—"

He holds up his hand and glances toward the door. "But I also know Gabriel is your best chance right now. I'll make him see this plan is crazy. We'll work something else out. Until then, you need his protection. I'll do whatever you need me to . . . whatever I can to protect you." His face darkens and his eyes shift to the door again. "I'll do anything."

I can't help feeling relieved when I understand that what he means by "anything" is that he'll stay here with Gabe and me. I know how hard that is for him.

I look up into his tortured obsidian eyes and see myself reflected there, the way I was when he loved me, before everything went so horribly wrong. For an instant, I let myself remember what it was to give myself to him completely—to tear down the walls and let him into my heart. I let myself remember the rush of the fall.

It was terrifying.

And amazing.

It was like he was the only one who ever knew the real me. I told him everything—things I'd never dared tell another living soul.

The whole ugly truth.

And he loved me anyway. Not because he had to, like Gabe, but because he wanted to.

I lift my hand to his face. My palm glides over the stubble on his cheek as my thumb traces his lips. He closes his eyes and sighs deeply.

When he pulls me close again, I let him. But only for a second. Because there's a war waging inside me. He just said everything I hoped he would. My heart should be soaring, but instead it's weeping. I ache to curl into his arms and pretend all of this away, to grab at this last chance for happiness.

But I can't.

It wouldn't be fair for a lot of reasons, the biggest being that I'm not gonna be alive at the end of this.

My heart throbs as I take his hand and lead him over to the couch, where we sit. I sink into the cushions and loll my head back. Something dark and ugly rolls through my insides and dread creeps into my heart. I close my eyes, pushing away my inner demons. I can't afford them. I have too many *real* demons to deal with. "I have no idea what's gonna happen now. I only know it isn't finished." I feel him push back into the cushions next to me and I lift my head to look at him. "Do you remember when I told you I thought I was meant for something?"

He looks at me, his gaze intense. His lips are parted just so, and I have the sudden aching need to kiss him. I take a deep breath and hold it for a second as he nods.

I look away before I lose it again. "Well, I feel it more now. It started like a pebble on my chest, but now it's growing into a boulder." I shake my head, knowing how stupid it sounds, but I feel it pressing in on me even as I say it. "A really big, sharp, nasty boulder that won't let me breathe. Something's coming. I don't know how I know, but—"

"No," he interrupts, "it doesn't matter how you know." He leans toward me and props his elbow on his knee, threading his fingers into mine. "If your gut is telling you something's coming, trust it."

I nod, suddenly knowing what I need to say. "So, I need your help."

Surprise flashes across his face, then his expression grows somber. "What do you need from me?"

This is hard, and all I can do is hope he understands. "I need your support, but I can't be . . . with you . . ." His eyes cloud and I quickly add, "*Either* of you . . . right now. I need to keep my head clear—to think. Which I can't do very well when we're . . . you know." Heat prickles my face at the memory of him pressed against me in his bed, the feel of his skin on mine, and I'm sure I'm beet red.

The hint of a wistful smile turns the corners of his lips and my heart feels suddenly lighter. I didn't realize how heavily all of this was weighing on me until just this second. But, if he understands . . . if we can at least be friends again . . .

And if I'm wrong, and at the end of this I'm actually still alive, maybe someday we can be more.

But not until I know for sure.

I shift closer to him on the couch and he looks up at me. He lifts his hand and smooths my tears away with the tips of his fingers.

"I love you." It's out of my mouth before I realize I mean to say it.

He closes his eyes and leans his forehead into mine, letting out a shaky breath.

"But I need to be on my own," I add, lower. "To figure things out."

His forehead shifts on mine, a nod. He pulls away and looks down at me, and there's the smallest of sad smiles on his face. "As you wish."

LUC

She pulls herself from my grasp, and, as much as it hurts, I force myself to let her go. "I'll get us something to eat," I say, standing from the couch. I head to the kitchen and make sandwiches, more for the distraction than out of any actual need for food, and then we eat at the table. We don't talk, but the whole time

Frannie keeps shooting glances my way—which I notice because I can't take my eyes off her.

When we get the dishes put away, she wipes down the counters as I ease into the couch and click on the TV. Surfing the channels, it becomes clear why I've never bothered with a TV before, and I punch it off, tossing the remote to the coffee table with a clatter.

I look at her as she settles into the couch next to me. "Make me want to turn that back on," I say.

Her face pulls into a puzzled squint. "What?"

I raise an eyebrow at her. "Your Sway. You need to practice." I feel a smile tick at my mouth. "Guinea pig at your service."

She nods, then stares at me intently. But what I feel isn't a compulsion to pick up the remote. What I feel is an overpowering need to stroke her face—to kiss her. I pull a shaky breath, and she notices.

The look on her face is all the confirmation I need that I wasn't crazy. She wanted that as much as I did. I buzz all over with my need to scoop her into my arms and carry her into the bedroom. But what she said earlier is true. This isn't the right time.

Her eyes drop to her hands. "Sorry."

"I'm not," I answer and offer up a reassuring smile.

"I really suck at this." She doesn't look up as she says it.

"You know your Sway is strongest when it comes from your heart. For now, while you're learning, if you tie what you need to have happen to something you care about, it will be easier."

"Or someone?" Her eyes lift to mine and a shudder sweeps through me.

I nod. "Or someone."

"I think you're right. When it worked on that little boy on the beach earlier, I was thinking of my sisters."

"It comes from here," I say, lifting my hand and laying my fingertips over her heart. "If you remember that, you'll be fine."

She reaches up and grasps my hand, holding my eyes with hers. "Do you think I can do what Gabe wants me to?"

I've thought about that. As crazy as Gabriel's plan is, with a little more practice, I think Frannie could probably pull off her end of it. But there's no way Gabriel will be able to destroy Lucifer. He'll fail utterly and get Frannie killed in the process. "I think you can do anything you set your heart to."

She swallows hard and nods before dropping my hand. She pulls a deep breath and stands. "I just need some time . . ."

But time is the one thing I'm fairly certain we don't have. I gain my feet and look down into her eyes, praying sincerely to God to help me see my role—how I can help her.

Something in her expression changes—loosens. But just as she opens her mouth to say something, the front door swings open and Gabriel strides through, Faith's arm in his tight grasp and a scowl on his face.

Faith looks freshly showered, her hair still damp and dangling around her shoulders. She offers a strained smile when she sees us.

"Luc is going to stay at Faith's," Gabriel announces.

"Oh . . . um . . ." Frannie trails off and splits a tentative glance between Faith and me.

I fight the smile I feel pulling at my mouth, but I'm not entirely successful as I catch Frannie's eye. "Thanks for the offer, Faith, but that won't be necessary."

"Explain," Gabriel presses, shooting me a glare.

I shrug and my smile widens. "Love conquers all?"

Frannie bursts out a nervous laugh, and Gabriel's eyes shift between us, assessing. "This is what you want, Frannie?"

Her gaze grows concerned as it falls on me. "Maybe you should—" she starts, but I stop her with my best "don't even think about it" stare.

Gabriel rolls his eyes and settles into the seat on the couch that I just vacated. "You two need to make up your mind whether you love each other or hate each other." He doesn't even try to hide the venom in his words as he glares at me.

Faith settles into the couch next to Gabriel. It's clear from the look on her face that she's totally uncomfortable in the middle of this. "Um . . . thanks for the run, Luc. It was great to have someone to push me."

I nod and pull a chair over from the kitchen table as Frannie drops into the armchair under the window.

Gabriel settles back into the cushions. "Since the Luc thing," he says with a punctuating glare in my direction, "seems to be settled, Faith needs to give you the rundown."

Frannie quirks a quizzical frown at him. "What rundown?"

"Just about the people around here, so you'll know if anything is . . . off," Faith answers.

She proceeds to give Frannie the lowdown on everyone who lives within a half mile. Finally she starts winding down. "Oh! And old man Butler, third house on the right," she says, pointing down the beach, "is a stealth groper. He'll pretend to help you pick up your beach bag, or your towel or something, and cop a feel in the process." Her face pinches. "I'll point him out to you. Stay far away."

By the time Faith is convinced that Frannie won't be taken by surprise by Mr. Butler, or any other of the neighbors, we decide to call for pizza.

"Jerry, the pizza guy." Faith says low in Frannie's ear as he approaches the door, "got his last two girlfriends pregnant. Also stay away."

"So . . . yeah." Frannie says, her face screwing up with disgust.

We slide into seats around the table and demolish two large pizzas. "Now's the perfect time to practice," Gabriel says to Frannie as we're finishing up.

Frannie goes a little pale. "My Sway?"

Out of the corner of my eye, I see Faith's eyes widen.

Gabriel nods. "Start small."

She shrugs. "Like what?"

"Use your imagination," he says, leaning back in his chair and lacing his fingers behind his head.

Frannie's eyes fall on me and narrow slightly with effort . . . and I discover I'm suddenly craving another piece of pizza, even though I just polished off most of a pie on my own.

She smiles when I pluck a slice from the box and bite off a hunk. I smile back once I've swallowed, even though I'm fairly certain I'm going to explode.

Faith and I suddenly feel the overwhelming urge to wash the dishes, so we do. And when we've finished, I find myself in the Jeep on the way to the ice cream shop.

When I return with a quart of mocha java lava, which I don't even like, it's dark. We scoop ice cream onto cones and head out to the beach, where we sit in silence and eat, watching the moonlight shimmer over the rolling waves.

Finally, Frannie stands. "I think I'm gonna crash. All this making Luc get ice cream has worn me out," she adds with a playful jab of her toes into my side.

I pull myself out of the sand and head inside with her, leaving Faith and Gabriel on the beach talking strategy.

She heads to the bathroom, and I cross the room to the kitchen, where I pour myself the last half-cup of coffee from the pot.

When she emerges five minutes later, her face is shiny and pink and her thick, sandy blond waves fall around her shoulders and down her back. She pauses at her bedroom door, then slowly turns to look at me where I'm still leaning against the counter near the sink. "Night."

I push away from the counter, wanting to go to her. I don't know if the compulsion is her Sway or just my need, but, either way, I fight it. "Good night."

She takes a step toward me and my insides flip, but then she hesitates. "Thanks for understanding."

I nod once, afraid to open my mouth. I do understand. I understand everything—what's at stake, why she can't be with me—probably better than she does. But that doesn't make it any easier. I root my feet to the floor to keep from going to her, but then Frannie moves slowly toward me and curls into my arms, sending my heart racing. She stretches onto her tiptoes, her face tipped up to mine, and I hold my breath as I lean down and kiss her.

There aren't words to describe the sensations rushing through me with her kiss. Her lips move on mine, tentatively at first, but when she presses deeper into me, all my insides explode in a burst of bliss. She draws me closer and it's everything I can do not to sweep her into my arms and love her properly. Finally, she pulls away. I close my eyes and we stand with our foreheads pressed together. Neither of us move for a long minute, but, finally, I hear her start to breathe again.

"When I get everything figured out . . ." she starts.

I want the end of that thought to be, "then we can be together," but I know the reason she trailed off is because even she doesn't know what the end of the thought is.

I loop my arms gently around her waist and pull her to my chest. I lean my face into her hair, living in this moment and hoping it won't end. But then the front door opens and Gabriel steps through.

Frannie pulls away and her whole face changes. She squeezes my hand. "See you in the morning."

"Good night," I say again as she disappears behind her door.

Gabriel stares me down, but I'm way too tired for this. I spin and head to my room, away from his inquiring gaze. Because even if I wanted to, I wouldn't know how to answer the question in his eyes.

8

✠

The Evil Eye

FRANNIE

I'm gasping for air, but I can't get a full breath. 'Cause his lips, so hot, are burning into mine. His hands are on me, but he's being careful to stay away from the most sensitive spots.

Too careful.

I take his hand and guide it under my shirt. I feel him smile into my lips as his fingers inch toward their target, and a deep, throbbing ache explodes through me.

Delanie will never believe this!

Delanie?

The thought shakes me from my restless sleep. And, just for a heartbeat, I see it. Bloodred eyes set in a pitch-black face.

I'm panting for breath as my eyes snap open. I stare at the ceiling and replay the scene in my head. I've had lots of dreams about Luc that left me totally breathless, but this was different. *Real*, my mind screams at me.

I roll on my side and choke on my own spit as I gasp. In the shadows near the door, a shape looms, darker against the dark of the room, black wings spread, a menacing smile on his otherwise angelic face.

Matt.

This time I'm sure of it.

Until I sit and look harder.

At nothing.

Moonlight shimmers over the wall, and what I thought were big black wings are nothing but shadow. There's nothing there.

I lay back on the pillow, my heart pounding. It's a long second before I can breathe again. Finally, I glance at the clock. Four. Too early to get up. I drag myself off the bed and move to the window, staring out over the rolling waves at the pale horizon of a day preparing to dawn. Slowly, my shaking stops. These nightmares and hallucinations have to stop or I'll go crazy.

Or maybe I'm already there.

What was that dream?

Maggie?

I was Maggie. Whether that was her dream, or I was seeing something real, I have no idea.

The Mage.

Luc said he'd show me things in my dreams. Why is he showing me Maggie? Especially Maggie doing *that*—making out with some boy?

I feel totally disgusting, like some kind of voyeur. But my

little sister doesn't even have a boyfriend. So what the hell was that I just saw?

No. It wasn't the Mage. I just miss my family, so I'm dreaming about them. That's all.

I rub my eyes and try to clear the fuzz from my head, then stand here listening to the silent house and the crash of the waves on the shore. I move to the middle of the room and close my eyes. I draw a deep cleansing breath and center myself.

I sorta dropped judo after Taylor died. I sorta dropped everything, really. As I start moving through my judo routine, I'm not sure what to expect. At first, it feels a little like trying to reconnect with an old friend—distant and awkward. But after a few minutes I sink effortlessly into the moves, and a serenity I haven't felt in a while settles over me.

Focus.

Balance.

Breathe.

I close my eyes and let my body go with the motion. Muscle memory takes over and my mind shuts down. I don't want to think. I breathe slow and deep with each shifting position, and it helps me feel almost normal again.

Almost.

When I'm done, I push my window all the way open and lean on the sill, staring up at the last of the constellations in the brightening sky, and breathing in the salt air. But just as I turn back to the room, I catch movement in the dark window of Faith's house. The curtains blow back in the breeze, and I see her there in the pink light of the dawning day, watching.

I'm in a goddamn goldfish bowl.

My judo-induced serenity is gone. I breathe a long, weary sigh and slump into the window frame.

The hum starts so softly that, at first, I don't distinguish it from the sound of the waves. But when I realize what I'm hearing, I turn slowly back to the room. He's standing there, silhouetted in the dark. For just an instant, I can't understand how Gabe got in here without me hearing. But it only takes a second, as I stare at him in the thin light, to realize it's not Gabe.

It's a beautiful boy with green eyes.

A boy I've seen before.

He looks young—my age—except for his eyes, which look very old . . . and sad, like he's carrying the weight of the world. My heart aches as those sad eyes lock on mine and he takes a hesitant step forward. He's still humming as he stops an arm's length from me and stands there, gazing down at me as though looking for something he's lost. And it's then that I realize I'm humming along.

When he holds out his hand, there's a ripple, like sun off asphalt, as his form starts to waver and shimmer. I reach up to take the proffered hand, but my fingers slip through air.

Nothing there.

Yet, I can see him, standing not two feet away. It's only when I'm this close that I realize how tall he is. And it's hard to miss how muscular he is, 'cause he's wearing nothing but a pair of faded jeans—same as when we were on the beach. His long sun-gold hair falls nearly to his shoulders, framing a strong, proud face. But, as amazing as his face and body are, it's the beautiful white wings—three pair—that spread from his back and the way his golden skin contrasts with them that holds my attention. Staring at him, everything else seems to fade away. Time and space are meaningless.

His expression is soft and his eyes bright as he reaches up and drops a thin leather strap around my neck. I feel the weight of an object thump against my chest, but I can't take my eyes off the boy long enough to see what it is.

I'm not scared.

Logic says I should be. After all, there's some creepy demon thing living in my dreams, and now the boy from my dreams is standing here, in my room. But this isn't a dream, and I can't find fear anywhere in me. I feel nothing but peace.

He stops humming and stares at me for a long moment. "I've found you," he finally says, his voice a soft, musical echo. He lifts a hand and his touch feels as insubstantial as the brush of butterfly wings when his fingers trace the leather strap along my collarbone.

I don't dare move. I don't even breathe. I don't want to break the spell.

He smiles down at me and I feel my heart breathe a sigh. "We'll be together. I promise."

And then he's gone.

"No! Come back!" I gasp, my hands swiping at the air in front of me.

My surroundings come back into focus then. I'm in my room. In the cottage. In the dark.

Alone.

GABE

I sit on the sofa. And sit. And sit. Then shift and sit some more. I pull myself off the sofa and pace, closer and closer to Frannie's door. Finally, I knock. "Frannie?"

I push the door open and stick my head through, expecting to find her asleep, but instead, she's standing next to her bed, out of breath and flushed.

"Are you okay?" I ask, my heart hammering.

When she sees me she tries to smile, but it's strained. "Yeah, just a dream," she answers as if trying to convince herself. Her eyes lift to me and widen a little. "All of it," she says. "Just a dream."

"Can I come in?" I try to keep my voice calm, but something in her expression is scaring me.

Her eyes are still a little wide when she nods and I push through the door, closing it behind me. I move through the room to the open window and look out at the ocean, scanning the surrounding beach. "You're sure you're okay?"

I look back at her as she lowers herself onto the bed. I move to the edge and sit next to her. "Tell me about your dream."

That gets a nervous smile out of her. "Can't you just pick it out of my head?" she asks with feigned nonchalance.

The look in her eye tells me that she *really* doesn't want me to. Which makes me *really* want to.

"I'm trying to be a good boy. I won't pillage. But if you wanted to offer it up . . ."

Pink creeps into her cheeks as her hand gravitates to something hanging from a strap around her neck. "It was nothing . . . in a sorta embarrassing way."

I sit and brush the hair off her face with my fingers. There's pressure in my chest as my heart speeds up. As wrong as I know it is, I can't help hoping her dream was about me.

I shake my head. *Quite the Dominion.*

"It wasn't the Mage?"

She shrugs. "I don't know for sure. I don't remember seeing him this time."

"What *did* you see?" I press.

She blushes. "Maggie . . . and a boy."

I consider that for a moment. "It could be the Mage showing you something he wants you to see."

"I thought of that. But why would he show me Maggie making out with some boy?"

"I don't know." Still, something doesn't feel right. I pat the bed between us. "Do you mind if I stay here for the rest of the night?"

She breathes deep. "If you must."

"I must." I reach out and squeeze her hand. "You might talk in your sleep and accidentally divulge all your deep, dark secrets."

She yanks her hand away and smacks me across the shoulder. "Just for that, you can sleep on the floor. With earplugs." She shoves me, but when I start to push off the bed, she grabs my hand and slides over, pulling me in next to her.

I tell myself it's my sense of duty that won't let me stay away, but as I sit here, staring at Frannie—the soft light of dawn dancing over her features—I know it's more. My heart thrums.

She rolls over, her back to me, and I lie down with some space between us. I stroke her hair, resisting the urge to tuck up tight behind her and bury my face in it. I breathe her in, drawing energy from the connection.

"Gabe?"

"Huh?"

There's nothing for a long minute, then she says, "Thanks."

"Go to sleep."

"'Kay."

Her voice is thick with sleep a few minutes later when she says, "Gabe?"

"Yes."

She rolls on her back without opening her eyes. "I'm sorry."

"Go to sleep," I whisper again.

"'Kay."

Her breathing slows and she twitches and jerks as her memories assault her in her dreams. But for the moment, those are the only demons I detect. Finally, when her sleep seems more peaceful, I focus on the pink streaks of a dawning day streaming through the window, then close my eyes and give myself up to the Light.

But not before brushing my lips gently across hers.

For a moment, nothing happens, but then the raw, stinging burn is almost unbearable as it sears through me. I clutch myself and cry out as I shift into the Collective.

My eyes open to a smirking Aaron.

He takes a slow lap around me, down on one knee, then raises his eyebrows. "Are you injured?"

I stand and straighten up as the pain passes, then I look him in the eye. Aaron is the last celestial I need digging into my personal business. "I'm fine. It's nothing."

"You're sure? Because you look a little . . . green." His eyes narrow suspiciously. "Are you developing motion sickness?"

Among other things.

"I'm fine," I repeat, turning to the Board and looking it over. "What's Daniel's status?"

Aaron presses into the post that materializes at his shoulder, his arms folded tightly across his chest. "You're lucky I'm feeling charitable. I'd let you burn on this one just to prove a point, but sacrificing all of humanity seems a bit extreme."

I'm able to keep my groan internal as I drop back into a chair and rest my throbbing head in my hand. "What did you find out?"

I don't need to look at him to hear the derision in his voice. "What's wrong, oh omnipotent one? Too much pressure? Job too big for you?"

I lift my head and stare him down. "What did you find out?" I repeat in syllables.

He shrugs off the post and it disappears. "Marchosias has only made casual contact with the family, but he's using his usual tactics."

"Which are . . . ?"

His expression is pure condescension as he looks down his nose at me. "Where have you been all these millennia? Under a rock?" He smiles, cold and sharp. "No. That would be the company you're keeping. I think the demon's rubbing off on you, Gabriel. You're looking a little ragged around the edges."

I haul myself out of the chair, not wanting to think about what I have in common with Luc, and step up within a foot of him. "Is there any chance of getting a straight answer out of you?"

He leans in, his face inches from mine. "Is there any chance of getting someone competent in your job?" He puffs out his chest as he steps back.

"The path you're treading has been trod before," I say, struggling to keep my voice even. "And it didn't work out so well for Him. Pride is a dangerous thing, Aaron." I drop back into the chair. "Marchosias?" I bark, fed up. An unintended wave of power erupts from me with the word, knocking Aaron back a step.

He fights for balance and, when he has it, he looks down at me, eyes wide. "He's been following the youngest two."

I bound from the chair. My aching body protests, but I swallow the groan. "Grace and Maggie?" Frannie would never forgive me if anything happened to her younger sisters. "What is their status?"

The surprise clears from his face and is replaced with ubiquitous contempt. "Grace knows what he is, of course, so she's shied away from him, but Maggie is intrigued. Apparently, she harbors some feelings for her older sister's . . ." his face twists with disgust, ". . . friend, and thinks Marchosias bears some resemblance, which, obviously, he does. So how would you like to handle this, oh great one?"

"You know why I sent you in the first place. I need someone with your experience to protect that family. I want you on Maggie."

"Already done," he says.

I cut him a hard look. "Despite what you think of me, you know how important this is, and I trust that you won't let our . . . history . . . interfere with your doing your job."

"I don't need any coaching from you on how to do my job," he jabs. "I've been doing it longer than you've existed."

"Then go do it," I say, wearily, hoping he doesn't notice.

He glares me a dagger as he fades out. I just stand here for a long moment trying to get myself together and steel myself for the shift back to Frannie.

I can't fully contain the groan as I slide back into corporeal form and grasp Frannie to me. She stirs and I loosen my grip and kiss her forehead.

She's flushed and clammy, her face twisted in pain with some image or memory.

I stroke her hair and let my peace wash over her. But I've noticed it doesn't seem as effective as it used to be, because she continues to twitch, then lets out a groan and her eyes flutter open.

"Gabe," she rasps and reaches for me.

"I'm here, Frannie."

She pulls me closer and I hold her as she shakes. Her breathing becomes deeper, slower, and her breath on my neck is driving me insane.

I fight the feeling. I know what it is, but it's only recently that I've allowed myself to acknowledge it. But when she burrows tighter into me, and I feel her body—so close—I give in to it and press myself closer. I rub her back and the contented moan that purrs up from her chest drives me to want her more.

She settles deeper into me, mostly asleep, and I distract myself by turning my mind to what our next step is. I need to know Lucifer's weakness, and Frannie's the only one who can get that information. We need to hone her Sway, fine-tune it and sharpen it to a point. And we don't have long to do it.

I'm wrenched from my thoughts as Frannie's hand glides up my chest. I breathe back the wave of desire.

Think, Gabriel.

"My angel," Frannie whispers, and when I look into her face, her eyes are still closed, but she's smiling.

I trace my finger over the lines of her jaw. "I'm here."

Her lips are on mine before I have time to pull away. Soft. Warm.

Everything inside me explodes. My breathing is rapid and irregular as I struggle for oxygen. My head swims with the sensation of my need. Her hands are on me, burning me with the intensity of her touch.

Father above. Help me.

If He hears me, He doesn't answer, because the only thing I feel stir inside of me is insatiable earthly desire. I deepen our kiss as her fingers trace a burning path over my back, lifting my T-shirt as they go. I yank it off, then let my hands wander over her body, every stroke taking me deeper into the maelstrom of my own self-destruction.

But it's beyond my control now.

This was inevitable. I was foolish to think I could stop it.

Our lips part for a moment and I stare down at her. I lift my hand and trail a finger down her cheek, her neck, taking it all in. She shudders and I have just enough time to think to myself: *If this is the end of me, so be it.*

And then I notice it.

With every rise and fall of her chest, it glints in the pink light slanting through the open window. A darkened metal pendant on a thin leather lash, resting on her chest, next to Luc's crucifix.

I lift my head to get a closer look and feel the press of cold dread on my chest. It's a symbol I've seen only a few times since my creation. An Udjat. Not the Egyptian adaptation that satanic cults flaunt, but the true Udjat—a spiral eye. The mark of Lucifer Himself.

I grab it, meaning to rip it from her neck, but it scorches my hand and I pull away. The scent of burnt flesh hangs in the air as I shake her. "Frannie!"

She opens her eyes with a gasp and springs to a sit. "What . . . ?" she says, her expression a mask of shock.

"Where did you get that?" I say, pushing up onto an elbow.

"What?"

"The pendant around your neck—where did you get it?"

She grasps the crucifix. "Luc," she says, confused.

"No. The other one."

Her hand gravitates to the Udjat and her eyes widen slightly as something registers. "A boy," she says, her brow creased. She shakes her head. "I don't know. I had a dream and when I woke up, it was there." She lays back into the pillows and scans my bare chest with her eyes, full of trepidation.

I tuck the sheets around her. "I need to know about this dream."

"I . . . it was just what I said," she says. "I was Maggie—or in her head, at least."

"What else?"

"I don't know . . . maybe the Mage was there . . . and then

there was a boy." She shakes her head again. "I don't know." It's almost a plea. But then her eyes lower from mine, and she shudders again as she lifts a hand and lays it over my thrumming heart. "What happened, Gabe? Just now—with us?"

LUC

Gabriel's not on the couch when I emerge from my room, and I only need one guess as to where he is. I'm staring into the depths of a cold cup of coffee half an hour later when Frannie's bedroom door cracks open and Gabriel slips through into the family room. In the bright morning light streaming through the living room windows, I take in his bedhead and rumpled clothes. A part of me can't help feeling relieved that they look slept in—which means he probably didn't take them off.

"You're even starting to *act* human. You didn't need to use the door," I say with a tip of my head toward Frannie's room.

He glances up at me and shrugs, but there's guilt painted all over his face, making him appear far less than angelic—and making my blood boil. Rage rips through me like a shotgun blast at the thought of him in there with her—in her bed, where I'm not welcome anymore.

"I think you're enjoying your bedroom privileges a little too much, cherub," I spit. "Wouldn't be taking advantage of the situation, would you? I'd hate to think of the consequences. They're not pretty." I've seen them firsthand—Matt's wings being ripped from his body by the avengers is an image I'll never be able to forget.

He looks away and I know I've hit a nerve, making me wonder just what *is* going on behind that closed door at night. She told me she couldn't be with either of us, and I believe she meant it. But Gabriel has resources—ways of influencing her. Just as I once did. If he decided to cheat, she wouldn't stand a snowball's chance in Hell.

He makes his way to a kitchen chair where he sits. "We have a problem," he says, studying his bare foot where it presses into the leg of the table.

"Only one?" I join him at the table, sliding into the chair opposite him, and glower at him, drumming my fingers on the wooden tabletop.

His eyes lift to mine. "No."

"Okay. So give me the list."

In answer, he swings something onto the table by a strap. A heavily tarnished metal pendant.

It takes me a second to register what I'm seeing, then the chair topples over as I spring from it. "Sweet sin of Satan. Where did that come from?"

His eyes narrow almost imperceptibly as he shakes his head. "She doesn't remember. Something about a boy and a dream." He looks up at me. "Could the Mage have given it to her?"

I shake my head. "Mages don't have corporeal form. They can't exist that way in the physical world, so they can't carry anything solid."

"So, if it wasn't the Mage . . ." he looks at me through eyes full of trepidation, ". . . He's found her."

"But if He's only found her through the Mage, He may not

have seen enough to figure out where we are." I want this to be true, but the hope in my voice rings hollow.

Gabriel fixes me in a hard stare. "Even so, it's only a matter of time. Days at best. Maybe hours. If I'm going to have any shot at destroying Him, it has to be now, when it's just Him in this form—before He sends His legions."

Dread sits like a burning stone in my gut as I right the chair and slide back into it. "So this is it."

He nods gravely.

"Will she be ready?"

He just stares at me.

I glance toward Frannie's door and bound to my feet again when I hear her scream.

9

✝

Hell's Angel

FRANNIE

I pull on my jeans under my Hendrix T-shirt, thinking about what happened with Gabe. I remember every bit of it, but in my mind, it wasn't Gabe I was kissing. It was Luc. It was the strangest dream. He was still Luc, but lighter. An angel.

I felt too ashamed to tell Gabe, though, so I just apologized, like that's gonna fix anything.

A shiver ripples over my skin at the memory of his body against mine, his breath in my hair . . . but I turn off my mind and toss out the thought. 'Cause it can't happen again. There's nowhere in the world that feels as safe as Gabe's arms, and now I'm afraid I've ruined it.

I stand and move to the window. Pushing it all the way open, I lean out into the damp morning air and breathe deep.

I am so totally losing it.

I shift my hip onto the sill and just sit here, afraid to follow Gabe into the family room, not sure what to say to him. I look across the way and see Faith has gone from the window. For an instant it occurs to me that I don't know if Grigori need to sleep. It's not something I ever thought to ask my dad.

I pull myself off the sill and close the window behind me, but I'm not halfway across the room when there's a loud tap—or more of a scratch, like fingernails on a blackboard. I turn and scowl out the window, expecting Faith . . .

And scream when it's Matt that I see standing there. Solid. Real. Black wings tucked neatly behind his back.

An instant later, there's a crash of the door against the wall, and Gabe and Luc are standing inside the opening to my room, both wild-eyed and breathless.

I spin back to my window and find nothing but beach. Where I was sure Matt was standing a second ago, there's nothing.

Am I losing my mind?

Gabe rushes to me, but Luc holds back, hanging in the doorway. His gaze falls on my shocked face, and I see the question in his eyes. He doesn't miss anything. That's the one thing I can always count on.

Gabe guides me to the armchair in the opposite corner of the room, where he kneels in front of me, cautious not to touch me. "What happened?"

"Nothing. I just thought I saw someone outside my window."

Luc moves to the window and peers out.

"Who?" Gabe asks.

That's a question I'm not prepared to answer. Partly 'cause, if it was truly Matt I saw, that scares the snot out of me. But, if it wasn't, that's almost as scary. "It was no one. Just a shadow or something."

It's obvious Gabe doesn't believe me. Luc looks back over his shoulder at me as he stands in the window and I can't read his expression. Does he know?

"Matt," I say, lowering my eyes. "I think I saw Matt."

GABE

My heart stalls in my chest. "Was it a dream? Did you see the Mage?"

She scowls at me. "No, Gabe. I'm wide awake."

With a glance out the window, I grab her hand and pull her to the family room, sitting her on the couch. "Tell me everything."

"I have," she says, exasperated. "I looked out the window and thought I saw Matt standing on the dune. When I looked again, he wasn't there. That's it."

I'd believe her, but she looks as if she's trying to convince herself. And, with the Udjat showing up out of nowhere . . . "Frannie, I need to . . ."

Mercifully, she nods, so I'm not forced to finish the thought. I overstepped physically already this morning, and now I'm asking to do the same thing mentally.

But I need to know.

I slip into Frannie's thoughts, and under the pervading confusion and fear, there are images. I understand her confusion when the image of Matt surfaces—ethereal, without substance—

floating over the dune. From just her memory, it's hard to tell if he was really there at all.

Behind that image, others start to surface. There's something shadowy, just at the edge of perception—the Mage, maybe? Then the Udjat, without a sense of where it came from.

And then *me*.

The image of me in her arms is strong and laced with conflicting emotion: shame, love, guilt, and the strongest: desire. Heat prickles up my neck to my face as my own desires flare at the memory.

Desires of the flesh are a tricky thing, I'm discovering. Once they wax, it's hard to make them wane.

"Push me out," I say to Frannie.

"What?"

"Push me out of your thoughts. You need to learn how."

I wait, and feel her train of thought shift to me, here on the couch, right now. But it's only a second before it slips back to us, in her bed.

"Try harder, Frannie. Focus on grounding yourself," I say. "Clear your emotions and feel your physical body."

This doesn't help. Her thoughts *do* shift to a physical body. Mine.

I can almost feel her hands gliding over my skin. My heart throbs painfully in my chest and my breathing is erratic.

I snap myself from her thoughts just as the front door slams. I look around the room and Luc is gone. Through the window, I see him stride to the edge of the water and stand, staring out over the waves, with his hands laced over his head.

"I'm sorry," she says, rubbing her red face with her hand, too embarrassed to even look at me.

"It's going to take some practice, but we're short on time. Lucifer has found you, Frannie. He may not know exactly where you are yet." I shake my head. "Or maybe He does. Maybe that's why Matt's here. I don't know. All I know for sure is that He's in your head."

"He's not in my head, Gabe," she says, and there's a defensive edge to her words. "I remember what He looks like . . . what He *feels* like," she adds with a shudder. "If He was in my dreams, I'd know it."

I pin her in my gaze. "Then how do you explain the Udjat?"

"The what?"

"The pendant."

At the mention of the pendant, her face changes—hardens. "It didn't come from Lucifer, if that's what you're thinking."

"Frannie . . ."

Her jaw grinds and she folds her arms tightly across her chest. "Seriously, Gabe," she says, looking like she wants to slap me. "I've been in the same room as Lucifer. He's touched me. I know what He is."

I sink deeper into the couch and scrutinize her. "Either way, I need something from you. If this plan is going to work, I need to know His vulnerabilities. When Lucifer shows up in your dreams, I need you to find His weakness."

"Weakness?" she asks. "Does He have one?"

My insides clench into a tight ball. "Everything depends on it."

"So what do I do? How am I going to find it?"

"First, you need to learn to block Him from your mind. You won't be safe until you do. He can do the same thing you can. He can influence people to do things they might not do otherwise. If you let Him into your mind, there's no telling what He could convince you of."

"So I block Him. Then what? How am I gonna know what His weakness is?"

I feel sick at the thought of Lucifer anywhere near Frannie. But I dig deep and remind myself that this is the only way. She's a soldier. "You're going to have to get Him to tell you."

She turns white. "Why would He tell me?"

"That's where your Sway comes in. You're going to have to master it. In the battle of wills, you're going to have to be stronger than Him."

"Okay," she says, taking a deep breath, steeling herself. "Try to get into my head again."

I nod, then let myself slip back into her thoughts.

Her fear is still there, but there's also a sense of determination. I press deeper and the images are fuzzy, no one specific thought springing to the forefront.

"Better," I say.

But at my voice, her thoughts slip back to this morning. A shudder runs through me and I pull out of her mind before she takes me there again.

The front door snaps open and Luc steps through, sand stuck to his bare feet. Frannie looks up at him, her eyes pleading, and my heart contracts.

She loves Luc. I can see it clearly on her face every time she looks at him. And he loves her—so much that he's rejected everything he's ever known to be with her. I know that her feelings for me aren't the same. What we share is different—more seated in necessity than love. She wants me for how I make her feel, not because she loves me. I have to get myself under control—remember my place.

But it's so hard not to love her . . . or hate him.

10

✦

Harbinger

FRANNIE

Luc strides across the room with only a cursory glance in our direction. His eyes scan the table before he looks at Gabe. "Let me see the Udjat. There's a way I can tell if it's one of His originals."

"It's there," Gabe answers, jutting his chin in Luc's direction.

"It's not," Luc says, alarm in his expression.

And I can feel his alarm pulling at my chest, a raw, sucking feeling bordering on panic. When Gabe mentioned the pendant, for a split second, a piece of me hated him for taking it from me.

That same piece wants it back.

Gabe stands and crosses to the table with a sense of urgency. "I didn't touch it." He looks up at Luc with wide eyes. "I can't."

My heart kicks as I realize, just at that instant, that I can feel the weight of it in my pocket, pressing against my thigh. My pulse pounds in my temples as I try to make sense of this.

Luc and Gabe exchange a wary glance and I feel goose bumps prick my skin.

"It seemed solid, though I couldn't actually touch it. But the strap was leather. Could it just vanish?" Gabe asks.

Luc's head shakes pensively. "Maybe . . . if He called it back." He rubs his chin, still thinking. Then he turns to me. "Where did it come from, Frannie?" His voice is insistent, and I can't look at him, because I know now. With it on me, in my possession, I can see him—the boy who gave it to me.

"I don't know," I lie.

"Keep me out," Gabe says, and I know this is more than a training exercise. He knows I'm lying and he wants an excuse to go in looking for my green-eyed angel.

But I'm not ready to share him.

I feel Gabe rooting through my head and I try to do what he said: focus on my body, the physical world. I imagine a wall in my mind, rough, dark stone with a thick iron core, rising high, surrounding me and protecting me.

After a minute, he sighs. "That was better," he says, and I'm instantly relieved. But then I catch the edge to his words as he adds, "But that wall looked a little too familiar."

Both his gaze and his voice are hard and I don't know what to think.

"What do you mean?" I ask cautiously.

He turns his sharp gaze on Luc. "She's using the Walls of Hell to defend her mind."

The only sound in the silence that follows is the beginnings of a summer shower, tapping on the roof—then a knock at the front door. And that's when I remember Faith.

I leap from the couch, thankful for the interruption. "That's Faith." I run to my room as Gabe moves to the door. "Tell her I'll be ready in a second."

I duck into my room and stand with my back against the door for a minute, trying to catch my breath. When I can think, I rifle through my stuff and pull out my warm-ups. Not perfect for judo, but I didn't bring my workout stuff. I tie my hair back into a knot and wrap a ponytail holder over it. When I come out of my room, Faith is standing in the family room with Gabe.

". . . not letting her out of my sight," Gabe finishes, his voice raised.

"You said I could go, Gabe," I say, trying to forget the only reason he said it in the first place was 'cause I accidentally Swayed him.

"He can only find her while she's sleeping, right? I can guarantee you she won't be sleeping." Faith shoots a smirk at me. "It's impossible to sleep when you're getting your butt kicked."

"Dream on," I say, feeling lighter already.

"She needs this. Let her go." Luc's voice comes from the table, where he's leaning, his arms crossed over his chest.

Gabe looks me over, then Faith. "Fine. I'll come with you," he says.

Faith lifts her eyebrow at Gabe in a challenge, as one corner of her mouth pulls into an amused smile. "You go, you better be ready to fight."

He leans onto the back of a chair and folds his arms, and I can tell he's not giving in.

So I do it again.

It will be fine. I push the thought with my mind and watch Gabe's face.

"You can work out on the beach," he says, demonstrating just how useless my Sway is when I'm trying to use it on purpose.

"She needs a real workout," Faith argues.

Let me go. I'll be fine, I push again.

Gabe looks hard at me for a long minute, fighting some internal battle. "One hour," he finally concedes. "But any sign of Lucifer's crew and you're out of there."

Faith gives me a knuckle-bump.

"Kick some ass," Luc says, pushing away from the table.

A smile tugs at his lips and my heart flutters, remembering our judo lessons and where they usually led. I almost ask him if he wants to come, wanting the excuse to touch him, but decide that would probably be a bad idea. "Okay. See you later."

He smiles at me again and nods once.

"Be safe," Gabe says as I collect Faith on the way out the door. "And drive carefully!" he calls after us as the door slams.

LUC

I watch her go as Gabriel blinks at the door then looks at me.

I move to the window and watch after Frannie and Faith as they pull out. "Her Sway is getting stronger."

I hear his sigh. "A double-edged sword."

I bark out a laugh. "Be careful what you wish for."

When I turn back to face him, his expression is strained. "Tell me more about the Udjat. How does it work?" he says.

Acid churns in my gut at the thought of Frannie with an Udjat. "Lucifer forged six Udjat in the Lake of Fire, one for Himself and one for each of the five archangels who fell with Him. Each one is bound to its owner. Once in its owner's possession, if lost or removed, it will always return." I walk to the kitchen and lower myself into a chair. "The story goes, Lucifer did it to reward the archangels' loyalty by enhancing their power." I can't stop the mirthless laugh that escapes my chest "But He's a control freak. I think He did it to keep them in line—to control them. He didn't create the archangels, after all, so they missed out on His special loyalty perks programming."

"So, if He brought it through the Shadowlands, then it's able to cross planes," Gabriel says. "If He called it back, it's possible that it could have, what . . . grown legs?"

I lean into the table. "Each Udjat contains a sliver of His essence. They're alive, for all practical purposes."

He drops into a chair across from me, head in hands, thinking.

"You can't be serious about using her to lure Lucifer here."

He jerks his head up and glares. "I'm dead serious."

"I'm not going to let you do that." I want to rip him out of the chair and shake some sense into him, but seeing as the cherub has had issues controlling his temper lately, that would likely be counterproductive. Instead, I stand and walk back to the window as rain starts to pelt the glass. "There has to be another way."

"You know this won't end until either Frannie is dead and one side has her soul or Lucifer is gone. I prefer the second option, and the only way I can figure to get there is to bring Him here where I can handle Him."

I turn back to him. "But therein lies the problem, Gabriel. You *can't* handle Him. In the end you won't get either option. What you'll get is Frannie in Lucifer's grasp and you, me, and most of humanity dead and burning in the Inferno. So, if that's what you're going for . . ."

He's on me in a flash, slamming me back into the wall.

"She can do this. She has to!"

I shove him back. "If she had months to learn to use her Sway, maybe. But even then it would be a long shot. We're talking about Lucifer."

"You just said it. Her Sway is getting stronger. She'll be ready." He pushes me again and spins toward the kitchen.

"She won't, and neither will you."

He sends up a roar and the wood splinters as he puts his fist through the cupboard door next to the sink.

"What the Hell is wrong with you?"

He turns back slowly and stares at me for a long moment before storming past me to the door. He flings it open and, as it slams behind him, I catch his parting growl.

I sink into the couch and try to sort this out. If I hadn't seen the Udjat with my own eyes, I wouldn't believe it. But the fact that she had it confirms that she's been found. Not only that, but in order to deliver it, either the Mage or Lucifer Himself has found his way into the corporeal world.

Our world.

Which means time is running out.

I head to my room and change into shorts. I need to run. Since I've been mortal, I've discovered it's the only time I can think clearly. I push out the door into the storm and launch myself up the beach. I run—and think.

Gabriel is insane. He's going to get Frannie killed. I can't let that happen.

I run faster, feeling the driving rain sting my face.

I have to get her out of here.

We're leaving. Tonight. Leaving is dangerous, but not as dangerous as staying. It's the only thing I can think to do to protect her from Gabriel. I never thought it would come to this, but he can't be trusted.

I need to distract Faith and slip Frannie past Gabriel. When she gets home I'll tell her. She'll trust me.

She has to.

FRANNIE

"How far is it?" I ask.

"About a half hour." Faith clicks on the windshield wipers against the rain, pouring in sheets from the slate sky. They tap out a constant rhythm as we pull onto the weather-beaten road that leads from our little beach community to the highway.

I try not to stare as she skillfully navigates her worn-out Impala around potholes, but she's the only Grigori I've met other than my father, and I can't help wondering if there's something I should notice. I never thought there was anything strange about my dad, well . . . other than his liking brussels sprouts. But now I know different.

"So . . . you're Grigori?"

A smile tugs at her mouth. "I thought we already established that."

For a while I don't say anything. I have so many questions, but I don't want to seem nosy.

"Was there something you wanted to know?" she volunteers.

I look at her in time to see her glance in my direction.

"What's it like?" I ask.

The gears grind as she downshifts and negotiates the narrow road. "What? Heaven?"

"No. What's it like to fall?"

Her eyes shift to mine for a heartbeat, then she looks back out the windshield. "It's . . . hard."

"Why did you choose to become Grigori?"

"Because the alternative sucks."

"But some angels choose it."

She nods, her expression becoming solemn. "They do."

"Did Gabe tell you about my brother?" I ask, my chest tightening.

"Matt," she says without looking at me.

"Did you know him?"

"No. We never met." Her eyes flit to mine. "Gabriel said he was your guardian. That's really unusual."

I nod, then lean into the window, trying to find air through my closing throat. It was a mistake to bring this up. I'm totally torn between needing to know everything and being terrified of what I might find out.

Her hand is on my back. "I'm sorry, Frannie."

I hunch for a moment longer, until I can breathe again. "I'm okay," I say, pulling myself upright. "It's just . . . I don't understand why he would choose that."

She shrugs. "It's hard to think straight. First of all, it really hurts . . . losing our wings." She grimaces with the memory. "And second, it's hard to accept that if we stay on Earth, we'll lose almost all our power. The only thing that saved me was that I couldn't imagine never returning." She glances toward me. "When mortals think of fallen angels, they think we've fallen from Heaven, but really, we've fallen from His grace. That's the unbearable part—and the part I want to earn back."

I pick at some fuzz on the seat belt. "Is there any chance Matt could ever come back? Could he change his mind?" I don't dare look at her, but I know by her hesitation that the answer is no.

"I'm really sorry, Frannie," she says, her voice just audible over the beating wipers and pelting rain.

There's a sharp pinch in my chest, and I wonder for a second if I'm having a heart attack. But it fades slowly. "I have to get him back," I say.

I hate the sympathy in Faith's face when I look at her. She turns back toward the road. "I've never heard of that happening before. Once an angel chooses Lucifer, there's no reason He would let them go."

"Just 'cause you've never heard of it, doesn't mean it can't happen," I say, thinking of Luc.

She breathes deep. "What else?" she asks after a minute into the awkward silence, her voice full of false cheer.

I shrug and stare out the windshield. "Do you have to sleep?"

She laughs. "Yes."

"But I saw you sitting in your window this morning, watching me." I realize how accusatory that sounds only after it's out of my mouth.

She pulls onto the highway and guns the engine, causing the rear wheels to lose traction on the wet pavement for a rotation. "It's my job. When you were home, your father did the same thing."

"He never sat outside watching my window!" I know this because Luc did, and Dad wasn't out there.

"No, but he was awake."

I slump into the seat. "So, if you're awake all night watching me, when do you sleep?"

"Mostly during the day, when you're with Gabriel."

I pick at a loose thread at the hem of my sweatshirt. "How does it work?"

"What?"

"My dad. And my mom. They're together . . . married." I'm not sure how to word what I'm trying to ask.

"So you want to know if we fall in love?"

"Yeah . . . and, I don't know . . . how you're so . . . human, I guess, that no one knows you're really angel."

Her face is serious and edged with sadness as she glances sideways at me. "We're not angel, Frannie. Not anymore." She sighs and doesn't say anything else for a long minute. "We do fall in love," she finally offers. "Not all of us, but some of us." She glances at me again. "It's allowed." Her eyes slide back to the road. "As far as the seeming human thing, we age slower than humans, but we still do age, and that's how long we get to earn our wings back. If we haven't earned them back within our Grigori life span, then we die and are judged as any mortal soul would be. But even if we're judged worthy of Heaven, it's a long haul in Purgatory first."

I think about that for a moment. "What do you have to do to earn your wings back?"

"Something exceptionally celestial."

"Like?"

She smirks at me, reminding me of Taylor again. "If I knew that, I would have done it."

"Oh," I say, slumping deeper into my seat. "Have you ever been in love?" I blurt.

"That's a little personal, don't you think?" she snaps.

"Sorry."

She stares out the windshield and her expression softens. "I am," she says in a low tone. "It's why I fell."

I sit here for a minute, stunned, but then I feel anger tighten my jaw. "They throw angels out of Heaven for being in love? That's just wrong."

"We are supposed to love man above all else. It is our directive."

I shake my head. "Still, it doesn't seem fair." I glance at her. "It must be amazing, though, to be so in love you'd give up Heaven to be together."

She shrugs and her mouth pulls into a hard line. "Not so amazing. He barely knows I exist."

"Oh," I say. I was so caught up in how romantic this all was that it hadn't occurred to me he might not love her back. "Have you told him how you feel?"

"I can't."

Anger flares, a pressure in my chest. "That is such bullshit. If you love him, you should tell him. Especially if you gave up everything to be with him. He should know that." No sooner are the words out of my mouth than my throat tightens. I'm such a hypocrite.

Her breathing isn't quite even and I wonder if she's going to cry. "It wouldn't matter."

I breathe deep and look at her. "You're gorgeous. If he knew . . ."

She blushes. "He's got bigger things to worry about at the moment." Her gaze shifts to me for a second and there's something dark there. "And I think he's in love with someone else."

"Well, that sucks."

"It does," she agrees, gripping the steering wheel a little tighter.

The rain picks up as she turns off the highway and weaves through the narrow streets of a quiet little town. The town seems mostly abandoned, probably 'cause of the weather. We pull into a decrepit industrial area and she glides into a parking spot near a few other cars next to a rusty blue warehouse.

"This is it," she says, her mood lifting.

We're soaked when we burst through the steel door into the dimly lit space. It's cavernous—nothing like the cozy studio back home. There are dirty mirrors on one wall with mats spread below them, and on the other side of the space bags hang from steel rafters. Despite the muggy summer heat outside, it's freezing.

A well-built Asian man with broad shoulders and a limp approaches as we step deeper into the space. "Faith! You brought us fresh meat." A grin spreads across his face and he pulls Faith into a bear hug.

She struggles against his grasp. His grin becomes playfully challenging. They twist and turn in some wild dance as she works herself free, and I hear her laughing. When she finally extricates herself a full minute later, she turns to me, her face pink with exertion.

"Colby Black. Judo," she says by way of introduction, and it takes me a second to remember that's me.

The man looks me over. "Welcome to the jungle."

Faith glances around the warehouse. "Pretty sparse today. Who do we have to put up against her?"

He shrugs and waves an arm toward the back corner. "Phil is warming up."

"Be serious, John. Phil is, like, sixty or something."

John cracks a huge grin. "Well, that leaves you or me." He looks at me. "What level?"

"Sixth," I say.

His eyes widen. "Black?"

I nod.

"Really . . ." He looks me up and down, unbelieving, then a wily smile slips across his face. "Let's put you up against George."

Faith looks around. "Who?"

"He's new. Get warmed up," he says, gesturing to the bags.

Faith watches John walk away. "George." She turns to me and shrugs. "Sounds pretty harmless."

"I don't want harmless," I mutter. I'm really looking forward to kicking the shit out of someone. Too many days of pent-up frustration.

"We'll see," she says, hooking my arm and leading me to the mats.

We stretch and then head for the bags. For a minute, I wonder if I've made a mistake. I'm having trouble finding my rhythm with the bag. But, little by little, it comes back to me and my body starts to move on its own. When I'm ready, I step away.

Faith turns from her bag. "You want to spar? To warm up for George?"

"Sure," I say.

We move to a small mat by itself in the corner and stand in the middle. She bows and so do I.

"Ready?" she asks.

"Ready," I say.

She crouches and circles around me, and I counter, in a defensive position, not sure what to expect. When she lashes out with a kick, I block it, but I immediately know she's no beginner. We continue to circle and I maintain my defensive stance and throw an occasional punch to feel her out. I keep my eyes open for her weakness. Everybody has one.

And then I see it.

She doesn't stay low enough when she moves to her right. She circles to her left and throws a kick that grazes my ribs. I jump back but immediately regain my balance. She sends another punch my direction and I block it and drive her to her right with a kick to her hip. As she shuffles to her right, I unleash another kick, which she blocks, followed immediately with a punch to her shoulder, which connects and throws her off balance. I take the opening to lunge and twist her into an arm lock, throwing her to the mat.

"Aww!" she cries. At first I'm afraid I've hurt her and let go. But when she rolls toward me, rage etching lines in her face, I realize it was a cry of frustation. She takes a deep breath and pulls herself to her feet. Her face softens as she raises her eyebrows. "You're ready," she pants. "Let's find John."

I grab my duffel and we head across the empty center of the dank warehouse to the back corner, where there are three regulation-sized mats set up along the far wall. Two of them are occupied. An older guy with a belly spars with an athletic-looking African American woman in her thirties. Next to them, there's no trace of John's limp as he dances over the mat with a smaller man, exchanging blows. I stand for a minute, analyzing their choices, and I watch the smaller man make his fatal mistake. John's kick comes in low and fast, and the smaller man isn't able to deflect it. He loses focus—and his balance—just long enough for John to lunge in for the arm lock and slam him to the mat, pinning him.

"You're up, Blondie," he says as he releases the man under him.

I look around. "Me?"

"You," he answers. "George!"

I follow his gaze to see a seven-foot mountainous man in his early twenties saunter out of the shadows in the corner. He's in the traditional loose black pants, but he's bare-chested and built, with auburn hair, dark eyes, and intricate black tattooing in a web pattern all across his right shoulder and down his arm.

"Rhen," I whisper.

11

Forbidden Fruit

FRANNIE

"John. Be real. She's like five feet tall," Faith says, and I can see the fear behind the glance she shoots me. She knows what Rhen is.

I shake my head, my eyes locked on Rhen's as he smirks at me from the other side of the mat. "It's okay." I'm shocked to feel a smile tug at my lips, but the thing is, I know I can take him. I have before. And best of all, he might even put up a reasonable fight as I kick the shit out of him and make him tell me everything he knows.

"Frannie! Be serious," she hisses in my ear. "I promised Gabriel. We're out of here!"

"No. He doesn't want to hurt me." Faith grips my arm, but I drop my bag and pull out of her grasp, stepping onto the mat. Rhen and I pace to the center and bow. I smile at him and ask, "George?"

A smirk flickers over his strong, handsome face. "I'm incognito . . ." He raises his eyebrow. "Colby."

I roll my eyes. "So, what now?"

A lazy smile pulls at his lips as he lowers his bulk into a crouch. "I win, you make me mortal."

"And if I win?"

"You make me mortal," he says, his eye narrowing to slits.

"I'm not seeing the up side, Rhen."

"George," he corrects, no humor in his voice.

"Whatever," I groan. "How about this? I win, you don't tell anyone where I am."

A slow, sharp smile flickers across his face. "You trust me to keep my word? Such a naïve girl."

I have a sudden flash of Luc calling me the same thing before I knew what he was. It feels like a lifetime ago. I *was* naïve then, but not anymore. "What I trust is that if all Hell knows where to find me, you won't get what you want. It's not in your best interest to share."

"If you two are just going to chat, there's a Starbucks down the street," John taunts from the edge of the mat.

I drop to a crouch and swing out with my leg, but Rhen deflects my kick easily.

"I'm rusty," I mutter under my breath as he grins.

He counters with a punch to my sternum, but I deflect it and spin, connecting with a kick to his knee.

"How did you find me?" I ask as he turns and lowers back into his crouch. We trade a few punches.

He smirks, then swings out with his leg, buckling my knee and dropping me to the mat. "Trade secret."

He lunges for me, smelling blood in the water, but in one quick motion I roll backward over my shoulder and spring to my feet. I unleash a kick that connects with his ribs, rocking him back on his heels. "Tell me and I won't embarrass you too badly," I add, landing the backup punch to his sternum.

He stares hard into my eyes as he regains his balance. "No can do. But you know I'm on your side, mostly."

"So you're, like, a double agent," I say, blocking a punch to my face.

"Something like that," he says, missing with his follow-up punch as I duck to my right.

"Tell me how you found me," I warn.

"Or what?"

I deflect his punch then swing my foot into his chest. "Or I'll make you squeal like a little girl."

Something passes over his face as he stumbles back from my blow, and I can see him contemplating whether to tell me— maybe remembering when I took him down in Luc's parking lot the day we left Haden. He opens his mouth but then lunges for my arm. He tries to spin me into an arm lock, but he's too slow. I rip his hand off my arm and throw him over my shoulder. He hits with a thud and looks up at me, startled, before bounding to his feet.

I could have finished him right there. It would have been too easy to twist him into an arm lock and pin him to the mat. But I have to admit, I'm having too much fun. This feels really, *really* good. My eyes flick to the small crowd gathered at the edge of the mat as someone hollers, "Crush the bastard."

I'm pretty sure Rhen doesn't want to kill me, and, even if he did, I don't think he'd do it with witnesses. But getting back into my routine, breaking a real sweat, is doing wonders for my mood.

I raise my eyebrows at him as he circles to my right. "So?"

He breathes a sigh then sends a punch at my face. "While Marc was busy trying to blow you out of the sky, I opted for a better plan."

I duck under his punch and he deflects my retaliating kick. "Such as?"

"Bribery," he says with a grunt, unleashing a kick to my chest.

I spin and grab his leg, throwing him to the ground by it, then roll and flip him onto his back in a leg lock, pinning him. "Who?"

He leers up at me.

"Ha!" John yells from across the mat. "We need to find you some tougher competition."

"Who?" I ask again in Rhen's ear, tightening the lock.

He grinds his jaw and glares up at me.

Then John and Faith are standing next to us.

I untangle my legs from around Rhen and we both stand and bow. "Thanks, George," I say, walking off the mat. I scoop up my bag and keep walking toward the door.

"I'll be seeing you," he calls after me, a smirk in his voice.

I glance over my shoulder at him. "Not if I see you first."

"What did he say?" Faith asks when we're tucked back into the Impala.

"Nothing," I lie.

I need to figure out how to play this. How can I get Rhen to work with us instead of against us? Before we left Haden, he said there was an uprising in Hell. How can I help him, other than turning him human, which I'm quite sure I can't do? And who did he bribe to find me?

I turn and look at the only person who knows we're here. "Have you ever met that guy before?"

"The demon? No." She shakes her head as she turns the key. The ignition chugs, then catches. "Gabriel is going to kill me."

"Not if he doesn't know."

She shoots me a look. "You are seriously out of your mind, Frannie. You know he can read your thoughts."

"He won't go looking unless he thinks there's a reason to, and I'm getting better at blocking him."

She glances at me, and I'd swear she was fighting tears. "You can't keep this from him. He's trying to keep you safe. It's all he cares about!"

The ache in her voice totally gives her away, and my heart skips as it hits me. "You're in love with Gabe." Jealousy kicks me in the gut, and instantly I hate myself for it I have no claim to him. I have to stop acting like I do.

She continues to stare out the windshield as the rain pelts the roof of the car, but she doesn't answer.

"If Gabe knows I've been found, we'll leave." I feel bad using my newfound knowledge to my advantage, but I need time to figure this out.

Her jaw grinds tight. "And you should."

I stare out at the passing ghost town, then take a deep

breath. "Faith, listen to me. That demon doesn't want to hurt me. He wants me to make him human so he can lead an uprising in Hell."

She turns to look at me with "you're crazy" plastered all over her face. "That makes no sense. How could you turn a demon human?" Her eyes shift back out the windshield as she swerves around a pothole the size of a crater in the center of the road, but can't miss the smaller one just beyond. "And what good would that do him even if you could?" she asks, her voice jarring as we bump through the hole.

I pull my hair out of the ponytail holder and scratch my head, debating if I've already said too much. "How much did Gabe tell you about us?"

"About the two of you?" Her eyes flare as she shoots me a look, and I wonder how much she knows.

"I really meant me," I say with a grimace, trying to block the memory of kissing Gabe this morning. "Did he tell you why we're here?"

She stares out the windshield, her hand tightening on the steering wheel. "He said you were his first priority, and he brought you here so he could protect you."

"Did you know that Luc is a demon?"

"Luc is *not* a demon," she says, incredulous. "I'd be able to tell."

"You're right, he's not—anymore."

Her expression becomes suspicious, creases forming at the corners of her eyes as they narrow. "Are you trying to make me believe that you turned him human?" Her gaze flicks to me. "Because that's ridiculous."

"Is it? You're sure?"

She turns back to the road and is silent for a minute. "Okay, so, even if I believed you could do that, how would that help this George demon with an uprising?"

I shrug. "He says that no one has ever been able to stand up to Lucifer until Luc did it. He thinks something in Luc's infernal wiring short-circuited when he was human or something."

"You lost me."

I breathe an irritated sigh. "Just take my word for it. Please? Rhen doesn't want Lucifer to get me. As a matter of fact, I think he'd work with us to be sure He doesn't."

"Who's Rhen?"

I roll my eyes and groan. "George."

"This is so confusing," she laments, clicking the windshield wipers up a notch as we pull onto the highway.

I slump into the seat. "So, are you gonna tell or not?"

She hesitates too long.

I sigh again. "How long have you been in love with Gabe?"

A bitter snort escapes her. "Forever."

I glance her direction. "And you never told him?"

She shakes her head. "When I died, he was . . ." she trails off and I wait, but she doesn't continue. Instead she stares out the windshield, her jaw clenched and her hand white on the wheel.

"How did you die?" I finally ask.

"I was murdered." She shoots me a tight glance. "By my step-father."

I feel suddenly cold, and a shiver races up my spine as all the blood drains from my face. Why did I ask? Did I really want to know that? "How old were you?"

"Sixteen. He knew I was going to tell, so he . . ." She trails off and looks as though she's fighting tears.

Anger flares to life inside me, first a flicker, then a blaze, imagining what she must have gone through. How could no one have helped her?

She breathes in a long, slow breath and holds it for a minute. "When you get to Heaven, they sort you into your group. I guess, because of all the years my stepfather . . ." She trails off again and swallows hard. "They put me with the guardians," she finally finishes.

"That's how you met Gabe?"

She nods. "I was terrified and he was so kind. And patient." Her gaze flits to me, and, despite her moist eyes, there's just the hint of a smile in them. "I screwed up a lot, which is why I was in training so long." She looks miles away. "He taught me so much . . . starting with the fact that what happened to me wasn't my fault. And eventually . . . I realized I was in love with him."

I find *I'm* fighting tears when I swallow and feel the wet lump in the back of my throat. "Whose guardian were you?" I ask.

Her eyes go dark again. "No one's. I didn't make it that far. I fell before I ever finished training."

I feel something twist painfully in my chest as the pieces click together in my head. "You fell because you loved Gabe," I say.

She nods, even though it wasn't a question.

Her eyes flick to me and hope flashes there. "You said you made Luc human." She turns back to the road. "Could you make Gabriel human too?"

The memory of being wrapped around Gabe in my bed the night of Taylor's funeral intrudes on my thoughts. At that moment, I would have given anything for him to be mortal. But now, knowing what Faith gave up for him, I can't believe how selfish I've been. "No." I sink deeper into the seat and close my eyes, listening as the hammer of the raindrops on the roof starts to slow.

When we sputter to a stop in Faith's driveway, I open my eyes and find the rain has nearly stopped. I climb out of the Impala and gaze across the beach at the angry waves, threatening to take the beach with them as they roll back into the gray ocean.

"Thanks," I say over the top of the car as Faith pulls herself out.

She holds my gaze. "I won't say anything for now. But if I see that demon anywhere near you again, that's it."

I nod as a plump raindrop splashes in my hair. "See you later."

I jog across the dune between Faith's cottage and ours, and when I reach the porch, I see a dark form moving toward me over the gray beach, coming from the other direction. I push through the door into the empty living room, afraid to wait and see who that form turns into as it approaches.

Matt? Rhen?

I head to my bedroom and reach for the handle just as Luc bursts through the front door, breathing hard. He presses it closed against a gust of wind and turns to face me. His bare feet are caked with sand and his black athletic shorts and gray T-shirt are plastered to his body and dripping puddles on the hardwood floor.

"You went running in the rain?" I ask.

He smiles, but it's strained. "Why not?"

I shrug. "No reason, I guess." I point to the bathroom. "Do you want to shower first?"

He looks down at his drenched clothes and pulls his T-shirt away from where it's stuck to the contours of his chest. "That'd probably be a good idea, if you don't mind."

"No problem," I say. "Just knock when you're done."

He grabs a pair of jeans off the chair in the corner and hesitates as he passes me on the way to the bathroom. He lifts his hand and loops a lock of stray hair behind my ear, his eyes storming as he looks down into mine. "Where's Gabriel?"

I shrug. "He wasn't here when I came in."

His eyes scan the room once then fall on mine again. "I need to get you out of here."

"What?" I couldn't have heard him right.

"We're leaving."

"Leaving?"

"There's something . . . not right with Gabriel. It's not safe for you here anymore."

My heart throbs in my throat. "You want to ditch Gabe? But . . ." This isn't making any sense.

"I know it's dangerous, but Gabriel's plan, it's insane. I can't let him . . ." He trails off as his face twists into a pained grimace.

"But you said he was my best chance."

He shakes his head slowly. "I was mistaken. He's not . . . himself."

I can't think. Gabe . . . Luc . . . how do I decide what's right? "So what are we going to do?"

"Pack your things while I'm in the shower," he says. "Then we'll figure it out."

My heart pounds at the thought of leaving with Luc. But how can I leave Gabe? He's kept me safe all along. He doesn't want anything to happen to me.

Luc lifts his hand again, threading his fingers into my hair, and for a second I think he's gonna kiss me. But he squeezes the back of my neck gently and gazes down at me with fire in his eyes. "Trust me, Frannie. Please."

I reach for my doorknob as he slips through the bathroom door. He pushes the door shut, but the latch doesn't catch and the hinges spring open an inch. The showerhead hisses to life as Luc turns the water on, and I wait for him to push the door closed.

He doesn't.

My hand is still on my doorknob, but I can't take my eyes off the bathroom door.

I know I told him I couldn't be with him. I know I was right when I said it. But my heart aches more every minute that we're together, but not together. I want to feel his arms around me. I want things to be how they were.

I think of Faith. To love someone so much for so long, but not be able to be with him . . .

I'm still an emotional wreck from everything she told me. I know that's what the tear trickling over my lashes is about as I pace slowly across the room. I slide up to the bathroom door and hear the change in the pulsing water as Luc steps into the shower. I think I mean to close the door for him, but instead, I just stand here, wanting so badly to push it open and join him.

What would he say? Would he be embarrassed? Ask me to leave?

Wrap me in his arms and love me?

Adrenaline thunders through my veins as I stare through the crack in the door and pull my sweatshirt over my head. I can make out Luc's form, moving behind the shower curtain, and my pulse pounds deafeningly in my ears. My hands start to shake as I slide off my warm-up pants. I take a shaky breath, grasping the hem of my tank top, and lift it off.

My heart slams like a caged animal against my ribs as I push open the door.

12

Silver-tongued Devil

FRANNIE

The burning sensation in the center of my chest takes me by surprise and I gasp. When I reach for the spot, the pendant lying on my sternum buzzes with electric heat.

I grasp it tightly in my hand and glance at Luc's outline through the thin curtain, my heart aching. With one last longing glance at Luc, I back out of the bathroom, pulling the door shut, and scoop my clothes off the floor. I slip through the door to my room and drop into the armchair in the corner, clutching my clothes to my chest, my heart still hammering, just as the front door swings open.

"Frannie?" Gabe calls.

"I'm changing!" I call back from the safety of my room. "I'll be out in a minute!"

I draw a deep breath and hold it for a second, waiting to see if he knocks. He doesn't. I let out the breath and realize my hand is still curled around the metal object. There's a momentary pang of guilt as I pull it up by the leather strap and rub the pendant between my fingers for the hundredth time. I should tell Gabe it's back. But I'm desperate for him not to take it away again.

It's electric. I don't know how or why, but I can feel the buzz under my hand. It feels good. There's something comforting in it, and I feel safer just holding it—like I'm connected to something powerful.

I tug on my jeans from this morning, lying where I left them in a heap on the cool wood floor, and pull my tank top on, then sink back into the armchair and try to think.

I dangle the pendant in front of my face and poke at it with my finger. It twirls at the end of the strap, catching the few rays of muted afternoon sun managing to trail through the heavy cloud cover. Despite the dark, worn metal, it reflects the faint light with every turn, mesmerizing me.

I run my finger along the edge, which cuts through my skin like butter. Something in me knew it would—wanted it to. I watch, fascinated, as a bead of blood seeps onto the metal. I press my cut finger to my jeans as, with the other hand, I try to smear the blood off the pendant with my thumb. But before I can, it seems to absorb into the metal—as if the metal is drinking it in. And then there's a sound, so faint I can barely hear it, like the hum of a tuning fork. I cradle the pendant in my palm, feeling the hum, and bring it up to my ear, listening.

There's a noise outside my door, and I glance in that direction, feeling suddenly defensive. I listen to the sounds of the house—the creaking pipes and the beating water of the shower; the quiet drone of the TV that Gabe must have turned on. My senses are humming right along with the metal of my pendant, wary of any threat.

Gabe wants it.

But he can't have it.

I'm so dialed in, tuning into the faint sounds coming from outside my door, that the tap on my window makes me jump out of my skin. I loop the strap over my head and tuck the pendant quickly under my shirt.

I wait for a minute without breathing. Listening.

Nothing.

The rain.

It was just the rain on my window.

My heart is pounding, adrenaline sending it into a frenzy. I lean back into the chair and breathe, slow and deep. Just as I'm starting to relax, the second tap sends my heart leaping into my throat. I stand and inch slowly across the room to the window.

At first I see nothing, but the next instant, Matt's face is pressed up against the glass.

"Oh my God!" I gasp.

I rush the last few steps to the window and throw it open. "Matt!"

"Don't be scared, Frannie," he says softly, backing off a few feet.

Rain pelts my face as I lean out into the swirling darkness of the diminishing storm.

"Can I come in?" he asks.

"You never asked before," I say, a shake in my voice.

"I have to now," he answers, and something dark passes over his face.

"Um . . . okay." I back away from the window, but it turns out he's not coming through the window. He disappears from the dune, and then I hear him clear his throat behind me. I jump, my nerves totally shot, and spin in his direction.

"You're really here?" I breathe, unable to get any air behind the words.

"I am."

"What happened? Where have you been?" I'm pretty sure I know the answer, but I can't help but hope I might be wrong. In the dim light, I see those glowing red eyes regard me and I feel something cold claw up my spine.

"Hell."

Even though I expected it, I still gasp. I think about Luc in the bathroom and Gabe on the couch. One scream would bring them both.

I open my mouth, but then I feel the cold press of guilt.

Matt stares at me, his gaze intense and his smile angelic, and I'm suddenly crushed by what I've done to him. An image flashes in my head: seven-year-old Matt, twisted on the ground under our climbing tree, and it's like a dull knife is carving its way through my insides. I wrap my arms around myself and groan.

I can't scream.

I have to help him. There has to be something I can do—with my Sway, maybe—to help him get away from Lucifer.

At best, Gabe and Luc would scare Matt off. At worst, Gabe would blast him into oblivion.

"Wow," he says. "That's a whole lot of guilt."

I look up at him, still squeezing myself against the pain. "What?"

"I can sense it—your guilt," he says, and I get the feeling there's more to it. "It's a handy talent that I just found out I have." He looks hard into my eyes. "Don't feel guilty, Sis. Everything has worked out."

But as he says it, I see him with Lilith and the knife cuts deeper. I double over and hear a cross between a whimper and a gasp leave my throat. He lowers his gaze and the pain stops instantly.

I stare at him as I catch my breath, trying to figure out what just happened.

"It's okay, Sis. It wasn't *all* your fault." He reaches for my hand, but when he touches me, he's a thousand degrees.

My elbow cracks sharply into my dresser as I jerk my hand away, sending a jolt of zinging electric pain down my arm into my hand, which instantly goes numb. I rub my elbow and flex my fingers, slowly realizing that stuff like funny bone pain doesn't happen in dreams.

This is real. Matt is really here.

I wasn't sure until just this second.

I look back up at Matt, feeling a new kind of fear creep through my gut.

He moves closer. "Please don't be scared. I'm not going to hurt you."

"How did you find me?" My voice is stronger, but it still shakes.

He quirks a cocky smile. "I'm your brother. Your twin. I did what any brother would do. I spied on you."

"Spied on me?"

He nods. "How else was I supposed to follow you?"

"You followed me? Here?" And then I remember. In my dream . . . or at least what I convinced myself had been a dream, when I saw him here in my room and out on the dune, I'd thought I'd seen black wings.

"You can fly," I whisper.

He nods.

The image of a shadow gliding over the surface of the clouds below our plane skitters through my memory. I remember thinking it was our shadow, but it seemed too small. "You got your wings back?" I breathe.

His face darkens. "Not how you mean." When his eyes connect with mine, they're hopeful. "But I want to." He holds his hand out to me again and I take it lightly, getting used to his heat. "I really want to come back—to earn my real wings back."

"Faith said that once you chose—"

"I didn't say it was going to be easy," he snaps.

I breathe deep. "How?"

"Maggie needs our help. She's in . . . trouble."

"What's wrong with Maggie?" The words slip out of my mouth, but I barely hear them, 'cause suddenly there's a cyclone in my head. Whirring thoughts swirling with panic and fear and dread.

"It almost worked last time . . ." Matt trails off, his eyes troubled.

"*What?* What almost worked?"

"Marchosias," he says simply. "And Lili is helping him."

The image from my dream, Maggie and a boy, cuts through

my out-of-control emotions. "Marc has Maggie?" I hear the hysteria in my voice and know I'm on the edge of losing it.

Matt nods, his face solemn.

Oh, God. My baby sister.

Panic knots my chest. I can't breathe as the image of Taylor, bloody and dying in my arms, slaps my senses. "No," I whisper.

"She needs our help," Matt says, studying my reaction but making no move toward me.

"I need to go." The words are choked as they leave my mouth. "I have to help her." Maggie can't die.

"We both do," Matt answers.

"Gabe," I say, finally able to pull some air into my lungs.

"No, Frannie. He won't let you go." There's an unmistakable current of panic in his voice.

"We need his help, Matt!"

His eyes flare, bloodred. "He's known all along."

My stomach drops to my knees. "About Maggie? I don't believe you."

"Think about it. His job is to keep you away from danger." His eyes lock on mine, intense. "He won't let you go back. Now that I've found you, he'll drag you off to some other hidden place and keep you locked away."

"He wouldn't . . ." I start. But I trail off as I remember him saying he'd do exactly that. I drop my face into my hands and try to think. Gabe can't lie, but I've never asked him directly about my family. I've never asked if they were safe. And when I've asked him to look out for them, he's always said he would do what he could. No promises.

I start to move toward the door. "I need to talk to Gabe."

Matt's eyes flare again and his gaze becomes unbearable. "He can't know I'm here."

I look harder at Matt. He's different now. His blue eyes are dark, and he just seems coiled so tight. He's not an angel anymore. He's a demon. Demons lie. What if he's trying to lure me away from Gabe?

But as I think it, I feel the sharp stab in my gut as guilt takes over my thoughts again. I picture his wings being ripped from his body. "I won't tell him," I groan.

His expression becomes hard as stone, set and determined. "Then what's there to talk to him about? Just come with me."

The pain becomes sharper, more intense, as he stares into my eyes, and I sink onto the bed, wrapping my arms around myself. Every muscle in my body clenches as I strain against the pain. "I need to know . . . if he knew and . . . didn't tell me." I groan between pants. "If it's true . . . I'll come with you."

"He can read your thoughts, Frannie. If you go out there, he'll know."

"No, he won't. I've gotten better . . . at keeping him out," I say, clutching myself tighter. The pain is so intense I expect that any second my chest will rip open.

Matt turns his gaze out the window and suddenly the pain stops. "Fine. But make it quick."

I pant to catch my breath. "Were you doing that?" I ask.

He turns back to look at me. "What?" he asks with inquiring raised eyebrows.

"Nothing." I shake my head, wondering what I was thinking. I steel my mind, focusing on my dream about Maggie and nothing about Matt. With that dream fresh in my head, I slide past Matt and head for the door. He doesn't stop me, and I throw a glance over my shoulder as I pass through and close it behind me.

Gabe clicks off the TV when I step into the living room. His eyes pull wide and he's at my side in a flash. He starts to turn the knob to my door, but I grab his hand.

"What's wrong?" I say, pulling him back toward the couch.

He glances down at me, still vigilant. "I thought I sensed . . ." He trails off and looks around again, his eyes finally falling on the door to the bathroom. He blows out a sigh and drops his head before lifting his eyes back to mine. "Could Luc be turning back?" he asks tentatively.

"Into a demon?"

He just looks at me out from under long white lashes, his eyes questioning.

My eyes slide to the bathroom door and I shudder, remembering how much I wanted to be in there with him. "I don't know," I say just as the bathroom door cracks open and Luc steps out. His towel is thrown over his shoulder and he's in jeans and nothing else.

I just stare at him for a long moment. He wants me to leave with him. Would he take me home?

Gabe slides back onto the couch, bringing me with him. Normally, I'd settle into him, but right now it's taking everything I have to stay in control, and I don't want to let down, to let him into my head.

He squeezes my shoulder. "So what's wrong?"

"You're looking out for them, right? My family? Maggie?"

I feel him stiffen at Maggie's name and instantly know Matt

was telling the truth. I pull away and look him in the eye as I ask. "Is Maggie safe?"

His eyes drop from mine. I can see him struggling with his answer—how to frame it so I won't freak out.

But I'm already freaking out. "I have to go home!"

"No. That's not an option." Gabe's voice is calm, and I feel him trying to bury me in his summer snow, but I shake it off.

Frustration builds inside me, growing like a thunderhead, and I want to hit him. "How can you just sit there if my family is in danger?"

"Listen to me, Frannie. Everyone involved understands that you are the priority."

Rage erupts from my emotional black pit and I can't control the stream of words spilling from my lips. "Does Maggie know? Does *she* understand that I'm the priority? That she's being sacrificed for me?" I plant my hands on his chest and push him hard, rising from the couch. "*Does she?*"

"Frannie, no one is being sacrificed." Luc's voice is soft, and when I look at him, so are his eyes. But I don't want his sympathy.

I spin on Gabe. "Does he know too?"

"Not everything."

Gabe starts to pull himself to his feet, but I shove him back down. "*Everything?* What's everything?"

Luc steps closer and I flash him a glare. He stops moving toward us and holds up a hand. "I'll go back. I'll take care of Marc."

The air leaves my lungs, as if I was punched. He just told me to trust him, but I can't trust either of them. "You *did* know."

His eyes don't leave mine. "Not until just now."

I'm not sure if I believe him, but it doesn't matter. I spin back to Gabe. "You've got to take me back. I can maybe try my Sway on Maggie . . . or Marc . . ." I trail off as despair grips my heart and squeezes. My Sway. The reason for all of this. I throw a growl at the world. "What about the rest of my family. Riley, Trev? Will they go after everyone?"

Gabe pulls himself up again. "Honestly, I don't know." He already sounds spent—defeated.

Everyone I love is in danger 'cause of me. And it's never gonna stop. My heart totally caves in as I realize there's no way for me to protect them.

Unless I go back.

With me there, they'd have no use for my family. They'd come after me. And at this point, giving up doesn't sound like such a bad option. Not if it would mean they'd leave everyone else alone.

I look Gabe in the eye. "They know I'm here, so there's no reason not to go back."

He doesn't believe me. I can see it in his skeptical expression. "Lucifer may have found you in your dreams, but if He knew where you were, His legions would be parked at our doorstep."

"Rhen was at the gym today," I blurt, trying to keep the image of Matt waiting in my room out of my thoughts.

His eyes widen as his hands clench into fists. "How . . . ?"

"I don't know, but he was there."

"I knew that wasn't safe," he growls. I can see his wheels turning, plotting our next move.

I'm so furious at him that the next thing out of my mouth surprises even me. "Do you even know why Faith fell?" I spit.

He squints at me, confused. "She fell in love with another guardian," he answers. His face clears and he gives me a reassuring look. "But you can trust her, if that's what you're worried about. She has a good heart."

I almost spill the rest—that it was his fault. I'm *that* mad at him. But I don't, partly 'cause of what he just said, and partly 'cause it would hurt Faith more than him. And she's been hurt enough.

I breathe deep and stare him down. "We can run, but it won't matter. They found me here, they'll find me anywhere." I'm a little surprised at how calm I sound. My thoughts start to slip to Matt and I redirect them.

Luc falls back into the wall. "The Mage," he whispers. His eyes lift to mine. "This is my fault." His voice is heavy, like the weight of the world is pressing down on him. "In your dreams," he continues after a deep breath, "were you standing on the outside looking in, or were you seeing things through Maggie's eyes?"

Not only was I seeing things with Maggie's eyes but feeling them with her body. Again, I feel dirty just thinking about it. "Through Maggie's eyes. What does that mean?"

"The Mage is showing you what he wants you to see."

"He wanted me to know about Maggie and Marc—"

"To draw you out," Gabe interrupts. "But it's not true. Maggie is fine."

I glare up at him. "How do you know?"

Gabe slips an arm around my shoulder. "Daniel is handling it."

Dad. I hadn't thought about Dad. I sink into the couch. "What can he do? How much power does he have?" I shake my head, trying to think. "He couldn't protect me on his own. He needed you or Matt—" I catch myself before my thoughts wander behind my bedroom door.

"He's not on his own," Gabe says. "I've sent help."

I chew my lip, trying to keep from thinking about what comes next. What I'm about to do. "I'm too tired to think about this now, but I still think we need to go back."

"We'll figure it out, Frannie," Gabe says. But I know what he means is that *he'll* figure out how to keep me from going.

I drag myself off the couch and head to my door. "Fine." I glance back at Gabe and Luc, wanting so much to confide in them but knowing they'll never let me go. I swallow back tears and hurry through the door into my room.

I close the door and rush to my closet, pulling out my brown canvas duffel bag. "Matt!" I whisper.

"I was right," he declares.

When I turn back from the closet with my bag and a fistful of clothes, his face is framed in my window, a smug smile on his lips. But looking at him, something occurs to me. "I can't just phase. How are we gonna get home?"

He holds up his hand and shakes a key on a ring over his middle finger. "Got it covered."

I toss the duffel bag on my bed and stuff the clothes and my iPod speaker into it, then return to my closet for some shoes. In five minutes I'm as packed as I'm gonna be, considering I can't retrieve anything from the bathroom without going into the family room. I shove my bag out the window into Matt's waiting arms, then swing my leg through the opening and slide to the ground.

Luc told me we needed to leave, to get away from Gabe, and I am. Just not with him.

"Let's go," I say spinning to Matt and holding out my hands for the duffel bag.

But when I turn, my pounding heart leaps into my mouth.

It's Faith, not Matt, staring back at me.

"Going somewhere?" She stands on top of the small dune between our houses, still in her workout clothes, fists on her hips.

I glance around wildly for Matt, but he's nowhere.

"It's . . . I'm . . ." I stumble before I remember I have an advantage. I think about Matt, how much I want him to earn his wings back. "I'm just going for a walk."

She scowls at me. "A walk," she repeats, pointing at my bag. "You need a duffel bag for a walk."

I shift my thoughts to Maggie, and my heart pounds out my need to help her. "I need to think," I say, focusing that love on Faith.

Slowly, her expression goes blank. "To think . . ."

"So I'm going for a walk on the beach," I say. I move slowly toward her and touch her arm, focusing harder. "I may be gone for a while."

Then something occurs to me.

"If Gabe and Luc come looking for me, tell them you saw me on the beach. Tell them I said I needed some time to think. Tell them I'll come home when I'm ready, but they shouldn't come looking for me."

She blinks, and for a second I think I've lost her, but then she says, "Okay."

Again I look for Matt and find him standing at the road next to a blue Camaro, parked across the street. I turn and run full speed toward him without a backward glance.

13

✝

Living on a Prayer

GABE

Something's wrong. It started out as an itch under my skin that I chalked up to paranoia at my dwindling abilities, but the itch became a tug. I know it's more.

I focus on Frannie's room, and instantly, panic chokes my thoughts. I burst through her door without knocking, because I know it won't matter.

The room is empty.

"Damn!" I hiss under my breath, charging through the family room and onto the porch. There are a few groups clustered on the beach, but no Frannie.

I run to the side of the house and check her window. Open. And under it is tracks in the sand. One set leads toward the road and another heads to Faith's house. I follow the ones toward the road first but lose them on the pavement. At a jog, I cross the thirty feet or so to Faith's and pound on the door. A few seconds later, she's standing in the doorway.

"Hi Gabriel."

"Have you seen Frannie?"

She nods absently. "She went for a walk. Said she needed some time to think."

It makes sense. And sneaking out the window for some alone time is exactly something Frannie would do, but something nags at the back of my mind. "Where did she say she was going?"

"Just down the beach."

"Then why do her tracks disappear on the road?"

Her face scrunches as she thinks. "I swear I saw her go toward the beach."

"Was she alone?"

The creases in her forehead deepen as she shakes her head. "She needs time. You're not supposed to look for her."

Panic grips my pounding heart. "Who was she with, Faith?"

"No one."

"You're sure."

"I'm . . ." She hesitates, then shakes her head.

I'm running for the bungalow even before she's finished the word. When I get there, I tuck around the corner and press myself into the shingled side, asking the Light to take me. I have to get to the Board. But instead of transporting into the Collective, searing pain slices through me and I find myself in a heap on the ground.

"What's going on?"

I haul myself out of the sand and turn to find Luc standing on the porch, staring down at me.

I drag myself to my feet. "Frannie's gone," I pant through the pain.

He eyes me suspiciously, then hops the rail, landing next to me in the sand. "Go find her and tell me where to meet you." He holds out his hand for the keys to the Jeep.

I dig the keys out of my pocket and drop them into his hand. Summoning everything I can muster, I focus on Frannie, but all I pick up is a whisper of a trail. I walk across the street and stand for a moment on the spot where her tracks stop, opening myself up to anything. Finally, I take a breath and hold it before answering. "I don't know where to go. I can't find her."

Luc just stares, unbelieving. "You're joking."

I feel like my throat is closing, depriving my brain of oxygen. I can't think. Why can't I sense her? Is it my waning power or something the infernal are doing to block me? I look up at Luc. "Can the infernal Shield a mortal?"

He shakes his head. "Not that I'm aware of."

"Though that would be a handy trick."

The baritone voice behind me sends a ripple of dread up my spine.

Luc looks over my shoulder at the bungalow, drops his head, and exhales. "Rhenorian. Sweet sin of Satan."

"I missed you too, bro," he says, stepping out of the shadows of the house.

Luc looks up at him, his eyes narrow. "How did you find us?"

"Just my lucky day." He leans into the corner of the bungalow and grins. "And by that I mean your cheesy celestial Shield seems to be malfunctioning."

"Unholy Hell," Luc hisses as he shoves me hard into the side of the house, leaving his palm planted firmly on my pounding chest. Red rage is clear in his eyes even though he's still human. "How could you let this happen?" he finally says when he confirms his fear with the wild beating of my heart under his hand.

A heart I'm not supposed to have.

It's the same question I've been asking myself since we got here.

LUC

The crushing pressure of this is almost too much to bear, and I have to hold my breath against the pain as I realize what this means. *Everything* that it means. Frannie turned him human.

She wanted him *that* much.

I slam him back into the side of the house. "You son of a bitch. How could you let this happen?" I ask again.

He shoves me away, but he doesn't look up. "The same way you did."

I grab him with both hands and throw him harder into the side of the house. "But I wasn't her protector, damn it!"

Finally, he looks up at me. "Let me go so I can find her."

I throw him one last time into the house and back off. "If anything happens to her, I'll kill you myself."

Rhen's low chuckle from behind me is more than I can handle. Before I realize I've done it, I spin and my fist is ricocheting off Rhen's jaw.

His head snaps back, but then he turns to me with a grin. "There aren't even words to describe how pathetic that was."

I glare up at him and rub my hand. "Why are you here?"

"You've been a slippery little used-to-be demon," he answers, rubbing his jaw and looking me over.

"Can you find Frannie?" I ask, my heart in my throat, grasping at any possibility.

He chuckles again, a deep rumble from his enormous chest, and he fixes Gabriel in a cold stare. "I thought keeping track of the ninja was your job, cherub."

Gabriel shoots him a glare and, with an obvious effort of will and a growl that shakes the ground under my feet, he shifts.

I look at the empty space where he was, feeling the cold edge of dread cut through me, then turn back to Rhen. "I take that as a no."

The humor clears from his face, replaced by surprise. "You're serious? You don't know where she is?"

I stare him hard in the eye and ask again. "Can you find her?"

He backs off a step. "That wasn't our deal," he grumbles.

"Your deal?" I ask.

"Your girlfriend's ex-cherub brother." He pokes a finger into my chest. "I told you he was no fan of yours."

"That's how you found her? Matt?"

"It was a quid pro quo. He swore to me he could find her, and I swore to him I'd keep you and Ozone Head out of his way— and maybe make you scream a little in the process."

"But you didn't."

A grin stretches his face. "I lie. Figured if you slowed him down some it would give me time to get . . ." his grin pulls into a leer, ". . . close, shall we say, to your little friend." He steps forward, right up into my face. "Did she tell you we got sweaty together this morning?"

My nails dig into my palms as I work to contain my fury. "Can you find her?" I ask again through gritted teeth.

His brow furrows in concentration. Finally, he shakes his head. "No."

"Then Matt got the last laugh, didn't he?" I say shoving him back. I jog for the Jeep and hop in, fumbling the keys into the ignition with a shaking hand.

Rhen appears in the passenger seat. "Looks like your feather-faced friend is losing his touch."

"Looks like," I say, ignoring the pang in my heart. As much as I'm painfully aware that there are bigger issues at the moment, it nearly kills me that Frannie wanted Gabriel enough to do this to him. I should have destroyed him when I had the chance.

"Well, this bites," he says. "A lot of good a dried-up Dominion is going to do the uprising."

"The uprising," I repeat, a tickle of hope in my chest. I throw Rhenorian a sidelong glance as I crank the engine to life. "How's that working out for you?"

"It's not. We were counting on your and Ozone Head's help, but then you vanished off the face of the planet."

"We were on the planet," I say as the engine finally turns over. I pause, wondering just how far gone Gabriel is and admonishing myself for not seeing what was going on. It was right there in front of me—his temper swings and violent outbursts and the way he looked at Frannie, like a starving animal. "As a matter of fact, I'm pretty sure neither of us can leave it at the moment."

"How pathetic is that?" Rhen mutters. "All I need to know is how she does it."

In the next heartbeat, which I can easily count since mine is pounding out of my chest, I'm shoving him up against the door.

"You will not come within a mile of her, except to help me find her. I'm assuming since my Shield is ineffectual, Frannie's is too, in which case, if we get you close enough, you should be able to sense her." *You and every other demon on the coil,* I think as a thread of panic twists through my gut.

"You expect me to help a celestial?"

I glare at him. "I thought you just said you were counting on Gabriel's help. I'm sure you've heard the adage, what goes around comes around?"

"I'm not going to take orders from a used-up featherface. I can find her. And you're both useless now. I don't need your help."

"She can't help you, Rhen," I say.

"She *will* help me," he says. A depraved grin tugs at his face. "And then I'll help myself . . . to her soul."

I glance his way and he's gone. I floor the accelerator, not sure where I'm going except away from here, and nearly run over Faith, who appears out of nowhere in the road in front of me.

I slam on the brakes and she runs to my window. "Where are you going?"

"To find Frannie."

She runs to the passenger door and throws herself in. "I'm coming with you."

GABE

In all my existence, I've never felt so blind. I seem to be able to shift on the coil, barely, but each time I've tried to give myself up to the Light, it's like I hit an invisible barrier—as if I'm too human to be allowed back into Heaven, which might be exactly the case.

For hours I've searched, shifting along the Florida coast looking for a needle in a haystack, and each shift has taken a little more out of me. In the end, it's all been for nothing. I've yet to pick up any trace of Frannie.

Of two things I'm certain. One: she's not alone because she got into a car. Two: she left with whoever has her on the pretense of going home to help Maggie.

I'm standing at a rest area on the side of the highway north of Miami when the phone in my pocket buzzes. I pull it out and look at the caller ID, hoping for Frannie. Instead, it's Faith. "Yes," I answer.

"Gabriel!"

"What is it, Faith?"

"I think Frannie . . . I think I saw her get into a car with a boy."

"Tell me everything you remember."

She hesitates. "It's all just so foggy." I wait through her long pause. "She was outside her window . . . and she said she was going for a walk on the beach, but then she went toward the road and there was a car . . . and a boy."

"What did the boy look like?"

"He was kind of far away, but . . . I think he looked like Frannie—the same hair, anyway. Luc thinks it could have been Matt."

"Matt," I whisper under my breath. It makes sense. I'm not sure how he found her, but if anyone could convince her to go with him, it would be Matt.

"Thanks, Faith. This is a big help. Where is Luc?"

"We're at the airport."

"We?"

"I'm coming with him. This is my fault."

I shake my head at the guilt in her voice. Heaven knows I've done more than my share of screwing up. "I'll see you in Haden," I say as I disconnect. I breathe deep, mustering every ounce of celestial might I can, and shift to Frannie's house, knowing this shift might be my last. I know there's no guarantee that she'll ever get that far, but there's someone there who can get to the Board and find her.

I materialize on my hands and knees in the shadows next to Frannie's garage and can't stop the groan that erupts from my chest. I wipe beads of sweat off my face with the back of my hand as I haul myself to my feet and start when my wrist comes away bloody. I pull off my T-shirt and press it to my face to staunch the flow of blood from my nose, cursing myself under my breath.

"You stink of demon. I'd have thought the stench would have worn off your fiery friend by now."

Even though I broadcast that I was here, essentially calling him to me, I still jump at Aaron's voice behind me. I've been over and over this, trying to find another way. But, in the end, I don't have a better solution.

"Aaron," I say, tossing my bloody T-shirt aside without looking up. Even so, I can hear the smirk in his voice when he answers.

"To what do I owe the honor of your radiant presence, oh omnipotent one?"

I turn to look at him then. "What is the status here?"

"Are you checking up on me?" he says, his smarminess giving way to incredulity.

"I'm here to speak with Daniel." I brush past him on my way into the garage to look for something to wear. "But I need you to do something for me," I add, offhand.

"I'm not your errand boy, Gabriel. In case you've forgotten, I have a charge—"

I spin on him. "I'm shifting your assignment. I need you to watch Frannie for me."

He stares for a long moment, trying to read me. "Something's going on," he says slowly, looking me over more closely with narrowed eyes.

I do the best I can to look like I've got it together. "I just need you to check the Board for Frannie and keep an eye on her. Of course, if you can't manage that . . ."

"I hate the humidity in Florida," he says.

"She's not in Florida. I think she's on her way here." I realize my slip as soon as it's out of my mouth.

"You *think*? Isn't it your job to *know*?"

"Go! Or I'll find someone else who can handle it!"

He grumbles and fades out with a glare as sharp as a razor blade.

I jerk my head around at the rustle in the rhododendrons near the house, expecting Marc—or worse—and I breathe a sigh of relief when a cat streaks across the ten feet between the house and the detached garage, disappearing around the corner. My eyes glide up the white siding of the house and to the trees outside Frannie's second-story window. No sign of Marc.

I duck into the garage and come up with a sweatshirt hanging on a hook near the door. It's too small, but I pull it over my head anyway and push up the sleeves. I trot to the front door, every step jarring my broken body, and ring the bell, breathing hard.

When it opens, Grace's serious face is peering back at me. "Oh . . ." she says, her eyes widening.

"Hello, Grace. I need to speak with your father. Is he in?"

She just stares back, wide-eyed, for a long moment before blinking. "Oh, my . . . Um . . . okay. Come in."

I step through the door and she just stands a moment longer, staring.

I look down at her, and she inhales sharply when I touch her arm. "You know what I am, don't you?"

She nods.

"This is really important, Grace. Can you please get your father?"

She nods again and turns for the kitchen just as Maggie appears at the top of the stairs.

"Hi Gabe," she beams. She skips down the steps and stops in front of me. "You know Frannie's not here, right?"

"I do. I was hoping to speak with your father."

Her eyebrows shoot up into her dark bangs. "About Frannie?"

I smile at her. "I suppose so."

She scrunches her face. "You're not gonna ask him if you can, like, date her or anything? You know she's with Luc?"

"I've seen them," I say, then scrutinize her. "Maggie, have you met a boy named Marc?"

Her eyes widen slightly, and she glances past me at the family room. "How do you know about Marc?" she says in a near whisper.

"Listen, I know how this is going to sound. You barely know me and I'm about to go all big brother on you, but he's dangerous."

A smile ticks the corners of her mouth and she opens it to say something, but I nip it. She needs to know this is serious.

"You know what happened to Taylor," I say holding her gaze. She goes pale and nods.

"Marc was partly responsible for it. You need to steer clear of him, Maggie. I'm begging you." I work to keep my voice calm. No need to scare her more than necessary.

She backs off a step, wide-eyed and looking a little green. "Okay . . ."

"Okay," I repeat as Daniel strides across the living room, a sense of urgency in his step.

He glances between Maggie and me. "Hey, Maggs, sweetie. Why don't you go clean up your mess in the kitchen?"

She nods and heads to where Frannie's mom is perched in the kitchen doorway with Grace peeking around from behind her.

"Ma'am," I say with a nod.

Frannie's mother smiles, but her eyes are cautious.

"Gabriel's just checking in, Claire," Daniel says, reaching for the doorknob. "I'll be back in a few minutes."

He pulls the door open and we step through into the night.

"How much does she know?" I ask as soon as the door's closed behind us.

His expression is edged with guilt, but his words are defensive. "She needed to know."

I nod. "She did. Does she know how much danger Frannie is in?"

His eyes drop. "I didn't want to worry her too much." He sighs deeply and steels himself before looking back up. "Has something happened?"

"Have you heard anything from Frannie?" I try to keep my voice neutral, but I'm fairly certain that I don't succeed.

"Not for a few days," he says, his eyes searching my face. "Is everything okay?"

"She's missing. I need to know right away if you hear from her."

His eyes narrow. "What aren't you telling me? Why can't you just find her?"

I can't hold his gaze as I shake my head. "I don't know." Which isn't a lie. I don't know if it's because my powers are failing, or if she's being Shielded by the other side, somehow. "I'm fairly certain she's on her way back here." I don't add that, depending on who she's with, she might never make it. "I've got Aaron working on something, and I'm going to stay here until we're able to locate her."

The paternal concern is clear in his eyes. "Find her, Gabriel."

"I will," I say, and pray to God I'm not lying.

"I'm frightened for my girls." He stares at his shoes. "You know about Grace—her ability?" he asks.

I nod. "She can see auras."

"But, Maggie . . ." he starts, then trails off, at a loss for words.

"What about Maggie?" I ask, feeling dread sitting like a stone in my stomach.

He shakes his head. "I can't figure it out. Anytime she's upset, lightbulbs start popping." He shakes his head again, slower. "Something to do with electromagnetic fields, maybe?" he muses.

"Maybe," I say, trying not to be obvious as I scrutinize him. He clearly doesn't realize how unusual it is for even one Nephil child of a Grigori to have gifts. Forget three. Which leaves me wondering about this gene pool. "What about Mary and Kate?"

He shrugs. "Mary's a born peacekeeper, but I haven't noticed anything else. Kate . . ." He taps his finger on his chin as he thinks. "I've always found her draining—like she sucks all the energy out of a person." He squints at me. "Do you think there's something to that?"

"I don't know," I answer, but my bet is on yes.

He turns and, with one last pleading glance over his shoulder, disappears into the house.

I slide around back and call for Aaron, who appears at my side effortlessly and without his signature smirk.

"Where is she?" I ask, unable to keep the urgency out of my voice.

He shakes his head. "I don't know."

I just stare at him, unable to speak or even breathe as panic chokes me.

He shrugs. "I checked the Board. She's not on it."

14

✝

Hell Spawn

LUC

We're out of the airport in a heartbeat, and the taxi drops us at my apartment for the Shelby. I climb in, not sure where I mean to go.

"Where would she be?" Faith asks from the passenger seat.

I shake my head. "Home. She was worried about Maggie, so I'd expect she'd head that direction." As much as I want him dead, I'm more than a little concerned that I've heard nothing from Gabriel. He should be there already.

I drive like a bat out of Hell to Frannie's and find Gabriel pacing the sidewalk in the pale light of early dawn. I pull up to the curb and Faith springs out of the car before I can even roll down my window.

"Is she here?" I ask.

Gabriel leans in, looking more than slightly shaken. "She's not even on the Board."

Faith skids up next to Gabriel on the sidewalk. "How is that possible?"

But before the question's out of her mouth, I know the answer. If Frannie's soul is no longer on the mortal coil, she won't show up on the Board.

He must see it in my eyes. "She's not dead, Luc." At first I think the edge to his voice is directed at me, but then I realize it's sheer determination, as if he can make it so just by wanting it. "He wants her alive. If she's with Matt, they're probably headed here."

It should be a relief she's with her brother, but my chest tightens as I recall my last image of Matt, his wings being ripped from his body by the avengers.

"Are you sure there's no way they could be Shielding her?" he asks with a hint of desperation.

I think on that for a moment, just as desperate for it to be true. "It's not a skill He gives us at the time of our creation. Not even Mages . . ." But then I trail off, a horrible thought hitting me like a lightning bolt. "Unless she was wearing an Udjat."

Gabriel's pulls a slow breath and looks me in the eye. "I took it from her and then it disappeared. She doesn't have it."

I press back into my seat and try to think. "If she's wearing His mark . . ." Then she's under His control, and it may be in His power to Shield her. My heart goes dead in my chest. "Is Marchosias here?" I say, glancing past him at the house.

"Aaron says he's been lurking and has spoken to Maggie a few times, but he's been able to run interference to keep it from going any further."

"So Maggie's okay?"

"As far as anyone knows."

"Do you want me to stay with her?" Faith asks.

Gabriel nods distantly, his mind obviously still on Frannie. "I'll tell Daniel you're here."

I crank the ignition. "I'm going to check around and see if anyone's heard from Frannie."

I can see Gabriel struggling with whether to stay here or come with me. Finally, he steps back from the car and absently loops an arm over Faith's shoulders. She encircles him in both of hers, sinking into his side. "If she makes it this far, I have to believe she'll come here," he says.

I nod and pull away from the curb, struggling to keep it together. Because if Frannie's wearing His mark, if she's under His influence, it might be too late. Frannie's and Lucifer's powers are not all that different, and in a battle of wills, Frannie would be at a disadvantage. Lucifer's power may not work on the celestial, but He's had eons to perfect it on mortals, which, despite her potential, Frannie still is.

I'm across town in a matter of minutes. The neighborhood is quiet as I pull up to the curb in front of the small, blue, single-story house and cut the engine. My eyes scan the low, trimmed hedges and the trees for any sign of trouble. I walk up to the door but hesitate before raising my hand to knock.

The house is dark, but it's early. I'm sure Frannie's grandfather is still in bed. If I had my demon's sixth sense, I wouldn't need to wake him. I'd know if Frannie was here.

But I don't.

We needed more time in Florida—both Frannie and me. She needed time to master her Sway, and I needed time to change.

Neither of us got what we needed. My gut twists as I realize the only one of us who changed was Gabriel. I never dreamed she was turning him too. It never crossed my stupid mind. I foolishly thought he had things under control. I can't believe I was so blind.

I drop my hand and almost walk away, but then I raise it again and rap on the door.

At first, there's no response, and I hope maybe Ed has taken Frannie away to someplace safe.

But there is no such place.

I knock again, harder this time. A few minutes pass and I'm ready to turn for the Shelby, when a light flicks on deep within the house. A moment later, the porch light illuminates and I'm washed in a pale white glow as the fluorescent bulb gradually brightens. I hear a rustle against the inside of the door and know I'm being inspected through the peephole.

The door cracks open and Ed's face is staring out at me, his eyelids heavy with sleep and his gray fringe sticking up on one side. He pulls at the belt of his plaid bathrobe with one hand, tightening it against the early-morning chill. His other hand rests in his pocket. He makes no move toward extending a hand.

I nod and hold mine out. "Ed."

He still doesn't take my hand, but he opens the door a little wider. "What's wrong?" His voice isn't steady as he peers at me through narrowed eyes, trying to find answers.

I hold his gaze with mine. "I need to know if you've seen or heard from Frannie in the last twelve hours."

His focus blurs for a moment while he tries to decipher the

meaning behind my words or, hopefully, decides how much to tell me. "She's at college," he says warily, staring hard into my eyes. "In L.A."

My heart sinks, and I breathe deep against the panic rising in my chest, not realizing until this moment how much stock I was putting in her being here, safe with her grandfather. He must read it in my face.

"What the hell is goin' on?"

I brace my hand on the doorframe, feeling suddenly weak. "She was never in L.A."

Before I realize he's done it, he has hold of my arm and, with surprising strength, flings me into the small family room. The door slams behind me and I'm just catching my balance when he produces a gun from the pocket of his robe and aims it at my face.

"I don't got no silver bullets or nothin', so I'm probably at a disadvantage, but I'm thinkin' a hole through your head might slow ya down at least."

"In my current state, it'd do more than slow me down," I say, slumping back into the wall, almost wishing he'd just do it.

He looks at me for a long minute, then lowers the gun. "So if she's not at school, where is she?"

I blow out a sigh and then gesture to the couch. His eyes narrow, but then he backs toward the loveseat. I follow and drop into the couch, remembering when I sat in this exact spot not too many months ago, when Frannie told her grandfather I was a demon—or at least, had been.

"Frannie's been in danger from the minute I set foot in Haden," I start. I hesitate, trying to decide how much to tell him, before finally concluding that he deserves to know all of it. "She's been with Gabriel and me in hiding for the last week."

"Gabriel? That angel?"

I nod. "Yes, but now she's missing."

"*Missing?*" he says, rising from his seat.

"She snuck out last night—took some things and went out through the window of her room. We think . . ." I trail off, unable to say the next part.

He lowers himself back down, his expression still wary, his eyes narrow. "You think what?"

I rake a hand through my hair, trying to figure out how to say this. "Matt was Frannie's guardian angel." I pause and wait for it to sink in before continuing.

His brow creases. "I thought you said this Gabe was her . . ." But then he trails off as his eyes widen with surprised understanding. "Holy . . ." He trails off again. "You mean *our* Matt?"

I nod. "But he couldn't . . . he wasn't able to handle the responsibility."

Ed is on his feet again. "What the hell does that mean?"

"He let himself become distracted. Tempted." Involuntarily, I grimace, knowing that temptation firsthand.

"Just tell me what the hell is going on," he barks, standing ramrod straight, gun hand twitching.

"Matt fell. He's no longer an angel. We think he found Frannie somehow and convinced her to leave with him."

"That's okay, isn't it? If he was her guardian angel he wouldn't hurt—"

I stand, meeting his eyes. "He's a demon now. He's no longer an angel. He serves Lucifer."

He looks at me a moment longer, stunned. Then, as quick as lightning, the gun is in my face again. "You did this!" His hand shakes just the smallest bit, and I can see in his eyes that it's not from fear. He shakes with rage. "I never shoulda let ya near her after I knew what ya were. I was a stupid old fool, thinkin' I saw myself in ya. Thinkin' ya were like me and Frannie's grandma." He growls, mostly at himself, and looks as though he's about to pull the trigger.

I just stare at him, no longer caring either way. I still believe Frannie'd be better off with me gone. But I feel a weary sigh leave my chest at the realization that this would send her grandfather to Hell, and I owe it to both of them to see that that doesn't happen.

His hand shakes harder as rage and hatred twist across his features. And even though I no longer have my demonic sense of smell, I'd swear I catch the black pepper of his fury. He steps closer and thrusts the gun at me.

I hold his eyes. "Help me find her. Please," I say, my voice measured.

His jaw clenches and his eyes burn. The bed of the fingernail on his trigger finger blanches with the increasing pressure as it slowly pulls tighter on the trigger. I wait for the blast as the gun discharges, but I don't flinch. I continue to stare into his eyes. Finally, after what feels like an eternity, he drops his hand back to his side and starts to pace.

"So she left . . ." His eyes shoot back to mine and narrow. "Snuck out."

I nod.

"If she left, there was probably a reason."

I drop my eyes. "Maggie," I say, not wanting to see the look on his face. "Frannie thinks she's in trouble."

"Maggie," he repeats.

Gabriel insisted that Maggie was fine, and I know he can't lie, but I've started questioning his powers of perception. "There's a demon, Marchosias. Frannie thinks Maggie's been . . . spending time with him."

I lift my eyes warily and he's glaring at me, catching the full meaning to my words. "Claire and Daniel didn't say nothin' about Maggie seein' nobody."

"Her parents might not know."

"She's a goddamn kid!" he shouts. "Holy God almighty." He drops the gun on the end table next to the loveseat and rubs his forehead. His whole body softens as he leans on both arms on the back of the loveseat, his head hanging between his shoulders. "So Frannie thinks she can help Maggie," he says, his voice uneven but lower.

"Gabriel has been watching Maggie, hoping Frannie will show up at the house, but I'm afraid something's wrong." I don't add that I'm sure that "something" has to do with Matt.

"Jesus H. Christ," he mutters. "What're we gonna do?"

I step to the fireplace at the back of the small room and lean an elbow on the mantel, my head in my hand. I'm not sure if he's talking about Frannie or Maggie, but either way the answer is the same. "I don't know."

Between my fingers I glimpse a copy of the same picture of Frannie and Matt that she has in her room. They're seven and covered in grease after working with Ed in the garage. I lift my head and run a finger over the glass, wishing with everything I am that I could have kept her safe.

Absently, I scan the multitude of photos lining the mantel, crowding each other out, two and three deep in places. There are others of Frannie, mostly with her family, but then one tucked in the back catches my eye and I go instantly cold.

"Unholy Hell," I hear myself say.

Ed lifts his head and looks at me with anxious eyes. "What?"

I pull the framed picture from the mantel and hold it closer for a better look. The picture is old, the colors dull and faded. In it, a young woman crouches on the front porch of a brick house, and in her arms is a squirming little boy dressed in a white turtle-neck and dark pants. He's kicking at her full skirt in his effort to free himself from her grasp. But even so, she's smiling at him, contentment all over her face. And crouching next to her, the little boy's tiny fingers wrapped tightly around one of his, is someone I haven't seen in over half a century.

Every muscle in my body tenses and I spin on Ed. "Who is this?" I demand.

"Me," he answers simply, his eyes questioning me.

"You . . ." I stare back at the man in the picture. "Who else?"

"My parents."

Unholy Hell.

"These—" I say pointing to the photograph, "—are your parents?"

"So I've been told."

"What do you mean, 'so I've been told'?" My voice comes out as a harsh bark, and I see his eyes flit to the gun on the end table, easily within his reach.

"Pop died not long after that picture was taken, I don't remember him."

I look at the picture again. That face is unmistakable because it looks so much like mine. So much like all of our kind. I'm suddenly sure my legs won't hold me. The room spins. I bring the picture with me as I stumble to the couch. "Gringus," I whisper to myself as I sink into it.

"What the hell is going on?"

"You're sure that's your father," I say, holding up the photo for him to see.

"As sure as I can be. That's what my ma told me and I got no reason to think she was lyin'."

"What was his name?"

"Gus."

All the air leaves my lungs. "How is this possible? How did I not know?" I mutter, dropping my forehead into my hand.

"Are ya gonna tell me what's goin' on?"

I lift my head slowly and look hard at him. Imps have a tell—sulfur. I smell the air, heavy with pipe smoke. No sulfur. But despite that, I know it's all true. It explains so many things.

"I knew your father," I say, holding his eyes with mine.

At first, a cynical smile pulls at one side of his mouth, but then his face goes slack and his body goes rigid as he remembers what I am. "You mean . . ." he trails off, shaking his head. "Nope," he finally says. "Can't be."

"How can you be so sure?" I ask.

"'Cause he was killed in an explosion in his factory. You said demons don't die."

"But when they're posing as humans, there's lots of ways Hell

204

can make it appear as though they have. Most of them involve fire." I meet his eyes as he slides into the loveseat across from me, studying them. Studying *him*. Then I glance back at the picture . . . the man, his eyes trained on the boy, pride and pure joy plain on his face. Paternal pride. There's no mistaking that look—or the resemblance. I would have seen it earlier if I'd ever thought to look for it.

My memory flashes to the last time I saw Gringus. Marchosias had gotten word to me that he had been summoned and sentenced to the Pit. I got there just before his sentence was executed. He stood tall at the Pit, unapologetic. When I asked what happened, his eyes went cloudy—distant. "You wouldn't understand. Not now, anyway," he'd said. But then his eyes cleared. "But always remember, Lucifer. This—" he gestured around us, toward the Lake of Fire and the castle Pandemonium, "—isn't all there is." He brought his fist to his heart and tapped it there. "Sometimes you need to follow your own path." He dropped his hand from his chest and placed it on my shoulder, staring hard into my eyes. "And some things are worth dying for."

His execution was especially gruesome. Lucifer took his failure quite personally because Gringus wasn't just any demon. He'd been created as Lucifer's Left Hand. His Gabriel. I couldn't watch as Lucifer tried to break him, but I heard he never gave in. Finally, after weeks of torture, he was carved into pieces and thrown into the Pit.

Lucifer never replaced Gringus. Rumor was that He was afraid to give any one demon that much power after what happened. I doubted Lucifer was afraid of much, but I also knew He was paranoid. Once burned . . .

"How can *you* be so sure?" Ed counters, pulling me back to the room.

I rub my aching forehead, then look up at him. "Because I knew him well. He was my Consuasor. My mentor."

I close my eyes and loll my head on the back of the couch. *Frannie . . .*

I pull a deep breath then exhale slowly, trying to absorb all of this. Frannie is Nephilim—half angel. But if all this is true, which I'm quite convinced it is, she's also one-eighth demon.

Nephilim and Imps aren't unheard of. They are more common than one would think. But I would wager my left horn that this has never happened before. There may be others with both angel and demon blood. But Frannie and her siblings, I'm quite sure, are unique.

They're less than half human.

15

✝

A Bat Out of Hell

FRANNIE

The blue flashing lights behind us shouldn't be a surprise. Matt is doing at least 100, weaving through the sparse midnight New Jersey traffic. It's really more of a surprise that this is the first time we've been pulled over.

He turns to me with a roguish grin. "Yet another chance for you to practice that talent of yours."

I glare at him and my gut jumps a little when I see how easily we've slipped back into the banter. "You want me to Sway a cop?" I say.

Matt's intense gaze settles on me. "Considering I died before I got a driver's license, that might be a smart idea."

Guilt cuts through me again, shredding my insides. "I'll probably go to jail for this," I mutter.

"We'll both go to jail if you don't," he answers, his expression suddenly intense.

The pain in my gut stops as he turns and rolls down his window. The cop approaches warily, wielding his flashlight like a club.

"Hello, officer," Matt says.

"I clocked you at ninety-six back there, son. What's the rush?"

Matt eyes me, waiting.

Crap.

"Oh, um, no rush, sir," I stumble. "We were just . . . um . . ." I don't even know what to say, and even trying feels skanky, like I'm trying to flirt my way out of the ticket. Only this is worse than flirting.

"License and registration," he says before I can think.

"My sister was just about to explain to you that your equipment needs to be recalibrated because you dropped it," Matt says, his eyes trained on me.

My gut clenches tighter. "Oh, yeah. . . . Remember how it fell on the ground when you got out of the car?" I say, lamely.

The officer, a good-looking guy somewhere in his thirties, stoops lower to see past Matt to where I'm sitting. Matt tips his head toward me in a "go on" gesture.

I clear my throat. "So, you know how the manual says dropping it can cause it to malfunction."

He looks at me and, for a second, seems as though he might argue.

But then I think of Maggie and my heart speeds up, realizing every second we lose here may be the second it takes Marc to tag her. I feel a rush of desperation. I need to get to my family. *Now.*

The officer's face takes on a puzzled squint.

I take a breath to calm myself down so I can focus on his mind. "Especially 'cause you heard something rattling inside after it fell."

"Rattling . . ." he repeats.

"So it's probably broken," I say, gaining confidence.

He straightens up and rubs the stubble on his chin. "I should get it recalibrated."

"Yes," I agree.

"Thanks for bringing this to my attention, miss," he says, ducking down again and flashing me a dimpled smile. "You two have a nice day. And drive carefully," he adds, standing up and banging his palm on the roof.

"Thank you, officer," I say, my heart pounding.

We pull off the shoulder, leaving the cop standing there, staring after us.

"That was wrong in too many ways to count," I say, knowing that there was no other way. We have to get home.

"Listen, Frannie. Your Sway is part of who you are. The sooner you get that, the easier things are going to be for you."

I flash back on Luc saying the same thing not that long ago, and I feel my stomach lurch. Why me? Why did this have to happen to me? "I don't want this."

He glances sideways at me. "Well, you've got it."

I slump into Matt's shoulder and feel his heat. He's as hot as Luc ever was. My stomach rolls, remembering what he is. I pull away and look more closely at him, looking for any change.

"Matt?"

He grunts without looking at me.

"How did you . . ." My stomach knots and I can't say it.

He shoots me a glance. "What, Frannie?" The irritation in his voice is actually comforting. He sounds like the old Matt. My brother.

"How did you get wings?" I blurt.

His jaw clenches and he stares out the windshield. At first, I don't think he's going to answer. Finally, he says, "He gave them back to me."

"He . . . ?" I ask, afraid of the answer.

He turns his head and stares at me, and that's all the answer I get.

I can't hold his gaze, so I lean into his shoulder again. "Was it awful?"

"What?"

"When you lost your angel wings."

For a long time, there's silence, and my muscles ache with tension.

"I don't want to talk about it," he finally says, his voice tight.

I'm glad he's not looking at me when my face twists into a cringe. I shouldn't have asked. Of course it was awful. I swallow. "How much longer?"

"Forever," he replies, still staring out the windshield.

"I'd tell you to drive faster, but I don't think that's possible."

His eyes flash as he turns to me, but then they become sympathetic. "I'm trying to hurry. It'd be really rough if anything happens to Maggie before we get there," he says as he changes lanes. "I'd think after Taylor, that'd be pretty hard to live with."

My stomach has been churning as the same thought has been burrowing deeper and deeper into my brain, taking root there. This is all on me. Taylor is dead 'cause of me. If the same thing happens to Maggie, I don't know what I'll do.

As I think it, I feel a stab of shooting pain in my gut and my hands reflexively go to my stomach. I look over at Matt in time to see his face pull into a satisfied smirk as he turns back to the road ahead.

"Why are you helping me?" I say when the pain subsides.

He glances at me from under raised eyebrows, clearly offended. "She's my little sister too, Frannie."

I don't miss the derision in his voice and I decide not to push it. Why he's helping me doesn't matter. What *does* matter is that he was the only one who was willing to help me when I needed it.

GABE

Marchosias lurks in the shadows behind the garage at the side of the house. He's propped on the fence with a clear view of Maggie and Grace's window. A shadow lingers behind him, a form in the dark that I can't make out. It's not a demon—that much I know—so it's probably Lilith.

Faith is on my heels as I pace between Marc and the house while he leers, his eyes glowing out of the darkness.

"Just zap him," she whispers. "It would be justified."

"It wouldn't," I answer. "He isn't hurting anyone."

She throws a glance over her shoulder as we round the corner of the house into the backyard. "But he wants to."

"They all want to. It's what they do."

"Which is why the Almighty should just blow them all into oblivion. He could, you know. If He wanted to," she says conspiratorially, once we're out of Marc's line of sight.

I peer through the kitchen window at Claire as she frantically mops the kitchen floor, the worry etched into her pale face. She keeps glancing at the phone, then the door. Finally, she leans the mop on the table and drops into a chair, face in hands, weeping.

This is so supremely unfair, and for an instant I think Faith is right. If there were no Hell, how much better things would be. But then the cold truth intrudes on my thoughts. Even if there were no Hell, there would still be evil. Man is perfectly capable of manifesting that on his own, without any infernal help. Without the threat of Hell, there'd be no checks and balances. No consequences.

I turn to Faith, my jaw tight. "And then what? There needs to be balance."

She settles into the wicker loveseat under the overhang near the back door and pats the seat next to her.

I look back in the direction of Marchosias one more time and drop into it, feeling exhausted. I weave my fingers into my hair, elbows on knees, and try to think. After a minute, I feel Faith's hand on my back, stroking softly, raising goose bumps on my increasingly human skin.

"You know, the fate of the universe isn't all on you. Let us help you." Her voice is soft, soothing.

I lift my head and she gazes at me, her expression softening. She reaches up and strokes my cheek. "Let *me* help you."

She stares into my eyes for a long minute, her hand on my face, her expression hopeful.

I reach for her hand and gently lower it, backing away. "You *are* helping. You've been invaluable."

"Gabriel," she says, her fingers weaving into mine. "I want to be more than invaluable." She brings my hand to her mouth and glides my fingertips over her lips. "I love you," she says, hooking her other hand around my neck and pulling me into a kiss.

I feel myself start to shake as I turn my head to the side. Her lips slide off mine, but she doesn't let go of me.

"Please, Gabriel. She'll never love you like I do," she whispers into my cheek. "I gave up everything for you."

My heart spasms as I turn back to her. "You did *what*?"

She captures my eyes with hers. "It was you, Gabriel. It's always been you. You're the one I fell in love with."

I close my eyes and breathe, trying to process that, but it's impossible to think with her hands moving over my shoulders, caressing. "I'm sorry. I . . . I didn't know."

She pulls closer and I feel her breath, hot in my ear. "I love you. I've always loved you."

Her lips glide across my cheek, toward my mouth, and I fight to ward off the desire I feel stir deep inside me. "I can't, Faith."

Her lips brush mine. "You can," she breathes.

I force myself to pull away and look her in the eye, my jaw clenched and my breathing uneven. "You know that's not true."

"I know it *is*." Her eyes blaze as she stares into mine. "I saw you," she says, pressing closer. Her hand finds my chest and fireworks explode inside me. "I saw you in her bed. You were kissing her."

My heart sinks. But still, every nerve ending hums. Damn these hormones. "You shouldn't have seen that."

Faith stiffens next to me and her voice takes on a hard edge as her hand drops to my thigh. "It was my job to see that."

Despair opens a sinkhole in my chest, and I feel the weight of the world pressing down on it, threatening to cave it in. "It shouldn't have happened." But I wanted it to. I wanted more than kissing. I wanted all of her.

Frannie.

Frustration roils inside me like a building storm at the memory of Frannie in my arms. My muscles tense and heat prickles my skin. I ache all over with need, unbearable and unrelenting.

"Please, Gabriel." Faith presses into me, a tear trickling over her lashes. "Kiss me like that." Her lips move along the line of my jaw, working toward my mouth. "Pretend I'm her."

Her tears on my face are warm and wet. Her skin, silk. Her breath, hot. I close my eyes and draw a deep breath, fighting the feelings that I can't control.

And then her lips are on mine.

Insatiable desire erupts from the depths of my core, and I pull her closer, crushing her to me, devouring her with my kiss— needing her like I've never needed anything before.

She shifts onto my lap and the feel of her body pressing into mine is more than I can take. Her lips move with mine and her hands glide over my back, pulling me deeper. There's no escape. I'm drowning in her.

Her lips leave mine for an instant and I struggle for air. "Frannie," I whisper.

She stiffens and time stops as I realize what I said.

"Well, isn't this special."

Faith leaps from my lap at the sound of Aaron's voice.

"Aaron," I say, standing from the loveseat and turning to him, trying to quiet my pounding heart and stay focused. "Where are the girls?"

His smirk is a mile wide. "Upstairs."

"Faith." I turn toward her. "Would you go up and keep them company?"

Her eyes darken and her tone is sharp and cold as a steel blade as she says, "Whatever you want."

She stares at me a moment longer, pain and anger grappling for control of her expression. Finally, she turns and disappears around the corner, and a moment later I hear her and Daniel talking at the front door.

"Whatever you want," Aaron repeats in a trill, watching after Faith. He looks me over. "O ye of little . . . Faith." He chuckles under his breath at his pathetic burst of wit. "That takes on a whole new meaning."

"It's not your concern, Aaron," I say, my self-disgust eating me alive, making me feel sick. I can't understand how the avengers haven't come for me. I don't belong in His fold.

"Favors from the fallen?" He taps a finger on his temple. "That sounds like an abuse of power to me. Can you say sexual harassment?" He chuckles again. "That demon really is rubbing off on you. I'll have to send him a thank-you gift."

"Are you done?" I say, folding my arms across my chest, trying to hold myself together.

"Just keep giving in to temptation, Gabriel and *you'll* be

done. It's a good thing you're so comfortable with the fallen, because you'll be joining them soon and I'll have your job."

My self-loathing erupts and I turn it on him. "Not if you can't manage to do yours. Do *not* leave Maggie's side while Marchosias, or any other demon for that matter, is in her proximity."

"Yes, oh lusty one." The smirk doesn't leave his face as he fades out.

I lean into the house and rub my aching temples, weak with defeat. "Frannie. Where are you?" I whisper, my heart collapsing.

LUC

I spend most of the day at Ed's trying to sort through everything, the whole time hoping for a knock on the door or a call from Frannie. Finally, I leave Ed at the house with instructions to call me if Frannie shows up, and I head to Riley's. Gabriel was going to stay with Daniel, so her house is covered. With Taylor gone, this is the only other place I can think that Frannie would go. I step out of the Shelby onto the sidewalk and stride to Riley's door, then ring the bell and wait.

Riley appears at the door a minute later with Trevor at her side.

Her eyes widen in surprise. "Luc?"

I smile and try to stay calm. "Hello, Riley. Trevor," I add with a nod in his direction.

"What are you doing here? Aren't you supposed to be in L.A. with Frannie?"

I stare at her, wishing I had thought this through a little

more thoroughly. From her surprise, it's clear that she hasn't heard from Frannie. But if she does, I need to know about it.

"We actually haven't left yet," I say. "Problem with the flights. Frannie had some last-minute things to do and we were supposed to meet at her house," I continue, "but she's late. I was hoping she stopped here on her way?"

"No. I haven't seen her." She pulls her phone out of her pocket.

"I already tried her cell. She's not answering."

Her hand drops to her side. "Oh. Well . . ."

I smile at her. "So, if she stops by—"

"I'll tell her to get her butt home," she finishes for me with a smile.

"Thanks, Riley," I say with a nod and turn for the car. "See you, Trevor."

"Tell her I miss her already!" Riley calls after me.

I raise a hand in acknowledgment as I jog to the Shelby, slipping into the front seat. The instant I'm in the car, I know I'm not alone. The pungent stench of unbathed humanity almost drives me back out onto the street.

"Lose something?" The voice is female, but I don't recognize it. I look toward the passenger seat into a face that is totally unfamiliar. But the eyes . . . they draw me in . . . pulling at something deep and primal within me—pure animal need.

I automatically reach for the door handle and drop my gaze before Lilith can snare me. "I recognize you, so you can turn off the infernal tractor beam. I'm not going to fall for it again."

"I suppose if I said 'your loss' that wouldn't help my cause."

"*Nothing* is going to help your cause, Lilith," I say, my eyes flicking momentarily to her new face.

Her host would be pretty if she wasn't neglected and malnourished—too skinny, with sunken purple hollows under her eyes. Her shoulder-length carrot-red hair is matted in places, and her pallid skin is drawn tightly over protruding bone.

I almost feel sorry for her, wondering what in her life was so bad it drove her to drugs—and, most likely, worse. But then Lilith smiles, exposing brown, rotting teeth, and her eyes glint in the dim light as something lascivious slides across her face.

"I'm not here for *that* anyway," she says.

I realize she sounds different. Weary.

"Frannie is with Matt," I say. "Where are they?"

A wicked smile curves her cracked lips. "Not far."

My hand shoots out like a dart, clamping around her throat and pinning her against the passenger door. "Where?"

"She's on a rescue mission, Luc. You know where she's going."

I let go of her as I feel her seductive pull, and her form starts to flicker into something far more appealing. "Turn it off, Lilith," I warn.

She slumps back into the seat. "You're no fun," she laments.

"Get out."

She sighs, sinking deeper into the seat. "Do you remember when you told me I didn't need to be like this?" she says, gesturing with the wave of an arm at her emaciated body.

"Yes." The scene is all too vivid in my mind—Frannie's lifeless body on the bed with Gabriel hovering over her, and Lilith holding Frannie's and my souls hostage inside her host.

"Did you have an actual plan, or were you just blowing sunshine?"

I drop my gaze, because I was, in fact, blowing sunshine. I would have said anything to get her to let Frannie's soul go.

"I don't want this anymore," she says quietly. "And I think I know a way out."

My gaze snaps to her then. I can't help myself. "How?"

"It has to do with Frannie."

Where I was suspicious before, I feel my hackles rise. "You go anywhere near Frannie, I will kill you with my bare hands."

The smallest of smiles curls the corners of her lips. "That didn't work out so hot last time you tried."

My blood runs cold when I remember the park—how I had intended to kill Lilith/Angelique.

"My mistake. I won't make the same one twice," I bluff.

"As titillating as the thought of you making the same mistake twice is . . ." she says, reaching out to stroke my thigh. "I'm serious. I want out." With the last words, her casual façade slips and she looks dead serious and scared. "You got out, Lucifer. You're the only one ever to do it. Help me. Please."

The desperation in her eyes is unmistakable. And the fact that I can look into them for this long without needing to dive into them—dive into *her*, I think with chagrin—is all the proof I need that she means what she's saying. She's turned off the succubus siren.

I look at her more appraisingly. I gave up my immortality for love. She gave up her mortality for lust. When she had the choice all those eons ago, she chose eternity in the Abyss. Is it possible that she could change after all this time? She's spent a good chunk of those eons at King Lucifer's side. She could know things—His weaknesses, vulnerabilities. "Give me one reason why I should trust you."

"Because you were right. Once He has Frannie, He won't want me anymore. He's already obsessed with her. It's all He talks about." Her pale green eyes lock on mine. "I'll have nothing. I'll *be* nothing . . ." she slumps and trails off, defeated. Her eyes fall to her thigh where she picks at a large scab just below the hem of her short skirt. "You have to help me," she says, her voice so low I can barely hear her.

"What are you proposing?"

She lifts her eyes and stares at me out from under scraggly, matted red lashes. "You help me, I help you."

"That seems a bit lacking in the details department. Give me something specific."

She continues to hold my gaze. "I think Frannie's more than she seems. *He* thinks she is. It's not just her Sway He wants."

Again, I feel myself bristle. How much does He know? Because Frannie *is* more than she seems—angel, demon, and mortal rolled into one. Couple that with her Sway, and God only knows what she's capable of. "Frannie's not going to be any part of this," I growl.

"If you want to take Him down, she's going to have to be."

I feel a jolt of shock grip my gut. I never expected taking Him down to be on the table. It's not possible. But even if it were, I couldn't risk Frannie. "Then there's no deal. I'm not letting you—or Him—" I add with a shudder, "—within a mile of her."

But as I say it, I feel a hole open in my chest, realizing I don't know where "within a mile of her" is. She could be anywhere. And He could already be there with her.

There's a tap on the glass behind me and Lilith's face pinches. "Don't tell him," she hisses.

I turn to see Marc's face leering through the window at me. "Your boyfriend isn't in on the plan?"

She glares at me, a warning in her cold eyes.

When I roll down my window, Marc leans in. "Didn't get enough the first time?"

My stomach rolls and I glare up at him. "If you touch Maggie, I *will* kill you." He barks out a laugh as I reach across and push open Lilith's door. "Stay away from Frannie. Stay away from me."

She grins. "Or you'll what? Sic your celestial friend on me?" she says as she slides out of the Shelby. "You're even starting to smell bad," she adds, waving a hand in front of her face.

Coming from her, that's almost laughable. Though, even after she's gone, the scent of unwashed humanity lingers, and I realize it may not have all been her. She and Marc stand, watching, as I peel away from the curb. I head back to my apartment for a change of clothes and pray sincerely to God that Gabriel's had better luck than I have.

16

✠

Saving Grace

FRANNIE

We reach Haden in just over twenty-four hours, as the sun hits the horizon and the reds and purples of sunset take hold.

"Where are you going?" I ask when Matt misses our exit on the highway. "We need to get home."

"I think we need to scout it out before we go charging in there," he answers. He slows and moves into the right lane. "If Marc is with Maggie, it's only to get to you. I don't want you walking into a trap or anything."

For the hundredth time panic grips my heart as I wonder what the hell I'm thinking. *Please don't let me screw this up*, I pray. "But what if he's with her? What if he tags her before we get there?"

His eyes dart sideways at me. "I'll go see what's going on, then come back for you. But I need to leave you somewhere safe in the meantime."

"So, where are we going?" I ask through my tight throat, breathing against my exploding heart.

"Grandpa's."

I start. "You too?"

He smirks at me. "What do you think?"

"You have to come right back for me. Gabe will find me if we mess around too long. He'll keep me from helping Maggie."

"If Gabriel is anywhere, it's at the house. One more reason why I need to go first and check it out."

I look at him. "What are you going to do?"

"I just want to check in with my old guru. You know . . . catch up and stuff." He turns his attention back to the road as he takes the exit ramp.

I drum my fingers nervously on the armrest, my eyes darting around, as we enter Grandpa's neighborhood. He pulls up to the curb in front of Grandpa's. "Go inside. I'll be back as soon as I can. If Gabriel's there I'll have to figure out a way to sidetrack him, so it may not be until morning."

"Okay," I say. "But try to hurry." I step out of the car and stumble numbly up the walk. As the sun goes down over Grandpa's neighborhood, everything is deceptively calm. When I reach the door, I hear Matt pull away. I watch him disappear behind the trees, then I stand at the door for a long time before knocking, trying to work out my explanation.

But before I even lift my hand to knock, the door swings open and Grandpa is standing there. He reaches for my shoulder and pulls me quickly inside.

I stand with my arms wrapped tightly around him, afraid

to let go, and I can't stop the tears. "Grandpa," I sob into his shoulder. He's so warm—and his heat starts to thaw the chill in my heart.

He strokes my hair as I take in the familiar scent of sweet pipe smoke clinging to his shirt. "I got ya, Frannie." His sandpaper voice rumbles in his chest.

"Grandpa," I say again as the tears slow. As happy as I am to see him, my voice only sounds tired. I feel myself leaning harder into him as exhaustion takes me.

"I been waitin' for ya," he says, continuing to hold me, then he breaks his embrace and leads me into the warm and familiar living room. "Luc was here lookin' for ya. Almost shot him," he says as we settle into the couch. He loops an arm behind my shoulders and squeezes. "Probably shoulda."

I feel myself start to shake and lay my head on Grandpa's shoulder. "Luc was here?" I look down at my fidgeting hands. I was so mad when I left. I just wanted to get away from both Luc and Gabe. But my heart struggles to keep a rhythm as I remember the look on Luc's face when he said he wanted to leave, just the two of us. "What did he want?"

"You. He thought ya might end up here." He shifts and looks at me. "What're ya runnin' from, Frannie?"

"Not from." I pull a deep breath. "To. Is everything okay at home?"

His brow creases. "Far as I know."

All of a sudden I'm confused. Matt was so sure. "So Maggie's okay?"

"Luc asked the same thing." The crease in his brow deepens. "What's goin' on, Frannie?"

I exhale a tense sigh. "There are a lot of things going on right now. I can't tell you everything. It would be dangerous for you."

"Don't ya dare be worryin' about me." He tries to keep his voice light, but I can hear the concern behind the words. "I can take care of myself."

I shift under his arm and look up at him. "I know, but . . ." I hesitate, not sure how much to tell him. He already knows so much, but at the same time, so little. "I didn't really leave for college."

"I figured. But ya went somewhere with Luc."

"And Gabe," I say.

His eyes harden. "The angel."

I nod.

He looks me square in the eye. "Seems to me like this angel and Luc done nothing but put ya in danger and steer ya wrong."

I shake my head. "No, Grandpa. All the screwups have been mine." I think about Taylor and Matt again and feel sick, despite the fact that my stomach couldn't be more empty.

He must hear it growl, because he stands from the couch. "I'll get ya something to put in that stomach."

"'Kay," I say, trying to remember the last time I ate anything.

I sink deeper into the couch, and a few minutes later, Grandpa is back with a ham sandwich and a glass of milk.

"Thanks," I say, taking the plate and glass from his hands.

He sits next to me, watching, as I scarf down the sandwich and chug the milk, too starving to be self-conscious.

"Ya want another one?" he says, taking the plate from my hand when I'm done.

The feel of food in my stomach isn't exactly comfortable, seeing as I've gone so long without it, so even though I'm still a little hungry I decided to quit while I'm ahead. "No, Grandpa. But thanks."

He lays my dishes on the coffee table and hooks his arm over my shoulder. "You're stayin' here with me."

I tuck tighter into his side. "Ma—" I catch myself. "My friend might be coming back for me tonight. I really shouldn't stay here. If Luc was here—"

"The others'll come lookin' for ya too," he finishes for me.

I nod.

Grandpa's gaze becomes uncharacteristically intense, and I can almost feel heat radiating off his body. "What would happen if they found ya?"

I shrug to cover my shiver from the chill that fingers up my spine. "I don't know," I answer honestly.

"Do ya think whatever it is would be worse than spendin' the rest of your life lookin' over your shoulder?"

I shiver again, remembering how drawn I was to King Lucifer—how much I lusted for His power. "Yeah."

Something in Grandpa's eyes flash. "Are ya sure, 'cause it doesn't seem to me they're tryin' to kill ya . . ." I catch something in his voice that isn't exactly relief. It's bigger.

"I'm pretty sure He wants me alive." The shudder is stronger this time as I realize I've shifted Grandpa's "they" into the "He" that I can't get out of my mind now that I've thought of Him. The pendant lying against my chest starts to tingle, then burn. I bring my hand up and lay it over my chest as my heart beats in rhythm with the pulsing of the metal on my skin.

"Well, as long as you're here, I'll keep you safe."

"I can't stay, Grandpa. It wouldn't be safe for *you*."

I'm surprised by the chuckle that I feel more than hear. I look up into his face.

"Nothin's gonna touch ya here," he says, a smile still on his lips. He pulls himself from the couch and holds his hand out to me. "Why don't ya get some rest? We can talk about what's gonna happen tomorrow, tomorrow."

I glance at the clock and it's barely nine. "It's pretty early . . ."

He chuckles again as I take his hand and let him pull me out of the couch. "Not for an old man like me."

"'Kay, Grandpa." I turn for the short corridor that leads to the guest bedroom and he follows me up the hall. "Thanks for letting me stay here. Please don't say anything to Mom or Dad. It's safer for them if they don't know where I am."

"My lips are sealed," he says, and just for an instant, I'd swear something in his face changes. The glint that's always in Grandpa's eyes turns to more of a burn. But the next instant it's gone, and I'm sure it was just my being paranoid.

I glance in the bedroom door at the bed. Matt will be back any minute, but in the meantime, a shower and a nap doesn't sound like such a bad idea. I think about telling Grandpa that Matt is coming for me but then decide telling him about Matt on top of everything else might be too much. "Someone might be coming for me," I finally say.

"You mean other than Luc and that *angel*?" His voice sharpens to a point on the last word and his eyes flare again.

How does he know about my beautiful angel?

"Um . . ."

"Luc said Gabriel was looking for you," he says, and my insides unclench.

"Yeah . . . I'm sure he is." My throat clicks as I swallow. "I was actually thinking of someone else. And when he comes, I'll have to go."

"Everybody wants a piece of you," he says, as he pulls me into a hug. And what I smell on his shirt isn't pipe smoke.

It's rotten eggs.

I push away and look into Grandpa's face, terrified of what I'm suddenly sure I'll see. But his blue eyes, though concerned, are soft. He leans in and kisses my forehead. "Night, Frannie."

And all I smell is the hint of sweet pipe smoke that always lingers around him. No brimstone.

I'm totally losing it.

"Night, Grandpa," I say, trying to keep the shake out of my voice. I slip through the door into the guest bedroom, flicking on the light.

Grandpa catches my eye just before the door closes. "You belong with me." The gravel tone of his voice starts to smooth into something softer and more musical. "I will always keep you safe."

GABE

The first time, I didn't think anything of the tickle running up my spine. The second time, however, it pulls me from my thoughts. I try to fade out, and I still can, but it takes a Herculean effort to keep my increasingly corporeal body invisible, so I give up.

As I stand and descend the two steps from the porch to the walk, a movement at the corner of my eye makes me spin. I look up to see the family room curtains sway from where Grace dropped them. I had hoped she'd stay with Faith and Maggie upstairs, but she's been sitting in the chair near the window off and on for most of the day, watching me.

Faith.

I can't stop thinking about what happened—what she said. She fell from Heaven because she loved me. How was I so blind as to not know that?

Because I didn't understand human love then.

But I do now. Now I know the power of it. I understand the lengths a person would go to in the name of love—the sacrifices they'd make.

I'd willingly give up my wings for you.

I'd said those words to Frannie before we left Haden, and, God help me, they're still true.

I pinch my forehead against the headache brewing there and walk around back, my guard up. Marchosias is gone for the moment, but that doesn't mean he won't be back. As I round the corner into the backyard, the door opens and Grace slides through onto the back porch, closing it quickly behind her. The darkness has made her braver.

"Hi," she says without looking up.

"Hello."

"Am I . . . bothering you?"

I walk slowly up the steps and slide into the wicker loveseat, motioning for her to join me. "Not at all."

"Because Dad said we should leave you alone."

I can't help but smile. "I could use some company."

She sits at the other end of the loveseat, a few feet from me, still looking at her feet. "Is Frannie an angel?"

If I didn't know about Grace's ability to see auras—a being's true essence—I'd think the question strange. "No."

"I didn't think so, but there's something different about her." Her eyes lift briefly to mine, then fall just as fast. "Something . . . not really angel . . . but Divine."

I think about that for a second, because she's describing exactly what I feel in Frannie—something celestial but not angelic. "What do you see when you look at an angel?"

She chews her lip for a minute before answering. "Anyone who's not human looks . . ." she trails off and shrugs. "There's not really a word. Shiny?" She shakes her head. "No. That's not right. It's more than shiny." She hesitates, searching, then her eyes light up and she looks into mine. "Luminescent. That's it. And sort of metallic. Angels are bright, like platinum, and demons are darker, like tarnished bronze." She nods her head, satisfied.

"And Frannie?"

Her lashes lower and she shifts in her seat. "She's . . . different but still luminescent. I can't really describe it." She shrugs. "It's like there's parts of both. Does platinum tarnish?"

I smile. "Not that I'm aware of."

She shrugs again. "That's the only way I can describe it."

"Grace, this is really important. Never approach a demon. If they sense your ability . . ." I trail off, not wanting to frighten her.

"It's okay," she says, chewing her lip again and watching her hands, folded in her lap. She peeks at me out of the corner of her eye. "I can make them go away."

My heart skips. "How?"

She looks at me then. "I pray. Ephesians six eleven seems to work the best."

I appraise her for a moment. Can she actually repel demons? That would be a useful tool.

"How old were you? The first time you saw an angel?"

Her eyes find mine again. "Six."

"Young," I say. "Were you frightened?"

"A little," she confesses. "It was in the hospital after Matt fell out of the tree. The nurse who came to the waiting room with the doctor to tell us they hadn't been able to save him was an angel. Because she was there, I believed Matt had gone to Heaven, and that made me feel a little better."

At Matt's name, I feel that tickle up my spine again.

She really looks at me for the first time. "Do angels eat? I could get you something."

"No, thank you. I'm fine."

"I made some lemonade . . ." she says.

I smile the most reassuring smile I can find. "Lemonade sounds great, Grace. Thanks."

There's a shy smile on her face as she pushes to her feet. I stand and turn to watch her head into the house.

Which is why I don't see the blast until it's knocked me flat on my back.

Too late, I throw up a field.

The smell of brimstone mingles with seared flesh as he stands over me, gloating. "Guardian angel protocol rule one. Never let down your guard, even for lemonade." Matt's eyes flash red heat.

I push to a sit and wince as pain slices through me. "Where is she?"

"Safe. . . . From you, anyway."

Hauling myself off the ground is harder than I anticipate, and I stagger and nearly fall again. "Where is she?" I repeat.

"Grandpa has her." He smirks, his face a toxic mixture of rage and amusement. "Though I don't think he's quite himself."

I muster everything I can find and launch into him. I'm sure the last thing he expects is a physical attack, and he falls under my weight before he can launch another blast of Hellfire. My hand is in his face as I pin his arm back.

He chuckles under his breath, taking me off guard. "Must be hard, carrying around all that guilt."

The mix of emotions that assaults me as I look down at him is hard to describe. I don't have the framework to put a name to all of them. But guilt is definitely in there. I'll always feel guilty about what happened to him. But looking into his hard eyes, full of hatred, it's clear that sentimentality will only get me killed. "Is there a point you're trying to make?"

"Why didn't you tell me I was special too? It's not just Frannie."

"You needed to find out for yourself when you were ready."

"Thankfully, others had more faith in me," he says. I feel his infernal energy pulse under me as if it has a life of its own. "I can feel it eating at you . . . all your doubt. Do you still belong? Will you ever be able to go back? Will you ever get into my sister's pants?" He turns his head to look at me and tsks. "Nasty angel."

Out of nowhere, all at the same instant, the sharp edge of guilt twists in my gut and a blast of Hellfire erupts from his whole body, throwing me back. I hit the ground and he bounds to his feet. He plants the sole of one shoe in my chest, his glowing fist pointed at my face. "Gotta love it when the holier-than-thou get what they deserve."

I twist out from under him just as a blast of Hellfire leaves a crater in the lawn where I was lying.

"Stop!"

The shout comes from the porch. I look up to find Grace standing there in the waning light, a glass of lemonade in each hand.

"Go inside, Grace," I call as panic crawls through my chest, but when I turn back to Matt, he's standing, arms hanging limply at his side, staring at Grace.

She squints back at him, a mix of repulsion and fear on her face, and drops the glasses where she stands. They explode in a shower of glass and lemonade when they hit the brick stairs. Her lips start to move in what sounds like a mumbled prayer.

Matt winces but doesn't break her gaze, almost as if she's holding him hypnotized. A second later, he's on his knees, hands over his ears. "I'm sorry, Grace. Please . . ."

Grace moves slowly toward Matt, her lips still moving in her murmured prayer.

I'm on my feet the next second, standing between them. Out of the corner of my eye I see Daniel and Claire pour out onto the back porch.

Daniel sprints down the stairs toward his daughter, crunching through broken glass, but I call him off with a raised hand.

"Grace," I say, reaching for her shoulder, but she keeps moving past me as if in a trance.

". . . having fastened on the belt of truth, and having put on the breastplate of righteousness . . ." she mutters.

"Grace," I say again, spinning her to face me and shaking her gently.

She blinks, then lifts her eyes to mine. For a second she doesn't seem to see me, but then her eyes well and she says, "I thought he went to Heaven."

"Go inside, Grace. Please."

I loop my arm around her and we start walking back the way she came. Claire takes her when we reach the porch and guides her through the door with a last glance back at Daniel. When I glance over my shoulder, Matt's gone, but Daniel is standing on the lawn, looking out to where Matt was, stunned.

"Matt?" he says, dazed.

I lay a hand on his shoulder and flood him with peace. "I'm so sorry, Daniel."

He drops his head. "He's chosen."

"I'm afraid so." I give him a pat on the back and head with him to the door. "Go check on the girls."

He nods, locking his eyes with mine in a silent plea, before ducking through the door.

"Well, that was interesting."

Aaron's simper from behind me does nothing for my shaky nerves. I turn to tell him to shut up and do his job, and find his hand raised in my direction, delicate white lightning dancing over the surface of his skin.

He shrugs and a cold smile cuts across his face. "Who would

have known a fallen could take down the great Gabriel?" he says, then his expression shifts to a mask of feigned grief. "It's just a shame I was too late to save you from him," he adds as a blinding streak of lightning erupts from his palm.

17

✝

Second Coming

FRANNIE

The door clicks closed and I just stand here in the bedroom for a second trying to remember what Grandpa said. My mind feels full of cotton candy. He said something about being safe, I think.

I give my head a last shake, then crack the door open. Grandpa is gone and the lights in the hall and family room are out. It's totally dark except for the yellow light slanting into the hall from the dim overhead fixture in my room. I make my way the few steps to the bathroom. It takes a second for the fluorescent bulb to flicker to life, and I realize I'm breathing too fast. As the fluorescent glow fills the room, I look in the mirror and almost gasp. My eyes are sunken and purple, and my skin is so pale I look dead.

But then my eyes are drawn to the metal pendant that I couldn't bear to remove. I trace my finger along its curved surface and feel it call to me.

I yank my eyes away from my reflection and pull open the medicine cabinet. Inside, I find a hotel toothbrush wrapped in plastic and a travel-size tube of Crest. I run the toothbrush over my teeth, then crank the shower on full blast. I pull off my clothes and step in, letting the warm water trickle through my hair and down my body. At first I just stand here, intending to take my time, but then I decide too much time alone with myself is dangerous, 'cause I have a sudden, overwhelming need to call for Gabe. I think of him and Luc. I'm sure they're looking for me, and it tugs at my heart that, for the first time in months, I don't have either of them at my side. I'm on my own, for better or worse.

Was this a mistake? What if I royally screwed up by coming here? Have I put Luc and Gabe in danger? The last time I ditched them, Taylor ended up dead. I feel suddenly cold and crank the hot water, then hurry through my routine and wrap myself in a towel, tucking it tightly around me. I chance one last glance at the dead girl in the mirror before flicking out the light and heading back to my room.

I lock the door behind me and cross to the window, where I look outside for Matt. When he's not there, I turn and lean against the window frame, trying to settle my nerves, and let my eyes wander over the familiar treasures on the heavy antique dresser. These things have been here all my life. I walk over and pick up a picture of all five of us kids with Santa when Maggie was only a baby.

I miss them so much.

Panic kicks in my chest. I have to get to them—to Maggie—before it's too late.

I feel all my muscles tense as the image of Maggie and Marc surfaces in my mind. What if it's true? What will I do if he's already hurt her?

I close my eyes, breathing back the threat of tears. She's going to be okay. I have to believe that.

I don't understand my Sway, what it is or how it works, but I'm starting to trust it, just like I trust my visions. I've seen it work. I can't deny it. And I also have the feeling Gabe is right. If I'm gonna have a chance, I need to learn to use it. It seems to come easiest when it comes from my heart, and when I try to force it, it doesn't seem to work at all.

I need it to work now.

I feel love for my family swell in my heart and send a message out to Maggie.

Be safe. Be safe. Be safe.

I focus on moving air in and out of my lungs as I put the picture down. I run my fingers over a lump of clay that Matt painted a smiley face on in kindergarten and gave to Grandma and Grandpa for Christmas. Next to it is a round tin with powder and a fluffy white puff that used to smell like jasmine, but now smells like dust. Grandma's silver brush with horsehair bristles and matching hand mirror is here too. I pick it up and bring it to my nose, but her smell is long gone from it. The assortment of bobby pins and hair clips in an old polished abalone shell sits next to the brush. I smile at the memory of my oldest sister, Mary. She thought she wanted to be a beautician when she was nine. We'd spend hours in here, Mary doing everyone's hair and makeup. Even Matt's.

My eyes slide to the small wooden jewelry box where all

Grandma's costume jewelry was stored—Mary's stash for accessorizing her younger siblings. I lift the box, remembering that, after we were all dolled up, we'd sit in here for hours playing games and listening to the tune from the jewelry box, stopping what we were doing every so often to wind it. I remember Matt telling me to stop playing it and grabbing it away.

"That's very old and delicate," Mom had scolded as she lifted it from his hand and placed it back into mine. "It can't take rough handling."

I stroke a finger over the carved lid, inlayed with some pure black stone. The stone has absolutely no shine, but it's not dull either. It seems almost alive, devouring the light around it. And, as I trace my finger around the spiral of the design, I feel the tip of it go numb.

I wind the tiny key at the back of the box and curl my fingers under the lid, lifting it ever so gently, heeding my mother's words from so long ago.

As the first notes waft up to meet me, I start. It's the tune from my dreams. This is why I recognized it. I close my eyes and start humming along, swaying gently to the old familiar tune. I only realize I'm gripping the pendant in my other hand when I feel the sharp edge cut into my finger.

I lift my palm to my face and watch thick crimson blood seep slowly from the wound on my finger and trickle down my hand. I'm mesmerized by the tune and the blood and barely hear the low rumble followed by a wet ripping sound.

Then a musical voice is humming with me to the comforting melody.

When I look up, the green-eyed angel is standing near my

door. He moves cautiously to stand next to me and looks at me in the mirror over the dresser. "I was waiting. I knew you would call."

I turn and raise my eyes to his, and he smiles down at me.

"You're wearing it," he says. He lifts a hand and traces a finger down the leather strap around my neck to the pendant lying on my chest, and I hear the tuning-fork hum come from it again. He smooths a finger gently over the metal and the skin under it tingles. "I made this for you."

I look down and the pattern—an eye-shaped spiral that flares at the edges—is exactly the same design as the black stone on the box.

His touch is soft, but it burns as his finger follows the leather strap up to my neck. He pulls away and locks me in his astonishing green gaze, holding me mesmerized. Myriad emotions pass over his face, finally settling on a mix of relieved anguish.

Tentatively, I lift my shaking hand, expecting my fingers to brush through air, as they did before when I tried to touch the green-eyed boy in my dreams. But instead, they contact warm flesh. The air charges with static electricity as I trace my finger over the back of his hand, leaving a thin trail of blood from my cut that vanishes into his skin. And that's when I see it. Red electricity skittering over my hand.

"You see," he says hooking his finger under my hand and inspecting the dance of red lightning across my knuckles. "You belong with us."

I'm struggling for air when I finally ask. "Who are you?"

He smiles. "Look deep within yourself and you'll find me there."

The rush of frustrated anticipation makes thinking straight difficult. I remember him slipping the pendant around my neck. I feel him cradling me, safe on the beach. But those were dreams.

His eyes glow with the light of a star, just as they did in my dream. I stare into them, mesmerized, and the pendant burns into my chest, pulsing with its own living energy.

His smile spreads, warm and genuine. "You recognize me from your dream—your morning star?"

Somewhere inside me terror takes hold as a deep corner of my brain registers what's happening—who He is. But the pendant pulses on my chest and I'm paralyzed, unable to even pull my hand away from His.

He gazes down at me, disappointment clear in His expression. "I hoped I wouldn't frighten you in this form."

I shudder as the image of His other form, huge, with black bat's wings and glowing green eyes in a jet-black face, surfaces in my mind, but I still can't move. But then I remember what Gabe said. Can He read my thoughts?

I focus and build the wall up around my mind.

He looks at me a moment, then a smile breaks over His face. "Very good." It's not until He squeezes my hand and releases it that I realize I hadn't let His hand go. "Gabriel has taught you to guard your mind. Wise, that."

Finally, I find the strength to close my eyes and back away. I'm shaking so hard I'm half surprised my legs don't collapse. I know I should run, but I'm not sure I could.

As I stand here, totally panicked, trying to figure out how to get not only me but also Grandpa out of here, it hits me.

This is it.

This is what I'm supposed to do—the thing I'm meant for.

He has come to me, and I feel a deep certainty that this is how it was supposed to be. Gabe wanted me to lure Him to me and find out His weakness. I can do this. Even if He doesn't have a weakness, maybe I can influence His thoughts. If He trusts me, maybe I can make the difference. *This* is what I'm supposed to do with my Sway.

It has to be.

"But . . . what is your *real* form?" I ask, setting my resolve and trying to find the courage inside me to follow through with this. I can't hide the shake in my voice, but I hold His gaze.

His smile fades and His face transforms into a mask of sadness. "My true form . . ." He says, pensively with a slow shake of His head. But then His eyes lift to mine, hopeful. "This is my true essence—my Heavenly form. This is what I was meant to be." There's a deep longing in His voice as He adds, "What I could be again if I were allowed to return to Heaven."

"You were an angel," I say, trying to sort this out. He was an angel before He fell. He wants to be an angel again. If He returned to Heaven . . . what would happen to Hell?

His wings ruffle behind Him. Without realizing I've done it, I find myself stepping closer. I lift a hand to brush my fingers over the edge of the feathers, feeling myself drawn to Him. But before I reach them, I catch His gaze, and what I see there makes me pull my hand back. Even though His gaze is soft, there's something hungry in it. I drop my hand and my wide eyes find His again. "Why did you change?"

He lowers His gaze and the anguish in His eyes is unmistakable. "Rage will change a being." He sounds suddenly old and very tired.

"Rage . . ." I repeat. "At what?"

He still doesn't look at me. "I'd never known loss like that . . ." The despair in His words wraps like a blanket around my heart and squeezes. But then His eyes lift back to mine. "I need you to understand me, Frannie. I'm not the monster that religion and warped histories have made me out to be."

"I . . . I want to understand . . ." I say, but it's a lie. I want to run.

But I can't. I need to find the strength to do this.

"Do you?" He shakes His head but then lifts His tortured gaze back to mine. "Do you know why He cast me out?"

"Pride . . . ?" It comes out as more of a question than I mean it to.

He regards me with deep green eyes and a sad smile lifts the corners of His mouth. "That's what they've led you to believe, isn't it?"

"All the stories . . . the Bible . . . they all say that."

He sighs. "Mortals are more comfortable when they have someone to blame. It makes them feel safer to compartmentalize everyone into good and evil. If they know where evil lives, they can avoid it. They want everything clear-cut. Black and white." His eyes meet mine and His voice hardens "Nothing is black and white. It's all shades of gray."

"I don't . . ." I trail off as He backs away from me and threads His fingers into His hair, frustration etching His face.

"Good and evil are not separate. They're two sides of the same coin. No single being is all good, just as no single being," He says, pounding His fist into His chest over His heart, "is all evil. I was cast out because I loved God above all others." His green eyes plead with me. "Does that make me evil?"

"But . . ."

I force myself to stand still as He moves closer, not sure what I'm feeling. This angel is Lucifer. I know that. But He *is* an angel. What if what He's saying is true? I can't help thinking that maybe He's not pure evil. As if to validate everything I'm feeling, His next words tear my heart wide open.

"Take Matt for example. He's not evil, Frannie. He's the same brother you've always known. He has your best interest at heart. He's trying to do the right thing by you."

I feel tears well in my eyes and I swallow back the throbbing lump in my throat.

"He's going to be fine. I won't let anything happen to him. And if I come back . . ." He says, His eyes locking on mine, "so does he."

I only realize I'm crying when I hear my breath hitch on a sob.

There's sympathy in His gaze, and for an instant I almost forget who He is. He lifts a hand toward me, but drops it again. "I'm sorry. I didn't mean to hurt you, but I need your help. Things can be as they were meant to be. Just one word, Frannie. That's all it will take." His voice is like cool silk, so enticing, and I feel myself becoming lost in it.

I'm mesmerized by His closeness—by the feel of the power coursing through Him into me. Filling me. I shudder, and that word, *yes*, is perched on my lips. "How were things meant to be? What are you asking me to do?"

He lays His hand softly on my shoulder and the pendant flares. "Bring me back."

18

✠

The Devil's Own

GABE

I duck and roll as Aaron's celestial blast, tenfold stronger than Matt's Hellfire, takes out the hedge to the left of the door. My field is designed to repel Hellfire, but it's useless against celestial attack. Because that's never supposed to happen.

"Think about this, Aaron," I say, gaining my feet.

"I have. More than you know. I've had a near eternity to think about it."

I summon my own power and the celestial energy coursing through me stings my mortal flesh, but it's a relief to know I can still manipulate it to my will. "Destroying me is not going to serve your purpose."

An icy grin slits his face. "But it will feel *so* good."

"So, then, you're ready to join Matt in Lucifer's kingdom? Because, if you do this, that's where you're headed."

"There are two mortals whose memories will tell a different story. The image of Matt attacking you is what He will receive." He shakes his head slowly. "And the only other witness is a Grigori, who will swear that I tried to protect you."

"Daniel will not lie for you," I say.

A confident smirk settles over his face. "I wasn't referring to Daniel," he says coolly as Faith steps from behind the maple tree in the back corner of the yard.

She stares at me for a long heartbeat with dark, dead eyes.

"Faith . . ."

Her beautiful face twists with pain. "I would have done anything for you." A tear leaks over her lashes and down her cheek.

Aaron chuckles. "You know what they say about a woman scorned."

I look at her, begging her with my eyes. "Please, Faith. Just go inside."

Instead, she tucks back behind the tree.

"We've had a little talk, and she sees you for what you are now. She understands how you manipulated her." A malevolent smirk twists his face. "As I said, there will be ample proof that Matthew is responsible for your death. So tragic when a pupil turns on his mentor." Aaron's hand lifts like a shot, and a blast of white lightning rips past my head as I roll to the side.

I hear Faith scream from behind the tree. "No!"

"Don't do this, Aaron," I say, regaining my feet.

My heart slams into my ribs as I see Faith slip out from behind the tree and move slowly in around Aaron, her eyes wild with fear. With a quick glance, I try to warn her back, but I don't dare do more and draw his attention to her.

"Aaron," I say, lifting my hand, hoping to keep his eyes trained on me. "This is a really bad plan. Even if He believed I was destroyed by Matt, you wouldn't be in line for my job. He'd want another Dominion."

"I've proven myself over and over. For eons I've done exactly as I was asked. He'll see that and reward me. I'm sure of it."

"What He'll see is your pride."

"No." He shakes his head violently, lightning crackling over his raised hand with the flare of his temper. "I've never put another above man. That's where Lucifer went wrong. It's because of my love of man that I want your job. His children need someone who can truly protect them against Lucifer." The hand at his side opens, gesturing around him. "And all anyone has to do is look at where we've ended up to know you're not up to the task."

I watch as Faith flanks his blind side. Before I can do anything, she jumps on his back, pulling him off balance. They fall to the ground and I fly at them as Aaron turns and lays his hand on Faith's arm. I wrap my arms around her mid-dive and pull her out of Aaron's grasp, but, just at that instant, there's an electric jolt that runs through her into me.

I groan and roll off Faith as the scent of burnt flesh hangs heavy in the humid night air. Faith convulses and then lies motionless on the ground.

I'm barely off the ground when he unleashes another bolt. This time I don't get out of the way quickly enough and his blast strikes my arm. In my celestial form, this would do little physical damage, but in my new pseudo-mortal body, it rips a chunk of flesh from my shoulder, leaving a bloody crater, and throws me to the ground.

Aaron's eyes pull wide as he sees the damage he's inflicted. His gaze flicks from the wound to my face. He raises his arm, very slowly, as his expression of disbelief shifts into triumph.

The slam of the back door draws his attention and, instead of unleashing his blast on me, the streak of lightning from his palm shoots toward Maggie, who stands wide-eyed on the back porch. She barely has time to flinch before the lightning consumes her.

My cry, "No!" morphs into a growl as I unleash a bolt of my own and the celestial charge rips through my flesh. Aaron screams and drops to the ground as my blast connects.

And then something slams into me, where I sit dazed on the ground. At first I think it's Faith—that she's not dead after all—but then I realize it's Maggie.

I can't understand how she's not a pile of ashes on the porch. I watched Aaron's bolt hit her. There's no way a mortal could survive a direct celestial blast.

"Get up!" she screams, tugging my arm, snapping me from my daze.

I gain my feet just as Aaron's retaliatory flash reaches us, but instead of incinerating us, it splinters around us as if it's hit an invisible barrier. I feel the distinct crackle of a field that isn't mine surrounding us.

When the lightning stops, I look into Maggie's terrified eyes. "What did you do?"

She starts shaking and steps closer to me. "I . . . I don't know."

I look down at Aaron, who glares up at me and fades out. Faith lies crumpled on the lawn, faint tendrils of white smoke curling around her.

I pull Maggie to my shoulder. "Are you okay?"

She nods, but she's staring past me at Faith, looking anything but okay.

"Where's your father?" I ask.

Her voice is shaky as she responds. "Inside. With Grace."

I reach out but am still unable to identify what the energy crackling around us is. It's definitely some sort of field, but it's not mine.

Something to do with electromagnetic fields? Daniel had mused about Maggie's power.

He was right.

Maggie is a human Shield.

A sigh heaves my chest. It's not just Frannie and Grace. There's much more to this family than being Nephilim.

My heart lifts and sinks all at the same time. Maggie and Grace will protect Frannie in ways even I can't. Grace can repel the nefarious, and Maggie can protect her from physical attack from both the infernal and celestial. But it means they've both just become soldiers in the war.

Maggie hugs me so hard I'm surprised, in my current state, that she doesn't crack a rib or two, but I don't let her go, and as I hold her, flooding her with peace, I feel the crackle of electricity soften and disappear as her shaking slows.

"Go inside. Find your father," I say, guiding her gently to the door.

Once Maggie's inside, I turn back to Faith. I kneel at her side, and for all the good it will do, I pray that it's a celestial that comes for her. I reach for her, but her form is already becoming less substantial as she starts to fade from this plane into the netherworld. I breathe away the ache in my chest and stay with her until she evaporates like fog. When she's gone, I kneel for a moment more before reaching for my phone and calling Luc.

LUC

I'm just climbing into the Shelby when the phone in my pocket vibrates. I snap it open.

"Frannie's at her grandfather's," Gabriel says. His voice is thick, and panic kicks hard in my chest.

"What's wrong? Is she okay?"

His voice hardens. "Just get to Ed's."

I'm peeling out of the parking lot before he's even finished the sentence. "I'm on my way."

"I'll meet you over there," he says, and then he's gone.

The drive feels like an eternity, even though it can't be more than five minutes. I race into the driveway and my door's open before I've stopped.

When I see Gabriel pounding on the door, I do a double take. His arm is in a makeshift sling and his shoulder is haphazardly bandaged.

I rush up next to him, adrenaline pounding through my veins. "Why are you knocking? Just shift in there."

"I can't," he snips. "There's some kind of field." He pounds again. "Frannie!" he yells.

"Why isn't Ed answering?"

He shakes his head. "Matt said something about him not being himself."

"Unholy Hell," I mutter. Panic kicks harder in my chest at the revelation that someone has managed to possess Ed and throw up a field that even Gabriel can't penetrate. "Keep trying," I say as I bound away from the door.

I skirt around the house and peer through the family room window. The room is dark, but as I watch, a light flicks on in the corner and Ed staggers slowly toward the door. He looks drunk—or postpossession, which can knock the Hell out of a mortal. He moves from one piece of furniture to the next for support as he makes his way to the door.

I jog back to the front of the house as he approaches the door and reach the porch just as he cracks it open, leaving the chain latched.

"What do ya want?"

"Ed," I say. "Frannie's here, and she's in danger. Please let us in."

His gruff scowl pulls into concern. "I told ya this mornin'. I haven't seen her."

I fight to stay calm. "Ed, listen to me. I know this doesn't make any sense right now, but I'm telling you the truth. She's here. She's in the house."

His eyes grow suspicious. "I'd know if she was here."

"Please trust us."

That's when his suspicious eyes shift to Gabriel. "Who's us?"

"This is Gabriel. Please let us in, Ed."

He takes in the sling and the bloody bandages under Gabriel's singed T-shirt. "You're *that* Gabriel?" he asks, skeptical. "The angel that's been helping Frannie?"

Gabriel nods, but guilt flits over his features.

He stares a moment longer, then the door slowly closes while Ed undoes the chain. For a second, I'm not convinced he's going to open it again and Gabriel shoots me a panicked glance, but then it swings wide and Ed stares us down a moment longer.

"She ain't here," he says, but he seems less adamant.

"It's a really long story," I say. "How are you feeling?"

He rubs his temple. "Like I've been trampled by the Budweiser Clydesdales."

"It'll pass," I say as Gabriel loses patience and pushes past Ed into the house.

"Frannie!" he calls just as a door in the hall opens and Frannie spills out.

FRANNIE

It sounds like a battering ram is coming through the front door.

Lucifer looks down on me, a hint of desperation in His eyes. "Say it, Frannie. Pledge yourself to me and make me what I was meant to be." His hand, which had been soft on my shoulder, tightens uncomfortably.

I hear Grandpa's bedroom door open, and I skirt around Lucifer toward the door, pulling out of His grasp. I remember that I'm naked except for the towel when I feel His fingers trail over my back. I yank on my jeans and a tank top and bolt for the door. Lucifer grabs me around the wrist before I make it.

"Do you believe in me?"

I turn and pull away from his grasp. "I do, but I need to go. Grandpa needs my help."

He shakes His head as a slow smile creeps across His lips. "It's nothing your grandfather can't handle."

He locks me in His gaze and His energy fills me, making me feel like all my insides are vibrating to His unique rhythm. The pendant vibrates to that same rhythm, and I bring my hand up and press it harder into my chest. I'm struck by how different this Lucifer feels. Nothing like the Lucifer from Luc's apartment. Could it be that when I met Him in Luc's apartment, He just became what I expected Him to be? What if *this* is the real Lucifer? What if everyone is wrong about Him?

I look into His eyes and something nags at the back of my mind. Even though I know my purpose now, what I'm meant to do . . . even though it's staring down at me, waiting for the promise that will start the change . . . something doesn't feel right.

I slide to the door. "I'll come right back. I promise."

As He lets me go, an electric charge pulses through me, and all the hair on my body stands on end. "Go. But don't let them make you question what you know to be true."

Gabe explodes into the living room just as I push through the door into the hall. He sees me and strides across the room. I almost don't recognize him. His eyes are sunken hollows, his arm is in a sling, and he's bleeding.

Angels don't bleed.

Oh, God. What did I do?

Everything inside me goes cold and I feel like I'm suffocating. I glance back over my shoulder toward the hall, not sure what I'm expecting to see there, not sure what's real anymore.

"Frannie—" Gabe starts, but Grandpa cuts him off. He stares at me as though I just materialized out of thin air.

"When did ya get here?" He turns away from the door as Luc steps through and closes it behind him.

I move slowly toward him, confused. "A while ago. You made me a sandwich. Remember?"

He shakes his head slowly. "I don't . . ." but trails off, his brow creasing deeply.

Luc steps past Gabe, his expression intense. His eyes flick beyond me, to the door of my bedroom. "Frannie. Are you okay?"

I nod, still staring at the bloody bandages on Gabe's shoulder. Luc looks me over. "Did Matt hurt you?"

"No. I'm fine."

"You're lucky, Frannie," Gabe says, his voice measured. I can see behind those tired eyes how mad he is, and I don't blame him.

I move closer. "No one wants to hurt me. I know what I'm meant for now."

The anger in his eyes mixes with dread and fear. "He's been here. You've seen Him."

I nod, even though it wasn't a question.

He draws a sharp breath and holds it for a second. "Your tag. You haven't . . . done anything . . . ?"

Luc is watching the exchange warily, his expression guarded.

My heart races. I need to make them see that everything is okay. Better than okay. I know my purpose now, and as long as Lucifer trusts me, I think I can pull it off. "No. But don't you see? This is it."

Gabe charges past me, not even hearing my words, and slams the bedroom door back. I cringe, expecting . . . something, but instead, he turns back to me. "We need to get you out of here."

I step up next to him and peer into the empty room. Relief

sweeps through me at the same time as I feel a tug of disappointment in my gut.

Gabe strides out of the room and I follow.

Grandpa is standing near the couch looking at me in total confusion. He steps forward and slides an arm around my shoulders pulling me to his side. We sit together on the loveseat. A wary smile pulls at his mouth. "Anything ya wanna tell your old grandpa?"

I shrug. "You really don't remember talking to me before?"

"He was possessed." Luc's voice comes from the corner, where he's leaning against the hearth.

Everything inside me goes cold. "Possessed?" But then I remember the hint of brimstone I caught and the way his voice seemed to change, and something in my gut tugs tight. "Oh, Grandpa. I'm so sorry. I shouldn't have come here."

Grandpa squeezes my shoulder. "Don't ya even think that."

But I can't help thinking that. No matter what I do, where I go, I put everyone in my path in danger.

Luc sees it in my eyes. He always does. "It's not your fault, Frannie. Ed is fine. He doesn't even remember it."

I want to scream, but then a sense of relief settles over me as I realize they didn't hurt him. Whoever possessed Grandpa didn't hurt him or me.

'Cause of Lucifer.

At the thought, understanding dawns.

You belong with me. I will always keep you safe.

Those weren't Grandpa's words. They were Lucifer's.

A flash of fury streaks through me like a red-hot meteor.

It was *Him*.

How could He! Grandpa is old. He could have killed him.

The next thought hits like a swift kick to my stomach.

Matt.

He was in on it. He left me here with Lucifer, never intending to come back. He never wanted to help Maggie. His only plan was to get me to his boss.

He has your best interest at heart. He's trying to do the right thing by you.

Lucifer's words run over in my mind, and I feel my head spin. I close my eyes against the wave of dizziness.

Luc shrugs away from the wall. "Frannie," he says. "What is it?"

His words wrench me from my thoughts and I realize how cold I feel. I'm sure I'm paper white. I pull my eyes from him. "Is Maggie okay? My family?"

"They're fine. Faith is with them," Luc says, earning a pained glance from Gabe.

Gabe slides into the couch across from us, and looks at me out from under thick, white lashes. "What did you mean, Frannie, when you said you know what you're meant for?"

I breathe back my fury and look up at him. When I think I can talk without my voice shaking, I start slowly and watch his face. "So . . . you know I've always believed I was supposed to be some kind of diplomat—to help people communicate and bring opposite sides together." I hesitate and Gabe nods for me to continue. I swallow hard and bite my cheek, unable to look at him as I finish. "What if the sides I'm supposed to bring together are Heaven and Hell?"

Grandpa's grip on my shoulder tightens slightly as he stiffens, and I so wish he wasn't here—that I hadn't come here and made him part of this. I glance up for Gabe's and Luc's reactions. They share a wary glance.

"If there's anyone who could do it, it's Frannie," Luc says with a flick of his eyes toward me.

"How do you figure?"

Luc lifts a framed picture from the hearth and gazes down at it. "She may be Nephilim, but a part of her belongs to Hell. It always has."

19

Revelations

FRANNIE

My mind reels. Grandpa sits on the loveseat with me in stunned silence as Luc explains.

"So, Frannie and her sisters are unique," he finishes. "Gus wasn't just any demon, so it stands to reason that Hell's claim to Frannie would be strong. Which explains a lot, if you think about it."

I *have* thought about it. As shocking as the fact that Grandpa—and therefore me, my mother, and all my sisters—is part demon is, I keep going back to what Lucifer said.

No single being is all evil.

I think for an instant about telling them, but I'm not ready to share that yet. I need to figure out what it means—how I can use it. I'm not sure how, but I know this is it. I can feel it.

This is the answer to everything. Maggie, Taylor, Matt. I can fix it all.

Gabe lifts his head from where it rests in his palm and stares Luc down. "We have to get her out of here."

"No!" I say, more forcefully than I mean to.

He turns his wary gaze on me. "You can't believe anything He's told you, Frannie."

I throw my hands up in exasperation. "What could be bigger, Gabe? Can you think of any bigger use for my Sway? This is it— the thing I was meant for. You've always said I could change the shape of Heaven and Hell."

He stands abruptly. "Not like this."

Luc pulls himself to a stand. "Think about this for a second, Gabriel. Frannie might be right."

"You're not serious!" Disgust twists Gabe's face. "You're supposed to love her. How can you just give her up to His control?"

Luc looks for a second like he's been punched in the stomach. His face pulls into a grimace but then clears. "This isn't easy for any of us." His eyes flit to mine then back to Gabe. "But can you imagine if Frannie can bring Him down? It will make Rhenorian's uprising look like a sandbox scuffle."

My stomach lurches. "I'm not bringing anyone down," I say through a dry mouth. "That's not what this is about. He wants to change . . . to come back to Heaven. I just need to negotiate a truce."

"A truce," Luc repeats warily, his eyes piercing me.

Gabe sinks into a chair and looks up at me. "You're not suggesting—"

"I shouldn't even need my Sway. It just makes sense. What greater good could I ever do than ... what ... ? Abolishing Hell, I guess. If I could convince ... Him ... God ... to let Lucifer come home, then everything will be fine—how it was before He fell."

"Everything was not *fine* before He fell, Frannie," Gabe says, his face set and his jaw clenched.

"How do you know? You told me you were created *after* the War."

"I was, but it was called *the War* for a reason. The War was a culmination of a struggle that started much earlier, the root of which was power and pride. Lucifer has had too much power for too long. He's not going to willingly give it up to return to the fold."

My mind races and I feel myself bristle. I don't want to use my Sway to convince them. And I shouldn't have to. This makes sense. Why can't Gabe and Luc see that? I can make this happen—no more Hell. This is what I was meant for. It's the only logical thing. I fix Gabe in a hard stare. "I think you're wrong."

Everyone, even Grandpa, looks at me like I've lost my mind.

Luc steps forward and very slowly lifts his hand to touch my arm. My breathing becomes uneven as he looks hard into my eyes and sweeps my hair back behind my shoulder with his other hand. "Don't do this, Frannie. Please. He's dangerous. You can't seriously believe He's going to change."

Everything in me clenches into a hard ball, partly in reaction to being this close to Luc and partly in response to his words. "*You* changed," I finally say and spin from the room, my heart aching.

LUC

She has a point.

I watch her hurry from the living room and realize I want to believe her. Frannie changed me—everything about me. Could she do the same to Lucifer? I pull a deep breath before turning to Gabriel. "Is it possible?"

He shakes his head as her bedroom door closes, his gaze still trained on the empty hall. "I don't know."

Ed, who had been uncharacteristically quiet up until now, looks at Gabriel in stunned disbelief from where he sits on the loveseat. "What's she talkin' about—negotiatin' a truce?"

I shake my head, not able to conceive what that would even look like.

"Frannie is far more than she appears," Gabriel answers, and I can see him considering the possibility.

But if she tries and doesn't succeed, I'm not sure any of us would survive it. Gabriel's troubled eyes find mine, and his expression is pained as he comes to the same conclusion I've drawn.

"It's 'cause of me bein' from Hell," Ed says.

I sink into the loveseat next to him. "No," I answer, even though it wasn't a question. "And you're not really from Hell, Ed."

"May as well be, for all the help I am to Frannie."

I rake a hand through my hair. "You might be able to get her to listen."

He stares at the floor and shakes his head. "You know she doesn't listen to anyone." His eyes lift to mine. "But what if she's right?"

"She's not right," Gabriel interjects, pulled from his own musings. But he doesn't say it with any real conviction.

Ed looks between us.

"Why would she be so convinced that Lucifer wants to return to Heaven?" Gabriel asks himself more than us.

I look hard at him. "You've heard of the silver-tongued devil? We're talking about the original. He can make almost anyone believe almost anything. He can't influence the celestial, but he's had eons to practice on mortals, which, despite her potential, Frannie still is."

"She wasn't ready," Gabriel says, his voice heavy. "We didn't have enough time." He looks up at me, desperate. "She's not blocking Him."

My heart squeezes into a hard knot.

Gabriel rips the sling from his neck with a wince and tosses it to the coffee table. He circles his shoulder as he massages it, looking weary. "How did this happen? She was tagged. *Shielded.* He shouldn't have been able to get to her."

There, the fault lies with me. "The Mage. I'm sure he led Lucifer in. All He had to do was lure Frannie away from your protection. He did that by using Maggie as bait, obviously. And here we are."

Ed glances toward the hall. "So, what do we do now?"

I fix Gabriel in a meaningful stare. "Pray for divine intervention."

FRANNIE

I pace through the room and head straight to the window. Everyone keeps telling me Maggie's okay, and I want to believe them, but until I can talk to her . . .

I'm totally torn between going home and staying here. Actually, I'm totally torn over a lot of things. Lucifer was here, and the way we left things, I'm pretty sure He'll be back. I'm also pretty sure I can't run from Him. And I'm not sure I want to. I don't think He'll hurt me. Maybe I can ask Him to call Hell off my family. Desperation takes hold and I look over my shoulder at the closed door and consider climbing out the window again.

No. I couldn't do that to Grandpa. Besides, I'm pretty sure Gabe would smite someone if he came in here and I was gone.

I pace my room, trying to calm down, but my breathing and heart rate just get faster. I can't stand waiting around. I pace another circle then give up. I fling my door open and march down the hall. "I'm going home," I announce. "I need to see Maggie."

Gabe shoots Luc a warning glance, and Luc hangs his head. Panic kicks in my chest. "What?"

Neither says anything.

"Is everything okay? You said Faith was there," I say, looking at Luc.

He glances at me then at Gabe, who won't look at me.

"Tell me what's going on!"

Finally, Gabe looks up. When he speaks, his voice is low and pained. "Faith is dead. Aaron killed her."

"No." It feels like someone kicked me in the stomach, and the word comes out in a whoosh. I close my eyes and focus on breathing. When I finally can, I say, "Everyone else is okay?" I know it's selfish, and I feel sick thinking about Faith, but I have to know about my family.

"Your family is safe," Gabe answers.

"What happened? Who's Aaron?"

Gabe presses into the wall and sighs, but his body remains tense, his muscles coiled tight. "The guardian I sent to protect Maggie."

His answer throws my thoughts into chaos. I can't make any sense of it. "A guardian *angel*? A guardian killed Faith?"

He nods, and I see it's taking an effort to keep himself together.

"Gabe?"

His fists clench and his face twists as he fights for control. He turns toward the window as a pained growl rips from his lungs. It hurts just to listen to it, and I know in that instant, from the despair in that sound, that she told him. He knows she loved him.

I don't dare say anything. I don't dare move.

He pulls a hand through his thick platinum waves and turns to look at me. "She trusted me, and I let her down," he says. "It's my fault. I killed her."

I move slowly toward him. Luc looks away as I wrap my arms around him and send him my heart. I don't want him to hurt. I want to do for him what he's always done for me.

After a few minutes, his breathing slows. He lifts a hand and strokes my hair. "Thanks."

I pull away and look up into his face. "I owe you about a thousand more."

His smile is small and sad. "Maggie's fine," he says, and I realize he's picked the still barely contained panic out of my head.

I'm afraid to say what I'm thinking, but he already knows I'm thinking it, so, "Is this Aaron still protecting her?"

He shakes his head. "Maggie can take care of herself."

I'm losing control of the panic. I feel it snaking its way up my throat. "What does that mean?"

He glances at Luc again then back at me. "She has her own gift. She's a human Shield."

"A what?" Grandpa and I say together. I look up and Grandpa's standing in the kitchen with a mug in his hand.

Gabe blows out a sigh. "She appears to be able to manipulate electromagnetic fields to form an energy field around herself—and anyone close to her—that functions as a Shield."

"How do you know?" I ask.

"Aaron attacked me. Well . . . actually, Matt attacked me first. Grace stopped him with some sort of prayer, and then Aaron decided to finish the job."

Fear swirls into the panic already climbing my throat as my last shred of hope for Matt evaporates like fog in a breeze. Still in a bit of a daze, I choke back the lump rising in my throat. "Grace . . . what?" I ask.

He closes his eyes and drops his head. "It appears your sisters have been given gifts that would be useful to your survival—and theirs."

I take a second to process that. I've always known there was something different about Grace. "What can Grace do?"

"She sees auras—a being's true essence," Gabe says warily, but then a cautious smile curves his lips. "And, handily enough, she can repel demons."

I take a deep breath. "Well, that explains a lot," I mutter.

"It does."

Everyone's heads snap to the silky disembodied voice in the darkest corner of the hall. Two green eyes glow out of the black.

20

✣

Not-So-Divine Intervention

FRANNIE

In a heartbeat, Luc has me behind him and Gabe is standing in front of us with white lightning crackling over the hand pointed in Lucifer's direction.

"Stop!" I say, wriggling out of Luc's grasp.

Lucifer steps down the hall and the dim light slanting through the bedroom door reflects off His golden hair, casting a halo around His head. A lazy smile quirks one side of His mouth and His eyes pierce mine. "We meet again, my lady."

"She's not your lady," Luc says, his tone measured. I can see that he's not afraid of his old king, but he pulls me behind him again.

Lucifer's eyes flash to Luc. "Oh, but she is. And yours too."

"Stop," I scream again, and push past Luc to Gabe, tugging on his raised arm.

Everyone freezes, and for a long heartbeat it's silent. Then I feel Grandpa's arm ease around me.

Lucifer peers over my shoulder at Grandpa. "Except for the blue eyes, the resemblance is uncanny," He says, then shifts His gaze to Luc. "Wouldn't you say?"

Luc doesn't respond but continues to stand between us, jaw ground tight and murder in his eyes.

Lucifer looks back at Grandpa. "He was my Left Hand, your father, and he gave it all up for you."

I can't read Grandpa's expression as he stares at Lucifer. "Frannie shouldn't have to pay for my sins," he finally says.

My heart collapses and I turn to him. "Grandpa. No. Don't ever think that." I wrap my arms around him. "This doesn't have anything to do with that."

Gabe still has his lightning hand pointed toward Lucifer, and Luc looks ready to spring at any second. I have to defuse this. There's no choice. I dig deep and push with my mind, "We're all on the same side," I say. "Let's talk about this."

Slowly, the crackle of electricity over Gabe's hand lessens as his arm lowers.

I turn to Grandpa and pull him deeper into the family room. "Go to your room and stay there," I whisper to him.

"I'm not leavin' ya with that—"

"Please, Grandpa. I can't let anything happen to you."

His eyes narrow and he moves to his old recliner and sits. My stubbornness came from somewhere. I hold my breath for a second then blow it out in a long sigh. I sit on the couch and turn to the boys. "Everyone sit."

Their eyes clash for a brutal moment and I brace myself for

all hell to break loose, but then Gabe and Luc come over to sit on either side of me.

Progress.

"As you wish, my lady," Lucifer says, dropping into the love-seat across from us.

I glower at Him. "First of all, stop calling me that. You're not helping."

He sinks deeper into the loveseat, lacing His hands behind His head as if settling in for a baseball game, and twitches me a private smile. "I'll call you whatever you'd like. But you need to understand that you're not a common mortal. You are much more than that."

Something inside me twists as both Luc and Gabe stiffen, and I hope my shake isn't very noticeable. My pulse pounds heavier with each passing moment and I ache from the tension.

"I am pleased, however, that your protectors are taking their duty so seriously." Lucifer's gaze shifts from Luc to Gabe and lingers over his bandaged shoulder. His green eyes spark. "Though I feel compelled to mention that they're both looking a little worse for wear."

"Then why did you use Matt to lure her away?" Gabe shoots.

"Because I needed a moment alone with her to get us to this point, where we can sit down and discuss this," He answers with raised eyebrows.

"So, we're here now," I interject. "How do we do this?"

Lucifer smiles. "We talk."

I inhale deeply and I think to myself, *here we go*. "Okay, so, Lucifer. You want to return to Heaven, yes?"

I decide I imagined the flash of His eyes and the minute pause 'cause, when He answers, His whole face brightens. "Yes, my lady."

"And you're willing to give up your power over Hell."

"My reign in the Underworld means nothing to me. To return to the Kingdom, I'd relinquish it without hesitation."

I glance sideways at Luc and Gabe. The look on their faces is not what I was hoping for. Luc is coiled tight, ready to spring, and Gabe has his twitching lightning hand on his knee as they stare Lucifer down with blatant distrust.

And that's when I realize how futile this is. A few words are not gonna break down eons of history.

I cringe away from the realization that the only way this is gonna happen is if I make it happen. I don't want to force them with my Sway. But . . .

I look back at Lucifer as I struggle with what to do. He gives me an "I'm trying" shrug. His devil-may-care expression hardens, however, when I reach for Gabe's and Luc's hands and give them a squeeze. I breathe deep to settle my nerves.

"This is real. Things are on the edge of changing forever. Do you see how big this is? How can this not be what I was meant for?" Trying not to think about it, I push the thought with my mind and ignore the knot in my gut. "This is what I'm meant for—to bring Heaven and Hell together."

Gabe's shake slows and Luc softens slightly. "How can you possibly know He's sincere?" Gabe asks, but it's no longer in anger. I can tell he's thinking about it.

I look across at Lucifer, who shrugs again.

"Give me something to show you mean it," I say.

Lucifer's brow lifts. "Whatever you wish. Name your peace offering."

"Taylor." Tiny shards of ice stab at my gut as I say her name, and I realize my request is spectacularly selfish, but it's what I want more than anything.

The king's face pinches into a grimace. "I'm not able to give you a condemned soul. For that, you'd have to go to your beloved Almighty. Would you accept a lost brother in lieu?"

"Matt," I whisper. "Could you make him an . . . angel?"

"Once again, his ultimate fate is not for me to decide, but I can release him from Hell's service. He'd be free to return to Earth as a Grigori."

I glance sideways at Gabe and don't miss the pain in his eyes. He feels responsible for Matt's fall. Would it ease his guilt if Matt had a second chance?

"If He gives us Matt, will you believe Him?" I ask.

Gabe's tortured eyes turn to mine, but he doesn't answer.

I look back at Lucifer and can't stop the glare. "And I want you to call Hell off my family. I want Marc and any other demon lurking around them gone."

An amused smile plays over His strong features as Lucifer rises from the loveseat and steps toward me. "Anything else, my lady? Maybe a cheeseburger and fries?"

"Stop calling me that," I answer through gritted teeth.

He holds out His hand and the boys are instantly on their feet glaring at Him. I glance between them and Lucifer's outstretched hand.

I need to keep His trust.

Luc and Gabe both stiffen as I reach for His hand and He

draws me to my feet. "I will return with your peace offering," He says, the heat of His gaze scorching me. Then, in a puff of sulfur, He's gone.

GABE

My head is cotton candy, and I know it's Frannie's Sway. I can't decide if I'm contemplating this because she wants me to or because in some little corner of my mind, I know what she's saying makes sense.

Since I first was asked to Shield her as a child, I've known she was meant for something big. Huge. And she's right. I can't think of anything bigger than bringing Lucifer back to the Kingdom. But believing that's possible entails a certain degree of trust in Lucifer, and that's where I get stuck. I didn't know Him as an angel. Sometime before the War there may have been some good in Him. But I'm certain that the Almighty was right in His decision to cast Lucifer down, which means any chance at redemption is long gone.

Frannie glances up at the clock, which reads nearly midnight. "I need to get home," she says.

"It's late," I say. "Your sisters are safe. They're sleeping behind your father's field."

I see the scrunch to her forehead that means she's preparing to argue.

"Frannie," I preempt. "Showing up now will only frighten them. They'll be fine until morning. We'll go first thing. Promise."

Her eyes narrow. "First thing," she repeats.

"First thing," I confirm.

She breathes deep and looks at me a moment longer. "C'mere," she says. "Let me change your bandages." She grasps my hand and turns for the bathroom.

I follow her and she closes the door and proceeds to pull gauze, tape, and antibiotic ointment out of one of the drawers. Tugging me over to the toilet by my shirt, she places the supplies on the edge of the counter and sits me on the toilet seat. She leans in to me as she gently slides my sweatshirt over my head.

"You have no idea how worried I was," I say to distract myself from her proximity, and her smell, and the way I want to pull her to me and never let her go.

She peels the tape back from my skin and grimaces. "I'm pretty sure I do."

"Why did you run?"

Something hardens in her expression as she dabs at the swollen red crater in my shoulder with a damp cloth. "You know why."

"I told you Maggie was fine. It's a miracle you got here in one piece," I say, all the pent-up anger, fear, and frustration of the last twenty-four hours bleeding through into my words.

"You wouldn't let me come back, and I had to see for myself," she answers, indignant as ever. "Plus, they'd found us anyway, so it wasn't like we could stay in Florida." She tosses the bloody cloth into the sink and smears some ointment on the gauze.

That much is true, but . . . "Coming back here probably wouldn't have been the next choice on my list."

She places the gauze on my shoulder and yanks the first-aid tape a little harder than necessary to tear it. "I had to see for myself," she repeats. She throws the sweatshirt in the trash.

We emerge from the bathroom to two sets of inquiring eyes.

"Do you have a T-shirt Gabe can have?" she asks Ed.

He scoots into the bedroom and comes back holding a black T-shirt with a red Mustang across the chest and tosses it to me.

I slide it over my head, careful of Frannie's bandages. "I'll take outside," I say to Luc. "You keep an eye out here." As I stride through the family room to the door, Luc's and Ed's eyes follow me. And so does Frannie, a scowl fixed firmly on her face. She's not done with me.

We step into the cool night and make our way out onto the damp grass.

"Am I crazy?"

That wasn't the question I was expecting and I pull up short, turning back to face her.

"About?"

"Lucifer."

I breathe a sigh. "You're trying to find your way—your purpose. I don't think you're crazy. A little misguided, maybe . . ." She looks up at me, her eyes pleading, and I feel that cotton candy brain again. "I can tell how badly you want this, but what I can't tell you is if this is the right thing. It's hard for me to accept that Lucifer is willing to change after all these millennia." I grasp her hand and gaze down into her astonishingly blue eyes. "But I've seen you do some pretty unbelievable things with that Sway of yours."

A smile touches her lips, and I smile back. But then her

smile is gone. She lifts a hand and runs a finger over my bandaged shoulder. "Like this?"

Finally, the question I was expecting. "You haven't left me totally unchanged, Frannie."

She tentatively leans in, laying her ear against my chest. Her breathing is shaky as she listens to my pounding heart. Finally, she peels herself back and looks up at me with glistening eyes. "I didn't mean . . . did I . . . ?" she stumbles.

"Did you give me a gift?" I finish for her, gazing down into her eyes. "Yes," I whisper.

Her stunned expression hasn't cleared. "When did you know? That I was changing you, I mean?" she says.

"That night." I can tell by the sudden flush of her cheeks that she knows exactly which night I'm talking about. The night in her bed after Taylor's funeral. The first time I felt desire so intense and all-consuming that I would have traded my wings for one night with her. I smile down at her. "And I didn't hate it."

She looks as though she doesn't know what to say. "Sorry?"

"I wasn't lying, Frannie. You've given me a gift. Beings of the upper spheres—the Seraphim—can't feel. Not really. Not the same as humans and the lower angels. We were never from the Earth—never part of humanity, and real emotion is uniquely human." I step closer and grasp her hand. "You've given me something unbelievable. Even if I lose it . . . if you stop . . ." I trail off.

"Loving you," she finishes for me. "I won't," she says as my eyes lift back to hers.

I smile again, but feel the stab of pain behind it. "You should," I breathe. "Even if I can't stay like this, I've tasted it . . . what it's like to feel something so . . . profound. I could have existed forever and never known what I was missing. You did that for me. But now I need to do my job." I feel my gut tighten and I can't look her in the eye. "I was trying to think of what I could say to make you hate me."

"I could never hate you." I hear the alarm in her voice and it confirms what I already know. There's no way out of this that isn't going to hurt both of us.

Instead of following my instinct—and my heart—and comforting her, I finally do what I should have been strong enough to do from the beginning. I step back. "It's gone on too long." I shake my head and look to the Heavens. "Heaven help me, *I've* let it go on too long."

She steps toward me, but I take another step back. Her lips press into a line as she locks up into my eyes. Finally, she swallows hard and nods. "I'm so sorry, Gabe. I never meant for this to happen."

I feel a lump rise in my throat watching her struggle against her tears. After several beats of my pounding heart, she steps forward and wraps her arms around me and, this time, I don't back away, because I know what this is.

She rests her forehead on my chest. "You mean so much to me, and I've been so unfair to you." She lifts her head off my chest and glances at the house. I can't help slipping into her mind, and in it I find what I know I should. Luc. She loves him completely. She has all along.

I give her hand a squeeze and her forehead a kiss, then she turns back to the house and disappears through the door.

"Good-bye, Frannie," I whisper after her.

FRANNIE

I watch the shadow of a moving figure pass outside the window. Gabe is keeping vigil outside tonight, and it's reassuring to see him pass by every few minutes.

I rub my pounding temples. I've been so selfish. After all my promises that I wouldn't want him, I changed him too. All I can think about is if I've put him in danger. Does he still have his powers?

I lay back and stare at the ceiling, worrying about Gabe, Luc, Matt, my family. I need to get home. I need to see for myself that everyone is okay. Gabe said Maggie and Grace can protect themselves, and part of me is totally relieved that I'm not the only freak in my family. But a bigger part of me is scared for them. I don't know what it is Maggie and Grace can do, but I'm scared that Heaven, Hell, or worse, *both*, will decide they want it. I shudder thinking about how my whole life changed when Luc showed up to tag my soul.

The momentary flash of anger gives way to other feelings. Deeper feelings. It wasn't his fault. He was just doing his job— the only job he'd ever known.

And he was doing it for Lucifer.

I'm having a lot of trouble reconciling the contradiction.

Lucifer started out as an angel. He couldn't have always been bad. He might even have been good once. And now He wants to go back, and maybe I can help Him.

As I think about Him, the pendant starts to throb hot against my skin. I pull it up by the strap and look at the pulsing red glow.

I made this for you.

I lift the strap over my neck, rubbing the pendant between my fingers like a lucky penny, and watch the red glow fade. I curl it into my palm and feel it pulse.

Luc said Lucifer wouldn't give up His power, but Gabe doesn't seem as sure. Am I being foolish to think this is my purpose? Is He trying to manipulate me? This stupid power I have is the most frustrating thing in the universe. It only works one way. If I can manipulate the thoughts of mortals and others, wouldn't it have been wise to make it so I could read those thoughts first? There are a few minds I'd love to read right about now.

Like Luc's.

I can picture him out on the couch. I'm sure he's not sleeping, even though I'm also sure he needs it after the ride I took them on over the last thirty hours.

And so do I. I focus on my breathing, making it slow and deep, and try to turn off my whirring mind. Sequentially, I concentrate on releasing the tension in my body. I make my feet relax, then my calves, my thighs, my hips. Little by little, my body becomes heavy and sinks into the bed. My torso, my shoulders, my arms. Finally, I soften my neck and my face. Sleep is coming, slowly taking me under.

Until the bolt of lightning short-circuits my brain.

21

✝

Original Sin

FRANNIE

I spring to a sit with a gasp, hold my searing head in my hands, and pay attention as the image forms. My heart contracts when I see Luc, lying pale and lifeless in a hospital bed, tubes poking out of every orifice in his body. An echo of a woman's voice bounces through my head. "Time of death, six-thirteen."

When the searing pain subsides enough that I can move without screaming, I slip out of the bed. I pull on my jeans, stuffing the pendant that's still clutched in my hand into my pocket, and tiptoe to the door, sure the pounding of my heart alone is enough to wake everyone.

The instant I crack the door open and look out into the hall, I realize I was wrong. Luc's not on the couch. He's sitting on the floor with his back against my door. He tumbles backward as the door disappears out from behind him and catches himself with an arm before he lands on my legs.

My relief at seeing him alive is indescribable.

He's on his feet like a shot, peering past me with keen eyes. There's not a hint of sleep in them. When I glance down and notice the coffee mug on the floor next to where he was sitting, I know why.

"Is everything okay?" he asks.

Yes. You're alive.

"I couldn't sleep," I say to my feet. "I . . ."

His fingers are on my cheek, tucking my hair behind my ear. "What, Frannie?"

I look up into his eyes and I can hardly breathe. "I saw you dead."

His eyes widen for an instant, then he nods, as if he already knew that's where all this was heading.

"You can't die. I won't let you."

The smallest of lopsided smiles pulls at his lips. "It's not my first choice either."

"Am I crazy for thinking I can do this?"

His eyebrows arch and he heaves a weary sigh. "Pretty much."

I stoop to pick up his coffee mug and take a long swallow then wince. "That's got a punch to it."

A smile tugs at his lips and suddenly I can't look anywhere else. "Ed brewed me something resembling jet fuel."

I turn and pad back into my room where I sit on the bed. "What am I doing?"

I feel Luc's weight sink into the bed next to me. "Well, at the moment, drinking my coffee."

"I'm gonna get everyone killed," I say, staring into the depths of the mug.

"Let's hope not."

I hear the tease in his voice and turn on him. "This is *so* not funny! I saw you dead!"

Despite the hint of a smile on his lips, his eyes are dead serious, and I get it. He knows that better than any of us.

I set the mug on the nightstand and lean my shoulder into his. I feel him stiffen slightly, but he doesn't pull away. "Sorry about biting your head off. And running away. And . . . everything else."

"The biting my head off is understandable. The running away thing, not so much. What were you thinking?" With his breath in my hair, goose bumps work their way up my neck into my scalp and I shiver.

"Matt lied to me," I say, and the pang in my heart makes me physically wince.

He looks at me for a long moment, considering. "He's chosen, Frannie. And I can tell you from experience that the team he's playing for now shows no deference for the mortal realm's quaint notions of right and wrong. They'll say anything. *Do* anything."

I've never asked Luc about the things he did as a demon. I guess I was afraid to know. I don't want to think of him like that—have that image in my head. But suddenly I need to know how Matt's head works now. "Like what?"

He surprises me by taking my hand. He stares at it soberly,

and his voice is laced with something dark as he says, "Think Andrus and Chax."

"And Marc?" I add, squeezing his hand.

His eyes lift to mine. "No," he snaps, his face twisted in disgust. "I was never like Marchosias."

I take his hand in both of mine and turn it over, tracing the lines of his palm. "Sorry."

He watches my finger intently but doesn't reply.

"Lucifer came to me today and I . . ."

He tenses, his fingers curling into mine, and I can tell he's holding his breath, waiting for the rest.

"I'm not stupid. I know He wants my power, but I can't help thinking that I'm supposed to make a difference . . . change how Heaven and Hell work."

"That could be true," he answers cautiously. "Probably is, as a matter of fact. But I can guarantee you it's not by convincing the Almighty to take Him back."

"You said He wouldn't give up His power. How do you know that for sure?"

"I've had seven thousand years to watch Him operate. He's a coward, sending His minions to do His dirty work on the coil. And He's power hungry, using every ploy to gain control of humanity and tempt mortals down the fiery path. The more death, destruction, and depravity it entails, the better. He's created an army . . . including me . . ." at this his voice hardens as his self-loathing emerges out from under the thin emotional blanket he keeps it hidden under, ". . . to do His bidding. And remember, that bidding includes wreaking all that death, destruction, and depravity." He pulls back and looks in my eyes. "You've seen firsthand what He demands of His legions."

Luc doesn't have to say Taylor's name. I know that's what he means.

A scowl twists his face. "But He doesn't have any trouble inflicting unspeakable atrocities on His obedient minions, who are hardwired not to be able to fight back—with no free will of their own." He shifts away from me and hangs his head, weaving his fingers into his black mop of hair.

I move closer and lean into his shoulder, not sure what to say, but then he jerks his head out of his hands. "That's it!"

"What's what?" I ask.

"Free will. God's gift to humanity." He taps his thumb on his knee, thinking. "Rhen . . ." he says, shaking his head. "They don't need to be human. They just need free will. When I turned human . . ." He looks at me then, reaching out for my hand and threading his fingers into mine again. "When *you* turned me human . . . I had free will that I didn't lose when I turned demon again."

He catches my wince.

"Which I never blamed you for, by the way," he adds.

I lower my gaze.

Luc cups my face in his hand and lifts my chin so I'm looking at him. "Frannie, please. You need to believe me."

It's only now, as my eyes search his face, devouring every bit of it, that I realize how much I've missed him. His gaze is deep, as if he's looking for my soul, and I can swear I see his in those deep obsidian pools. My eyes fall to the lines of his mouth and I feel myself leaning in, closing the distance between us.

I taste the coffee on his lips, which are slightly parted, but don't move. None of him moves. He sits very still and closes his eyes. But when he starts breathing again, it's shaky.

I pull back and look up at him as he opens his eyes. They burn with an intensity I haven't seen there since before we left Haden. I reach for his face, stroking my fingers over his cheek and tracing his lower lip with my thumb. "What's going to happen?" My voice is no more than a whisper.

His mouth pulls into a hard line and worry wrinkles the corners of his eyes as he shakes his head.

This time, when I lean in to kiss him, he cautiously slides his hands around my waist. His lips move ever so slightly on mine, as if he's afraid of making any sudden moves and scaring me away. I tilt my head, deepening our kiss, and I feel him respond, pulling me closer.

Something heavy lifts from my heart as the seemingly insurmountable wall that has existed between us since Lilith crumbles to the ground. His pulse pounds with mine as I wrap my arms around his neck, settling into him, and kiss him like there's no tomorrow. When our lips finally part, he pulls me into his lap and I press my forehead into his.

"Whatever it is, please, always remember that I love you," I say.

We cling to each other, but I don't dare speak, afraid of breaking whatever midnight spell has brought us back together. The world is quiet with sleep; still and seemingly unaware that, at any second, everything could end.

I lift Luc's T-shirt over his head as he gazes down at me, unsure. My fingers trail over his serpent tattoo and across his chest, and I feel his skin pebble with goose bumps at my touch. When I reach the thick, rough scab of the burn on his ribs, I lay my palm over it and he closes his eyes and sighs. I tug off my shirt and press myself into him, feeling the burn of our skin as we melt into each other.

As I sink into him, needing to be as close as humanly possible, I'm overwhelmed by the sudden sense that this is goodbye. My heart aches and silent tears flow as I smother him with my love. He loves me back, so quietly on the outside while, on the inside, a torrent erupts.

My eyes open to the pale morning sun, just beginning to stream through the window, signaling the start of a new day. But the first thing I see is Luc's lazy smile. His arms are around me and we're snuggled into the blankets.

"Morning, beautiful. Did you know you talk in your sleep?" he says.

I panic for a second, trying to remember what I dreamed. For the first time in weeks, it wasn't Taylor. It was Luc.

Time of death, six-thirteen.

A black hole forms in my heart as dread takes hold of it, but then the memory of last night—kissing Luc and what that lead to—creeps into my consciousness and heat washes through me as an involuntary smiles tugs at my lips.

We're both still here.

And Luc is very, *very* alive.

I sink into him, savoring the feeling of his heat warming the cold places deep inside me that I've kept locked away from him for the last few months. "Did you sleep?" I ask in a voice still thick with slumber.

"Some."

I slide up in his arms and trace a finger along the dark hollows under his eyes. He closes them and I gently kiss his eyelids, then the tip of his nose.

He heaves an epic sigh, and a contented "Mmm . . ." purrs up from his chest.

I smile then kiss my way slowly across his cheekbones and along the coarse stubble over his jaw, finally finding his mouth again.

I can't stop the giddy squeal and giggle as he grabs me and rolls us so I'm pinned under him.

"You might want to be careful, or your grandfather is going to find you in a very compromising position," he says quietly, his gaze burning through me and a wicked smile teasing his lips.

My heart thrums as Luc kisses me, pressing into me from above. I wonder how I was able to resist this for so long when I feel myself totally giving in to him, wanting nothing more than to be swept away by him and not have to think about any of the rest of it.

Luc isn't a distraction. He's my sanity—my escape.

My heart.

And my soul.

It nearly kills me, but I find the strength to push him away. "You need to go," I whisper. "Grandpa will be up soon."

He smiles again and melts my heart. I grab him and pull

him close. He kisses me once more, slow and deep, then pries himself out of my grasp. I watch him intently as he sorts through our clothes, pulling his from the pile on the floor. When he's dressed he leans over me and kisses me again, and I close my eyes and fight not to pull him back into the bed. He leans his forehead into mine. "You are killing me. I hope you know that."

My heart lurches as my eyes snap open and stare into his, but then I see the smile in them. His lips find mine again before he stands and slips through the door, leaving me aching for him.

Not long after, my mouth starts to water as the smell of frying bacon and coffee wafts into my room. I throw on my clothes and head to the family room, where Luc is now on the couch, wrapped in Grandma's throw, pretending to be asleep.

I sit on the edge of the couch and lean down to kiss him. His eyes slit open and a sly smile turns up his lips. "You're blowing my cover."

I giggle and then jump when someone clears his throat behind us. When I turn, Grandpa is peering at us from the kitchen. "If anyone's hungry, I've got pancakes and bacon ready. Nothin' like Luc's omelets, but it'll have to do," Grandpa adds, giving Luc the evil eye as he swings to a sit.

My face is on fire. "We were just—"

But at that instant, I grab my head as lightning tears through my brain. "Oh, God!" I cry, unable to stop myself.

'Cause this time the image isn't me or Luc. It's Grandpa, lying in a heap on a green lawn, his eyes staring lifelessly into the sky.

My empty stomach heaves with the pain in my head, but there's nothing to come up. When it settles, I bound off the couch and run to Grandpa, hugging him as tightly as I can. "I never should have come here."

I glance wildly at Luc, and I see my own horror mirrored in his eyes. In that glance, I can tell he understands. But I can't tell Grandpa.

"I ain't gonna let nothin' happen to ya, Frannie," Grandpa's sandpaper voice rumbles from his chest into my ear as I stand plastered against him.

I feel sick again, 'cause it's *me* who has to figure out how to keep anything from happening to *him*. I peel myself away from him. "Just promise me you won't go outside."

He smiles down at me. "Thought your angel had things under control out there."

I breathe deep. "Just promise."

"Fine," he says with an amused smile. "How 'bout those pancakes?"

I hug him for another second then back away a step.

"I'll round up the night patrol," Luc says with a tip of his head toward the front door.

Luc opens the door, but before he steps through he glances back to where I stand and offers me a reassuring smile. Despite my heavy heart and the dread in the pit of my stomach, I can't help smiling back as he slips through and closes it behind him.

Grandpa turns from the stove where he's pulling another batch of pancakes from the cast-iron skillet. "Is the plan still to head to your folks?"

"As soon as we can," I answer.

I hear the front door click open and Luc steps through. He just stares at me for a long moment.

"What?" I finally ask.

He glances back over his shoulder into the yard. "Gabriel is gone."

22

✝

Raising Hell

LUC

The pancakes and bacon sit uneaten in Ed's kitchen as we race across town to Frannie's. The cheer of the cobalt sky and white, puffy clouds are at odds with the air of doom hanging over our group.

"Gabe wouldn't just leave," Frannie muses from the backseat of the Shelby.

"No. He wouldn't." Dread sits like a stone in the pit of my stomach.

Ed gives me a wary look from the passenger seat but remains silent.

We bump into Frannie's driveway and I pull to the end, near the garage in back. Everything seems quiet—either a very *good* sign or a very *bad* sign.

It doesn't take long to find out which.

I've barely stopped before Frannie's shoving me out of the car and sliding my seat forward. She bounds from the car and pulls up short, staring into the backyard.

I follow her gaze . . . and find Maggie near the large oak tree in the corner of the yard—in Lilith's choke hold, a knife to her throat.

"Hi, Frannie," Lilith says. "I was hoping that was you. Shall we try this again?"

Frannie stands very still, pale as death, her eyes glued to the hand holding the knife at Maggie's throat. Maggie wears an expression that is something altogether different. She's straining to turn her head to look at Lilith, and her eyes are full of insatiable need. Her hand is grasping at Lilith's thigh, desperate for even that tiny piece of her.

I step in front of Frannie, careful not to look directly at Lilith now that she's got her siren song cranked. "Lilith, put the knife down."

"Lilith." Frannie's whispers comes from behind me. When I turn, I see her expression soften, then become hungry, and she takes a step forward. Ed stands on the other side of the car, staring over the top of it, mesmerized.

"Turn it off, Lilith," I say, reaching for Frannie. I grasp her gently by the shoulders and turn her to face me. Her eyes stay locked on Lilith, and I have to grasp her cheek to pull her face around. "Frannie. Look right here," I say.

She presses her eyes closed and winces. "Maggie," she whispers. She opens her eyes and looks into mine, and I can see all the nightmares behind her gaze.

"This isn't Taylor, Frannie. Maggie will be fine. She's not tagged for Hell."

She winces again at the mention of Taylor, even though she was clearly already thinking about her. "But she could still kill her anyway," she says in a strangled whisper.

She will if I can't figure out how to stop her. And, if she does, I can't imagine how I'll stop Frannie from retaliating . . . unless I do it myself.

"Did you talk to her, lover? Tell her the plan?" Lilith calls.

Frannie starts to turn back to her, but I hold her chin. "You have a plan?" she asks.

"No," I say, gazing deep into her eyes, showing her I'm not hiding anything. "No plan."

"She'll do it, Luc. She just needs a little encouragement." Lilith presses the knife tighter against Maggie's throat to punctuate her point.

Frannie struggles out of my grasp, desperation clear in her strained expression, and I swear I feel a rush of energy surge under my hands as she pulls away. "What will I do?"

"Take the king down." A depraved smile curves Lilith's mouth. "Or die trying. Either works for me." She chuckles, a raw, wet rasp that turns into a hacking cough. "Come over here and get your little sister, Frannie. Then we can all talk about it."

When she looks at Lilith, there's murder in her eyes. "You grab Maggie," she says. This time, I'm sure I don't imagine the skitter of red and white energy dancing over her skin.

Unholy Hell.

What does this mean? What's happening to her?

When I look back at Maggie, she's trying to spin in Lilith's grasp, causing the knife to graze her skin. A rivulet of blood courses a path from under her chin to the hollow of her collar-bone and pools there.

I grasp Frannie's arms gently and lean in. And I feel it, the buzz of an electric current running up my arm. "Go, Frannie," I whisper in her ear. "Go with Ed into the house." My lips brush her cheek as she backs away and I inhale deeply, taking in her currant and clove, needing to hold on to her in any way possible.

She looks up at me and the determination on her face scares me. "No."

"Go. Maggie and I will be right behind you," I say, my heart clenching at the realization that these might be my last words to Frannie—and, if so, a lie.

She stares at me for a long heartbeat, then starts to back away.

I watch her for a second then turn to Lilith. "It's just us."

But then, like a blur, someone shoots past my side, launching into Lilith and Maggie. Before I have time to register what's happening, Lilith and Maggie hit the ground, Frannie on top of them, grabbing for the knife.

Lilith wrenches herself out from under Frannie as I lunge for the group. She swings the knife and it slices into my shoulder as I grasp Frannie and try to pull her away. But I see my effort is only helping Lilith gain control. I pull Maggie back from the scuffle on the ground. She blinks, out from under Lilith's spell, then grasps me tightly around the neck.

"Ed!" I shout, and he's there in a second, pulling Maggie to her feet and supporting her. She wraps herself around her grand-father, who looks at me with desperate eyes.

I dive back toward Frannie and Lilith where they wrestle on the ground, and I smell it clearly: ozone mingling with brimstone. Lilith rolls to a sit and takes another swipe with the knife, this time at Frannie, but I lunge toward her and kick, and the tip of the knife lodges in the heel of my boot. I give it another hard kick and the knife flies out of Lilith's hand and skitters across the lawn to the base of a rosebush in the garden next to the garage.

"Go, Frannie!" I yell as I bound to my feet. Out of the corner of my eye I see her dart toward her family. I lunge for the knife and, when I come up with it, I turn to face Lilith, who is on her feet as well.

She waggles her fingers, encouraging me toward her. "Go ahead. Make my day." She grins, looking pleased with herself. "I've always wanted to say that."

Maggie's scream from behind me pulls my attention, and I spin to find Frannie thrown over Rhenorian's shoulder like a rag doll. She's clawing at his arm, trying to break free.

My heart climbs into my throat. "Rhen, stop. She can't make you mortal! Put her down!"

He turns and fixes me in a mournful gaze. "Sadly, I'm not here on my own behalf. I'm programmed to protect the king's interests." He hikes Frannie on his shoulder. "And right now your girlfriend is one of His interests."

Ed and Maggie huddle near the corner of the house.

"Ed, take Maggie and go!" I yell, sensing Lilith moving behind me but not daring to take my eyes off Rhenorian.

"Like hell!" Ed calls back, his eyes wide.

"It's not safe for you here! Go—" Lilith jumps on my back and locks her elbow around my neck, choking off my words.

"Luc!" Frannie cries as Rhenorian turns and lumbers off with her thrashing against his back.

I plunge the knife into Lilith's hip and throw her off as an inhuman shriek cuts through the air, then sprint to where Ed is moving to intercept Rhenorian.

"No! Stop, Rhenorian!" I yell as he lifts his free arm to backhand Ed out of the way. I skid to a stop a few feet from Ed. "If you want Frannie to help you, killing her grandfather would likely be counterproductive."

He lowers his arm and glares death at me. "I'm done being nice."

I sidle closer, trying to find an angle into Frannie. "Do you even know what that word means, Rhen?"

The ground rumbles and a banshee scream rips from behind me as a sickening wet ripping sound fills the air. I spin to see Lilith wielding the knife that I thoughtlessly left lodged in her leg. She holds it overhead in both hands as she rushes headlong toward Frannie, where she's hanging helplessly over Rhenorian's shoulder. I lunge for Lilith as Rhenorian drops Frannie and lifts a glowing fist in our direction. But I see him hesitate, torn between directives. He needs to protect his king's interests at all costs, but no one touches Lilith—other than Lucifer. To harm her would be the equivalent of suicide.

Next to him Frannie drops into a crouch and throws her hands in the air. White lightning crackles over the palm of her left hand as bursts of red energy surge over her right fist. Both hands are targeting Lilith.

I don't know what any of this means, but in that instant I register that this is still Lilith. Killing her human host, whether it be with a knife, celestial lightning, or Hellfire would likely reverse Frannie's tag . . . if that even applies anymore.

On instinct I launch myself at her, but Lilith has a head start. "Frannie! No!" I yell.

Her expression shifts from fury to utter shock as her hands drop to her side and her questioning eyes find me.

But I have no answers.

Knowing I can't reach her in time, I dive for Lilith's ankles at the same instant as a blast of Hellfire slams into her. Lilith has just enough time to shriek before she's reduced to a pile of crackling, electrified ashes. I look up and Rhenorian stands, slack-jawed, his glowing fist still poised for attack, staring.

Because it wasn't his blast that took Lilith down.

I wheel to locate the origin of the lethal discharge and find Lucifer leaning against the maple tree in the back corner of the yard. "I'm sorry for that. She was becoming a nuisance," He says, brushing His hands together and shrugging away from the tree. He slinks slowly toward us, like a panther approaching its prey, His eyes trained on Frannie. He stops a few feet from her. "That was magnificent."

I glance to Frannie, who looks terrified. But I don't believe her terror is directed at Lucifer, as it should be. She's staring at her own hands.

Rhen steps toward her, but Lucifer holds up His hand. "Leave her," he says, and Rhen instantly backs off. Lucifer's eyes turn to Frannie. "Are you injured?"

She shakes off her daze and looks up at Him. "Um . . . no. I'm . . ." But then she seems to register who it is she's talking to, because she backs away a step, then turns to where Maggie is huddled in her grandfather's arms. "Take Maggie inside, Grandpa," she says.

"You come with us." He looks between Lucifer, Rhenorian, and me.

She nods. "We'll be right there." She starts to herd them toward the back door, but the next instant Marchosias is standing between them and the house.

"Marc?" Maggie gasps, as Frannie pulls her grandfather back.

Marchosias leers at Maggie and surveys the gathered crowd. A lethal smile twitches at the corners of his mouth, and his eyes blaze. "Why am I just finding out now that the party's already started?"

"It's a testament to your popularity, Marc," I say, gliding to Frannie's side and grasping her arm.

His gaze falls to the blood seeping from the wound in my shoulder and an icy grin splits his face. "I see you're still rocking the flesh."

"Jealousy looks good on you, Marc," I answer. "Green is your color."

His eyebrow arches as his eyes slide over Frannie, devouring her. "There may be some truth in that."

"Enough!" King Lucifer's voice shakes the ground, and His glare is fixed on Marc. "Feel free to leave unless you have something meaningful to offer."

At that, Marc does turn an interesting shade of green as the smugness leaves his face.

Rhenorian snorts and Lucifer's appraising eye turns on him.

Frannie pulls out of my grip. "Speaking of offering things, you promised you'd keep your minions away from my family."

"For that," He says with a wave of His hand at the pile of Lilith's still crackling ashes, "I'm truly sorry. Lilith is sometimes unpredictable, and the fact that she's not demon makes her hard to control."

Frannie swallows hard. "You also promised me Matt."

Lucifer's face softens as He gazes down at Frannie. "Soon, my queen."

My stomach twists. "Your *what?*"

Lucifer's eyes shoot to me, and in them I see the ruthless king I've always known.

Daniel rounds the corner into the backyard in his pajamas, a newspaper in his hand. "Frannie!" He runs to her and folds her into his arms. "I thought I heard you back here. Where have you been?"

"Dad," she says, her voice shaking. She pulls herself out of his embrace and starts to push him back the way he came. "Go back inside. Please."

Daniel lifts his eyes and takes in the rest of the scene playing out in the yard. "Holy Father above," he gasps just as both Marc and Rhen turn their glowing fists on him.

FRANNIE

I wrap myself around Dad. "No!" I yell, as the yard shimmers out of focus and reality falls away.

I feel Luc press into me from behind, squeezing so tight that I can barely breath. But I don't want him to let go.

I feel all wrong. Like I don't belong in my skin. I don't know what happened just now with Lilith. She was gonna hurt Luc, and with all my soul I didn't want her to. I wanted to protect him. It wasn't till he called out to me that I realized there was lightning . . . inside me. Then I saw it on my hands.

Everything around us goes sepia, the colors fading to brown as the life drains from the grass and the trees. At first, I think it's 'cause I'm about to pass out, but when I hear Maggie's shaky "What's happening?" I know it's not just me.

It feels surreal, as if I've stepped into the beginning of *The Wizard of Oz*. The sky above, that had been intense cobalt, now swirls with grays and blacks, like boiling ink soup. Everything is shrouded in heavy, low fog, except the fog flickers with an internal electrical storm making all the hair on my body stand on end.

Grandpa, Dad, and Maggie huddle together as the earth under our feet rumbles and then begins to shake violently. I look up to see Mom, Grace, and Kate stagger out of the house onto the back lawn. They run to the huddled group just as there's a metallic groaning sound. I turn in time to watch my house collapse on itself as an earthquake rips a ginormous hole in the ground under it. The group stumbles back from the edge of the growing chasm, and the entire house and most of the yard disappear into it.

And suddenly the sharp sting of brimstone cuts through the air.

I can't see beyond the yard 'cause of the fog, but here there is nothing but silent, lifeless devastation, as if this was ground zero for a nuclear blast.

Luc pulls me tight to his chest and I try to focus on the beat of his heart, but I can't block out Lucifer's words. *My queen.*

They echo deep inside me as the Udjat pulses under my shirt. I don't remember putting it on this morning, but it's there and it's like every cell of my body is hardwired to Him somehow.

I don't understand what's happening to me. I feel energy pulsing through me, wanting to burst out of me. I'm shaking as I pull my face from Luc's chest and open my eyes.

He's there, Lucifer, my green-eyed angel. Terrible and beautiful. He seems forever away across a cavernous gorge where the house used to be, but impossibly close all at the same time. As I stare, shadowy black forms streak from the chasm and take up position behind Lucifer. Winged creatures, black and leathery, lift from the gorge, wings spread, and circle over His head. But I'm so transfixed by Him that I hardly register any of it. A shiver rips through me at the memory of His touch, His dark thoughts, and the Udjat pulses against my chest with His energy. I pull away from Luc and feel my feet start to move my body forward, but a hand on my shoulder stops my progress. Luc's voice is in my ear. "Do you see Him now for what He is?"

I've rarely heard this combination of fear and pain in Luc's voice, and it jolts me from my trance. I look back over my shoulder at him, and, as his eyes lock on mine, the love I see there makes me question everything. I look behind Luc, to where my entire family stands, clutching each other.

I'm completely torn. I want to go to Lucifer. I feel as though I *need* to go to Him. But my heart is screaming at me to stay here with Luc and my family.

"You asked for something from me and I have it for you." Lucifer stands at the edge of the gorge, looking across at me, His arm raised, beckoning me.

I step closer to the edge, grasping Luc's hand tightly. My eyes connect with Lucifer's and His pendant burns my skin.

"Accept my peace offering. Come to me." He sweeps an arm to the side and bows His head as Matt is lead through the black figures behind Him, beaten and broken. He drops to his hands and knees at Lucifer's feet, then tumbles onto his side, motionless.

At the sight of Matt, something in me explodes like a hand grenade, leaving my insides in shreds. "No!" I lift my gaze to see Lucifer's arms reaching for me. I glare across the gorge. "What did you do to him?"

Lucifer steps forward, up to the lip of the gorge and raises His eyebrows, chagrin twisting His beautiful face. "Not me, my queen. You can't believe I'd hurt someone you love."

I feel Luc's hand on my arm, but I pull away. "Then who?"

"Bring him forward," Lucifer commands. The blackness behind Him opens and a winged form is pushed through. Hellhounds snap at his heels as Marc jabs him forward. He staggers and Marc gives him a final shove that sends him sprawling to the ground in a bloody heap next to Matt.

Crimson streaks mar the perfect white of his wings, and they lay on his back at an awkward angle. At first, I think someone splashed them with red paint, until he lifts his head and stares at me from under caked blood.

"Gabe," I whisper, sinking to my knees. My insides turn to cold stone and stars flash in my eyes as all the blood drains from my head. "Oh, God."

A blinding bolt of white lightning rips through the cavern and strikes at my knees. Suddenly, I'm shrouded in cool mist. It feels just like when I was a kid and we went on a boat ride under Niagara Falls. The mist is so thick that I can't see anything, but I grasp tighter to Luc's hand as I feel it start to slip from mine.

The mist starts to lift into a shimmer of incandescent colors, and I find myself kneeling on the floor in Grandpa's family room with Luc at my side.

"You've been quite busy."

I'm dizzy and disoriented as the horror of the scene at the gorge is replaced by the warm familiarity of Grandpa's house. The wonderfully comforting, lilting voice lifts my pounding heart, and when I look across and see Grandma sitting on the couch I'm sure I must be dead. The white streaks in her sandy hair appear to glow, veiling her beautiful face in a misty sheen, and a warm smile crinkles the corners of her sapphire eyes.

"Grandma!" I'm off the floor and onto the couch in a flash, wrapping my arms around her neck.

She hugs me back and she feels exactly how I remember her, warm, soft, and smelling a sweet mix of peaches and Grandpa's pipe smoke.

"Oh, my child," she says pulling away. "Tell me everything."

I sit close to her. "Am I dead? How are you here?"

"No, child. You're not dead. I'm here because you called me."

"I . . ." But then I think about that. My cry "Oh, God" was a plea. I lift my head and look her in the eye. "I need to speak to . . . God." I feel a little stupid saying it out loud and my cheeks burn. When I glance to Luc for encouragement, I find him still on his knee, head bowed, which does nothing for my courage.

Her knowing smile shines like the sun, warming me right down to my aching heart. "So speak."

"Can you tell Him—"

She lifts a hand, laying it gently on my face and suddenly it's Gabe times a thousand. I close my eyes and throw my head back as the same sensation of peace that I've always craved from him floods me. But what I also feel is that this is the source of it. It's amazingly intense but incredibly soft all at the same time.

Heaven.

"Oh my . . ." I open my eyes and look at Grandma. ". . . *God?*"

23

✠

Oh My God

FRANNIE

She winks at me and Her eyes beam, alive with compassion, love, hope, as She nods.

"My grandma is *God*?" I ask again in disbelief.

"I take the form of your choosing, child. So what is it that we need to discuss?"

I just stare blindly at the wall for a moment, looking for words. "My grandma is God," I repeat, trying to wrap my mind around this.

"Everyone's grandmas are God," She replies.

I breathe deep and try to remember what I was gonna say. "I . . . can't think," I say, blinking as I look at Her again.

"Would you rather I took a different form? I'll be anything of your choosing."

"No!" I shout, not wanting Grandma to leave.

She chuckles the way She used to when I was little and would close my eyes to sneak spoonfuls of cookie dough figuring, if I couldn't see, then She couldn't either. She reaches for my hand, holding it in both of Hers. "You needed something from me, child."

I close my eyes to calm my whirring thoughts, then open them and start in on the words I'd rehearsed so carefully. "What if Lucifer wanted to come back to Heaven?"

"That's a big 'what if,'" She answers, Her face neutral.

I nod. "Huge. But I think it's true." I catch myself. If this is gonna work, I have to be more convincing. "No. I *know* it's true. He's changed. He wants forgiveness."

She brings a finger to the side of Her nose and taps it there. "You're quite sure about that?"

The pendant throbs on my chest. "Yes."

She looks at me a moment longer, familiar worry lines creasing Her brow, and I feel myself start to shake. Suddenly, I'm anything but sure. I feel the pendant's energy flare and it feels dirty and dark. I want it off. I lift my hand to pull it over my head but then stop. I don't want Grandma to see it . . . to know I have it.

"I don't know what I'm supposed to do." My words are a plea, and I don't realize I'm crying until Grandma lifts Her hand and wipes a tear off my cheek with Her fingers.

She stands from the couch and paces to the table next to Grandpa's worn recliner, where he keeps his pipe stand. "Your path is your own," She says, fingering the pipe with a melancholy smile. "And your strength is your own," She adds with a pointed glance at me, Her fingers drumming Her chest, just where the pendant lays on mine. "You have great potential, but how you use it is up to you."

"So . . . would you let Him come back?"

"My dear girl," She says, and I shudder hearing those old, familiar words coming from Her mouth again. "For eons, he's had the option to return."

"Seriously? He can come back? Just that easy?"

Her sad smile tells me it's anything but easy. Which means I was wrong. My purpose isn't convincing God to let Lucifer come home.

"What does He have to do to come back?"

"Forgiveness is the key to everything, but forgiveness can only be given to those who wish it."

Forgiveness is the key to everything. I flash back to Gabe saying those same words to me not that long ago.

"Gabe!" I gasp. "I put him in danger by making him think . . ." I grimace and drop my head. I was so stupid, using my Sway to try to persuade him Lucifer was good. How was I so easily convinced?

"Is Gabe . . . ?"

She glides over to me and strokes my cheek. "He can't be killed, but he's changed from the Gabriel you knew." Her hand travels to Luc's shoulder, where he's still kneeling on the carpet. "Rise, my son."

Luc stands, but still doesn't look at Her. I grasp his hand, but he doesn't squeeze back. His hand just lies limply in mine.

Her gaze falls heavily on me. "Lucifer is correct on one point. There does indeed need to be a shift in the balance, and you're the one who can bring that about . . . with a little help," she adds with a squeeze to Luc's shoulder.

"How?"

"Lucifer may rule Hell, but he did not create it."

"I don't understand."

"He is the self-proclaimed ruler of the Abyss, and under his guidance it has become something it was never meant to be." Her gaze softens as She brushes the backs of Her fingers over my cheek. "Do you understand the true purpose of Hell, Frannie? Why I created it?"

"To punish mortals who sinned in life?" I ask.

The doleful set to Her face makes Her look suddenly older. She shakes Her head slowly, and Luc speaks up.

"To redeem souls for Heaven through penitence," he says, his head still bowed, earning a soft smile from Grandma.

Grandma's whole face glows when She smiles. "This is true, young man."

"I thought that was Purgatory," I say, confused.

"Purgatory," She answers, "is where souls are sanctified for their entrance to Heaven. It's a place for those who have died in grace and are marked for Heaven to, as the name would imply, purge their sins and shed their biases in preparation for a life of eternal glory in the Kingdom. Those souls are already Heaven bound. The souls in Hell, however, can choose to stay there, or they can choose to earn their way to Purgatory." She pauses, lifting a finger to Her temple. "At least that's how it was supposed to work." She turns to Luc. "So, young man, do you recall Lucifer ever giving a soul up to Heaven?"

Luc slowly lifts his head and looks at Her. "No."

Grandma nods. "And he never will." Her expression is solemn. "Lucifer has corrupted Hell. He actively tempts mortals down the path, never intending to give them up to Heaven when they repent. There are souls in Hell who have been unjustly condemned."

Luc's head bows deeper and I hear him pull a long, shaky breath, making me wonder how many of those souls he's directly responsible for. His mournful eyes lift briefly to mine and the pain I see there crushes my heart.

Grandma kisses my forehead. "The time has come for you to make your choice, dear girl. You have a gift. It's within your power to right Lucifer's wrongs, but you have no less free will than any other of my children. You can choose to live your life, just as you have been, or you can become more." She smiles at Luc's bowed head. "But, whatever you choose, keep your young man close. You will need him."

Everything ripples, like heat off sun-baked pavement.

I reach out to Grandma. "No! Wait! What happens if I—"

But before I can finish the thought, lightning crackles all around me, making the hair on my arms stand on end, and Grandma is gone. Everything around me shifts in the mist and I'm back at the gorge, staring across at Gabe's and Matt's broken bodies.

LUC

"What do I do?" she says, staring across the Abyss at her brother. She turns to me. "Tell me what to do!" she pleads.

"The choice is yours, Frannie," I answer, knowing what my choice would be if I could make it for her. I'd get down on my knees and beg her to choose the safe course if I thought she'd listen. But I can tell by the determination in her eyes as she gazes across the chasm at her brother and Gabriel that, whether she knows it or not, she's already decided. It's right there to see. She's not taking the safe route.

She glances to me for an instant, and when she locks my gaze in hers I know I'm right. A fire burns behind her eyes that I've never seen there before. She squeezes my hand with a sad smile, and my heart crumbles as she lets me go and steps onto a jagged precipice that extends over the maw. I watch as she breathes deep and holds her arm out to Lucifer. "I'm coming," she calls.

She only hesitates for a heartbeat at the lip of the chasm before closing her eyes, drawing a deep breath, spreading her arms and stepping headlong into it.

I lunge for her, meaning to pull her back from the precipice, but I'm not quick enough. The gasp and murmur from the other side of the standoff is audible over the rumble of the ground that closes like a bridge in front of her with every step.

I gain my feet and start moving forward again.

"What's happening to her?"

Daniel's voice behind me is almost lost in the wind swirling up from the maw. As I turn to look at him I see he's got Claire in his arms, holding back her desperate attempt to cross the bridge and get to Frannie. The rest of his family is huddled together behind them. And beyond them, the cavern pulses with white energy. Four immense angels hover just above the ground, ageless and boundless, blinding me with their radiance.

The archangels.

Gabriel, the warrior and God's Left Hand, stands at point,

his triple wings spread as if ready to lead the charge at a moment's notice. Raphael and Uriel watch Frannie's progress closely. But Michael can't help taking a moment to spare me a disgusted smirk.

I swallow hard and turn back to Daniel, not sure how to answer his question. "Take your family back there," I say, moving toward Frannie's bridge. "Stay behind the archangels."

"The . . ." he starts, but trails off as he looks behind him at the spectacle.

Setting my resolve, I turn and move to the stone bridge Frannie leaves in her wake. As I step onto it, the Lake of Fire roils forever below, a kaleidoscope of gold, red, and indigo.

Home sweet home.

The smell of sulfur is stronger here above the chasm. It burns my nose and makes my eyes water. I move across the stone bridge behind Frannie, hoping beyond reason that I can be of some use to her. She must sense me behind her, because she turns and holds up her hand, warning me to stop, and I see them—tears streaking her face.

My heart is in my throat as I stand, not ten feet behind her, desperately searching for something I can do or say to keep her on this side of the maw.

Ahead, the blackness swirls, rife with anticipation at the Heavenly charge.

Frannie slows to a stop just feet from completing the bridge. "Lucifer," she calls, her voice heavy with tears but determined. "We had a deal."

His smile is sympathetic. "And I've acted in good faith. Our agreement was that I would return your brother to you."

He plants a bare foot on Gabriel's hip, where he's struggling to pull himself to his feet, and kicks, sending Gabriel sprawling onto his face. "This one must pay the consequences for his actions."

"No." Frannie says, her voice surprisingly even. "I want them both. We don't have an agreement otherwise."

"Come to me and we can renegotiate," Lucifer answers, a hungry smile flickering over His face.

There is an instant where everything is dead silent. Frannie brings her hand to her chest, gripping something under her shirt, then takes the last step to complete the bridge between Heaven and Hell. She glides slowly toward Lucifer. He holds His arms out to her and she only hesitates for a second as she passes Matt and Gabriel, glancing down at their broken bodies, before she walks right into His grasp.

My gut churns and something inside my chest collapses. I spin, hoping to find the archangels preparing to intervene, but they only continue to watch. What I also find is that Daniel is as good at following directions as Frannie. Frannie's family is standing in a cluster on the bridge behind me.

I step forward, and Rhenorian moves to intercept me, ranseur in hand.

"No!" I hear Frannie call and look up to see her standing in Lucifer's arms, glaring out at me. "Just let me do this," she says more quietly, her eyes locking on mine.

My heart lurches and nearly stops as a triumphant sneer creeps slowly over Lucifer's face. His grasp on Frannie becomes more possessive.

Maggie pushes past me and runs to Matt's side. Rhen steps

toward her but Lucifer waves him off. Daniel, Claire, and the rest of her family follow her across.

Frannie's voice pulls me back to the scene unfolding in front of us. She looks up at Lucifer, folded tightly into His grasp. "You said with me at your side you could return to your true essence, but if you want to return to Heaven, you have to ask forgiveness. Are you ready to do that?"

"I will do what is required, but what I require of you is your pledge. I have fulfilled my obligation . . ." He gestures toward Matt with a grand sweep of His arm. "Now it is your turn. One word, my queen, and everything will be as it should be."

She stares into His eyes and pulls something up by a strap around her neck.

Unholy Hell.

The Udjat. She still has it.

It pulses at the end of the strap, alive. A red eye—searching.

My blood runs cold. I push forward, but Rhenorian thrusts the tip of the ranseur into my chest. Hellfire crackles over the surface of it and my T-shirt smolders.

"No," Kate says, and before I realize she's done it, she's stepped forward and grasped the end of the ranseur.

And where it was scorching a hole in my shirt one second, the next it's cold as ice.

Rhenorian looks at her for an instant then throws the ranseur aside. Opting instead for the old-fashioned approach, he grasps my shirt and cocks his fist in front of my face.

"Stop! Call him off!" Frannie stands at Lucifer's side, white and red lightning dancing over her skin as she stares Lucifer down. Her gaze gravitates to Matt and Gabriel, broken on the ground. "I'll do what you want," she says, "but you have to let everyone go. Matt and Gabe too," she adds, her voice hard.

He looks at her for a long moment, as if assessing His options. "Very well," He says with a dismissive flick of His wrist.

I shoulder past Rhenorian as Frannie runs to Gabriel's side and skids to her knees. I lower myself to a knee beside her.

Gabriel's eyes crack open and he looks up at Frannie. "Hey, beautiful," he says with a strained smile. "Come here often?"

"Gabe." She leans in, rubbing blood off his cheek with her thumb. "What happened?"

He shudders just before a grimace twists his face. "Turns out I'm not indestructible after all." He groans and pain contorts his face.

A tear splashes onto Gabriel's forehead as Frannie leans over him. "I'm so sorry."

Out of nowhere, a blast of red Hellfire hits Gabriel and he convulses.

I bound to my feet, positioning myself between Frannie and the direction of the maw, where Aaron is standing at the precipice, red lightning crackling over a fist aimed in our direction.

Hell's newest celestial recruit.

A scorching flash of red Hellfire connects with Aaron, and I look down to see Matt propping himself on one arm and focusing everything he has on Aaron with the other. I watch Aaron's retaliatory streak of Hellfire splinter as Maggie screams and throws herself over Matt. But Daniel lunges in front of both his children and takes a direct hit.

I'm thrown to the side as something next to me explodes. Blasts of both Hellfire and celestial lightning flash past me toward the maw. I look up to find Aaron paralyzed, encased in intertwined streaks of red and white lightning. It crackles and pops all around him for a heartbeat, then seems to focus into a single point and shoot back toward us.

A guttural cry erupts from Frannie and I throw myself in front of her. The concentrated mix of celestial and infernal energy rips through me, tearing out my soul on its way to her.

Frannie slams into me from behind, but all I can see of her is her hand reaching past me on my right, and instantly the energy is no longer coursing through me. I watch her skin drink in the fierce, dancing, electric charge.

Aaron stands at the precipice, still as stone, and in my waning consciousness, I realize he *is* stone. Brimstone. Lucifer walks over and pushes Aaron's shoulder, sending him plummeting backward over the edge of the Abyss. Dimly, at the edge of my perception as I sink to the ground, unable to breathe, I hear the echo of stone pound off the walls of the chasm.

I lay on the ground, struggling for air, and look up into the face of an angel. A weak laugh, no more than a puff of air, leaves my chest at the image of Aaron plummeting into the depths of Hell at the same instant I, the ex-demon, am being lifted to Heaven.

But as I look closer, I realize it's not an angel I'm seeing. It's Frannie. She's more than an angel. She's shrouded in white light, with the flicker of Hellfire dancing over her luminescent skin. But her astonishing sapphire eyes are all hers as they gaze down into mine, golden tears streaking her iridescent face.

"Luc," she sobs.

I try to lift my hand and wipe her tears away. I try to tell her it's okay. But my body will not heed my mind's commands. I can feel my heart struggle to keep a rhythm, and I hold on to the image of her for as long as I can. My vision grays around the edges and goes blurry.

Frannie lays her head on my chest. "I love you, Luc."

I feel her words reverberate through my unresponsive body. I feel her touch, warm, soft, as my heart pounds out the message I can't make my mouth form. I feel her lips on mine for one excruciating moment.

Then nothing.

24

✣

Armageddon

FRANNIE

I don't know what just happened, but I *do* know it's my fault. I felt something burst out of me, and when I called it back, I killed Luc. He lays lifeless and pale next to Gabe on the ground, and a fist clenches my heart and squeezes as I realize I've killed them both.

Then I see Dad, crumpled on the ground next to Matt, my whole family hovering over him.

"Daddy," I whisper as my heart collapses under the pressure. "Oh, God. No."

There's a crackle of lightning and a girl materializes next to Gabe. She lays a hand on him, her copper hair swirling around her fair face in a gust of cool air. She looks at me with amber eyes and a golden tear slips over her lashes onto her cheek. She bows her head, and in that instant I realize it's the girl who protected the plane the night we left Haden. Celine.

She scoops Gabe into her arms, stretches her wings, and her long white gown flutters behind her as she takes flight, lifting Gabe off the ground and disappearing into the roiling black sky a minute later.

I look up at Lucifer, my heart in my stomach.

How did everything go so wrong?

"Come to me, my queen," he beckons with an outstretched hand.

Something burns into my chest, scorching me with demonic heat.

I look down and Lucifer's metal pendant lies over my shirt, glowing red. I pull it up by the strap and stand mesmerized as it spins in front of my face, the gray light refracting through it as if it was the reddest of blood rubies. Its power—His power—throbs from it, drawing me to Him.

I gain my feet and move toward my green-eyed angel as if in a dream.

"No!" Maggie's cry rips me from the trance. She lunges for me and grabs for the pendant. But before she can get it away from me, a burst of crimson explodes from it and the air is tinged with the smell of singed skin and sulfur as she pulls her burnt hand back.

Maggie looks at me, her eyes pleading with me through her terror and pain, and with the sense that I've been punched in the gut, I suddenly see clearly. I can't breathe as I turn to Lucifer. "You never meant to return to Heaven," I say, finally understanding that I've been wrong—about everything.

"But, you're mistaken, my queen," He answers. "I do intend to return." A tiny burst of Hellfire explodes out from the pendant, drawing my attention back to it. It's so beautiful.

I feel myself moving toward Him again, the visceral tug too insistent to ignore. It's as if I have no will of my own.

The thought rolls around lazily in the back of my head.

No will of my own.

No free will.

I don't know where she came from, but Kate is at my side. She grasps the pendant and it goes suddenly dead.

"No!" Lucifer bellows, as if in pain, and I hear Grace, mumbling behind me—something about the shield of righteousness. I grind my teeth tight, setting my nerve, then rip the leather strap from my neck and heave the pendant as hard as I can toward the Abyss.

Lucifer's bestial roar tears through my head, mingling with my own. I look at Him and, even though He is still in the form of the beautiful green-eyed angel, I suddenly see Him through Grace's eyes. It's as though a veil has been pulled back, showing me what I couldn't see before. I see His true essence.

Black.

Nothing but black.

I have to fight to block Him from my head. Because, what I know now, looking at the thing I thought was my angel, is that whatever He was before He fell, that part of Him is gone. He's never going to change.

Even though my mind is racing, I can start to see what I need to do. I'm not supposed to get Lucifer to come back to Heaven. I'm supposed to broker a truce between Heaven and Hell.

Without Him.

As if He read my mind, He unleashes a roar that shakes the ground under my feet. At the same instant, all around me, an electrical storm erupts, the smell of ozone overpowering the brimstone wafting up from the gorge. All my hair stands on end as the air lights up in tiny licks of static electricity. Suddenly I'm surrounded by hundreds of fluffy white wings—and the angels they're attached to. I stumble back and gawk, openmouthed. They're so beautiful. All of them.

A silver-haired girl who looks younger than me smiles in my direction. She gives her wings one flap. Her long white gown flutters behind her as she's lifted into the air. Above us, others hover all around.

I stare in disbelief.

This can't be real.

But even as I stare, my pounding heart starts to slow and my gasping breath calms as their angelic peace dulls my panic, helping me to think.

Three angels swoop in and scoop the lifeless forms of Luc, Matt, and Dad into their arms. My heart wrenches and tears leak over my lashes as I watch them take flight and disappear.

Other angels sweep in on the black mass surrounding Lucifer and all Hell breaks loose.

Adrenaline makes my senses hum as I take in the scene—the battle raging all around. Streaks of white lightning and flashes of red Hellfire light up the darkness; shouts erupt in a thunderous echo; singed angels; smoldering demons.

"No!" Lucifer snarls. He spins and stares black death at me. "You will be mine. *Heaven will be mine!*"

The ground under us shakes with His rage. Grandpa steps in front of me, making himself as wide as possible to block me from Lucifer's line of sight. "Git back to where ya come from," he shouts.

I hear a scream from behind me and turn to see Rhen pulling Maggie away from me. I spin and kick, connecting with his arm and breaking his grasp on Maggie. But before she can skitter away, he grabs a handful of her hair.

"Let her go, Rhen," I say.

"Sorry," he replies, and his eyes flick to Lucifer. "Protecting His interests."

My eyes flick to Lucifer and He gives me a sad smile, then He locks eyes with Grandpa. Instantly, Grandpa falls to the ground with a strangled cry.

"No!" I drop to my knees next to Grandpa but am pushed back as I try to touch him. The air around him ripples with some sort of electric field as he cries out again and convulses on the ground. "Grandpa," I sob. I press my hand to the field around him. "No . . ."

"I will spare him," Lucifer says, His voice close behind me. "It's up to you, my queen."

I'm shivering violently as I turn to Him, shards of ice running through my veins. "What do you want?"

His voice is low but potent. "It's not so much what I want, as what I'm *due*. I have waited patiently for you, and now you're here."

Without the pendant, thinking for myself is easier. I don't feel the same visceral draw to Him as I did when I was wearing it. I chance a glance toward Rhen as Maggie struggles against him. Her field shimmers around her, opalescent, but it doesn't seem to do anything to slow Rhen down.

Desperation grabs my gut and won't let go. I turn back to Lucifer. "I'll do anything. What do you want?"

Grandpa groans and rolls into a ball when the assault on him stops. Lucifer cuts a cold smile at me. "I only want what's rightfully mine. You will give me Heaven." The heat radiates off Him, burning me with its intensity.

"I can't do that." The words catch in my throat as I choke back a sob.

He steps closer, His voice low in my ear, seductive in its promises. "But you can, my queen. You will give me what I want and you will rule at my side, or your family dies."

I want to crumple into a ball and hide. All I can think is how stupid I've been. So many are dead 'cause of me. Luc, Dad, Taylor, Faith. Panic grips my heart as my gaze shifts between Grandpa, lying on the ground, his breathing labored, and Maggie, in Rhen's grip. I have to save them.

Rhen's expression is despondent, and his eyes plead with me.

He doesn't want this. He wants out from under Lucifer.

"I'm not your queen!" I yell. "Let them go!"

He peers down at me with raised eyebrows, His green eyes piercing mine, as if searching for my soul. "I've waited an eternity for you. You have the power to give me what I desire."

I glance wildly around the cavernous space. The air is charged with electric rage as angels and demons fight all around. Rock showers from the cavern walls with explosive force as flaming streaks of celestial lightning tear through the space. Demons go down, oozing black ichor. Angels rain from the sky, their wings ripped open by Hellfire.

My heart dies a little when I see Celine take a direct hit. She drops to the ground just a few feet away with a resounding thud, and a dark-haired angel with a singed left wing swoops past and scoops her up. But she's limp in his arms.

I have to stop this.

Think, Frannie.

How do I make this happen?

I wrack my brain frantically for the key. There's got to be a way.

My Sway?

What do I make Lucifer believe?

Desperate for the answer, I gaze at Him, proud and powerful—so sure of Himself—and suddenly I understand.

Not Lucifer.

That's not who I need to Sway.

I look at Rhen as he drags Maggie toward the precipice, and focus. "Don't do this," I say softly, pushing the thought.

He shoots a mournful glance at Lucifer but doesn't respond.

"You can make your own choices." I fill my heart with my love for Maggie, for my family, and push harder—so hard I feel like my head is gonna implode, making me suddenly nauseous. "You don't have to follow His orders."

Grandpa cries out and my gaze snaps to him as he convulses. A cold smile slips across Lucifer's face, contrasting with the intense heat He exudes. "Tread lightly," He hisses.

I push toward Grandpa again and am thrown back by Lucifer's field. "Stop!" I scream, wheeling on Lucifer.

"How far this goes is entirely up to you, my queen."

Maggie screams and I spin in her direction. Rhen stands at the edge of the gorge, looking as though he's about to toss her in.

"Rhen! No! You don't have to do this!"

A sad smile flickers at the corners of his mouth. "I wish that were true," he mutters so low I barely hear him.

In the back of my mind, I replay what I did to Aaron, trying to remember how I made that work. But even if I knew how it worked and could do it again, I need Rhen. He's the key to this whole uprising—the one who can bring it together and make it happen.

If I can figure out how to get him past Lucifer's hardwiring.

I've never been good under pressure. My brain is a whir of thoughts, not a single one coherent.

God.

Grandma.

God.

Me.

God.

God's gift to humanity.

Free will.

Luc's voice echoes in my mind.

They don't need to be human, they just need free will.

Is my Sway enough to give free will to Rhen? To all of them?

For a second, I hesitate at the thought that demons with free will might be a dangerous thing. But then Grandpa cries out again. His breath is coming in wet rasps, as if he's drowning. The sound sends icy terror pumping through my veins. I have to do something—*now*—and I don't have a better idea.

I think of Grandma—of God—and focus every ounce of strength I can find on Rhen. My body becomes electric, my synapses firing on overload, and when I look down, I'm actually glowing—like Gabe.

It scares me a little and I feel my resolve waver, but then Maggie screams.

I pull myself from my thoughts in time to see Rhen launch Maggie over the edge of the gorge. My own scream rips through the space as one of Rhen's security detail, a short, squatty demon with furry legs, a tail, and black horns unleashes a blast of Hell-fire at the angel that dives over the precipice after her. The angel reemerges with Maggie in his arms a moment later and lowers her to her feet then retaliates with a crackling bolt of white light-ning.

And that's when I see he's different from the others—much taller and with three shimmering pairs of white wings.

His bolt sends the demon plummeting over the edge of the gorge. He turns to me then and lowers to a knee, his head bowed and his long platinum waves falling in a face that reminds me so much of Gabe that tears sting my eyes. Then he's gone, back into battle.

Maggie runs to Grandpa and reaches out. There's a shower of sparks as her hand contacts the field around him.

"Maggie," I cry, and try to pull her away, but I can't budge her. It's as though she's bound to the field and it's pulling her in too. She closes her eyes in concentration, and, as I watch, her hand starts to shake and the skin of her palm takes on a red hue. The hue becomes a full-on glow as she sucks the energy from Lucifer's field into her hand. Her whole arm glows red for a second, and when she shakes her hand, a shower of sparks spray from her fingertips and wink out before they hit the ground.

I kneel next to Grandpa and touch his face. He's so cold. His eyes open just a sliver and a hint of a smile curls his pallid lips.

"Grandpa!" I lean down and hug him gently, afraid of hurting him. "Hold on, Grandpa. I'm going to get you some help."

His hand opens and squeezes my arm almost imperceptibly. "I'm sorry for . . ." he pauses to take a wet, rasping breath, ". . . not knowin' what I was."

"No, Grandpa. This isn't your fault." I sob the words, and I hate that he's hearing that, but I can't help it.

I look up to see the immense platinum-haired angel standing over us. His lips never move, but I feel him more than hear him in my head, a soft whisper telling me Grandpa will be loved in Heaven. Instantly I know it's the archangel Gabriel. He nods, and the next instant a golden-haired angel descends and sweeps Grandpa into his arms.

Grandpa looks into the face of the angel, and then into the sky beyond. "I'm comin' Vivvie," he says in a cracking voice so weak it's barely audible. His eyes flutter shut.

"No, Grandpa! You can't die," I cry, clutching at him with all my might.

His heavy lids open again and he looks at me with such peace and serenity as he says, "It's been a good life, Frannie, and this is a good death. I'm ready."

The golden-haired angel leaps into the air and Grandpa is gone.

I stand there, staring into the sky after them for a long moment, my heart bleeding and tears streaking my face. But then

Hellfire streaks past me and I smell the pungent scent of singed hair. I beat out the flame at the ends of my hair and look up.

A dark mass forms behind Lucifer, swirling to life—hundreds of shadowy black forms with bloodred eyes.

Mages.

I recognize the eyes from my dreams. I watch them sweep into the mêlée, slashing at the air with their clawed hands, and I hear the celestial screams that follow.

I spin, panic taking over my thoughts, as shrieks and explosions erupt from every direction.

What do I do?

Rhen. Free will. That was my plan.

I spin and find him advancing on me. "You are free to make your own choices," I say. I feel celestial energy erupt out of me like lava from a volcano. "You decide."

In a heartbeat, his fist is pointed squarely at me and I brace myself for his blast. But when he doesn't strike, I step forward. "Did it work?"

He looks at me wide-eyed for a second, then turns his fist on Lucifer, whose attention is focused on His Mages, directing them like a maestro would conduct an orchestra. Rhen's unexpected blast strikes Lucifer in the chest, sending Him wheeling.

"Looks that way," he answers, gaping at his fist as if he doesn't believe what he just did.

Closing my eyes, I focus on the infernal and shout at the top of my lungs, "You can choose!"

A bolus of energy leaves my body all at once, erupting out of me into the sudden silence and echoing off the canyon walls with a boom. I'm momentarily blinded by the intense flash of white light, but when my vision returns a moment later, Lucifer stands tall, looking to the white sky with arms raised overhead, as if calling on celestial forces.

But what He's calling is much darker, and there's nothing celestial about it.

Hellfire swirls all around Him in a dervish of red, yellow, gold, and blue, stronger every second.

His eyes focus on me. "You will belong to me, or you will belong to *no one!*" He bellows.

The whirl of Hellfire consumes Him, obscuring Him from my vision for a heartbeat. When He throws His arms forward, it shoots from His being with all His infernal command and streaks toward me. But instead of consuming me, it feeds me. I feel it swirl through me, becoming even stronger. Before I realize I've done anything, enormous blasts of lightning shoot from my hands, red from my right and white from my left.

As I watch, my green-eyed angel vanishes. He's replaced by an immense black demon with leathery wings that lift Him into the air. He struggles against my red and white electric cocoon, flapping His wings, but He can't break free. Then Rhen's power joins mine, a Hellfire blast from his ranseur, streaking toward Lucifer. Others from all around the cavern add theirs—hundreds of streaks of red Hellfire all converging on one spot.

Lucifer.

The cavern grows eerily quiet, the screams and explosions ceasing, until the only sound is the crackle of Hellfire.

Lucifer hovers in midair a moment longer, still as stone, before I pull my power back. But, along with my own energy, I pull back His. It enters me like a flaming missile. Lightning courses through my veins, searing through me, burning me alive. There's a thunderous crash, and as my eyes adjust to the sudden dimness after the intense blaze of the convergent Hellfire, I see Lucifer hit the ground in a cloud of brimstone dust, splintering into a million shards. I fall to the ground, my body seizing. The earth rumbles under me and a deafening sucking sound almost ruptures my eardrums.

My fingers curl into the coarse grass of my backyard, and when I open my eyes, maple leaves flutter overhead. Beyond, puffy white clouds float lazily through an azure sky.

This is it.

This is the image after the lightning that night at the airstrip— the reason I was so sure I was gonna die. This is what I felt— lightning not only in my head but consuming me, radiating out of me. The lightning *is* me. I'm burning alive.

My heart implodes as I close my eyes and see Luc's face.

Then everything fades and I'm gone.

25

Divine Intervention

FRANNIE

When I wake up from the strangest dream of my life, my body feels uneasy.

Twitchy.

Jittery.

I need to run.

I open my eyes and I'm staring at Grandpa's living room ceiling. When I push to a sit on the couch and look around, I'm suddenly certain I didn't wake up at all.

Grandma is sitting in front of me.

I stare at her, my heart in my throat. And then I remember.

Not Grandma.

God.

I stare at Her some more, unable to find words. I want to apologize for being so stupid and so blind about Lucifer, but it just feels too embarrassing to even bring up. And, even as I think of Him, knowing that He's gone, I feel some insidious tug at my insides.

I twitch in my skin, unable to shake the jitters.

Grandma stands and drifts toward me, settling into the love-seat next to me. She loops an arm through the crook of my elbow and I start to feel calmer—less like I want to bolt out the door.

"He could be quite persuasive," She says, and I cringe when I realize She can read my thoughts, just like Gabe.

I drop my eyes and pick at the fringe of my jeans. "I should have known. I just wanted it so bad."

"It wasn't wrong to hope, my dear." When I look up at Her, Her expression is soft and forgiving.

"But I *was* wrong, and because of it . . ." I can't even say Gabe's name, or Luc's, or Matt's. At the image of Dad lying life-less on the ground, my throat closes as grief claws at my heart. "Oh, God," I mutter into my hands. "Dad."

"Your father is fine, Frannie. As a matter of fact, he's waiting for you at home."

My heart leaps and I look up. "He's okay?"

The radiance of Her smile reminds me who She is. "He's more than okay. He's earned his wings back."

"Daddy? He's an angel again?"

She nods. "Your guardian angel."

The mix of emotions is so sudden and overwhelming that all I can do is stare at the wall and concentrate on breathing so I don't hyperventilate. "I don't want him," I finally say when I can speak. I can't do to him what I did to Matt.

She chuckles and I look up into Her iridescent face. "It's not your decision to make."

"I don't want to put him in danger."

"The decision was not made lightly. Gabriel consulted me, and we decided this is the best choice. He's well trained and has learned the pitfalls from personal experience. He won't make the same mistakes twice."

I hold my breath for a second before I ask, "Gabe decided?" daring to hope. "He's . . . ?"

"You will see your Gabe again, my child. Soon."

My eyes fly to Her face, searching.

A knowing smile flits over Her lips. "He's a Dominion. It is exceedingly difficult to destroy a Seraph's essence."

"Gabe is alive?" I whisper more to myself than to Her.

"In a manner of speaking." There's admonishment behind Her gaze and I look away.

"I didn't mean to tempt him. It's just that . . ." I don't know how to finish. What I really want to ask is if I ruined him, but I can't.

I don't have to. She hears it in my thoughts.

"He'll be fine, but . . ." She trails off and I look into Her face.

"He can't be with me anymore," I finish, reading the sadness in Her eyes. The truth is, I knew it already. Last night at Grandpa's, I knew that was what we'd decided, even though we hadn't come right out and said it.

"It's for the best."

I nod again, swallowing back the throbbing, wet lump in the back of my throat. "What about Luc?" I ask, my gut clenching against Her inevitable answer. Thanks to me, Luc was very mortal. And that means he's very dead.

Her eyes darken. "Would you like to see him?"

My heart kicks in my chest and relieved tears spill over onto my cheeks. "He's alive," I whisper, dropping my face into my hands.

"For the moment," She says grimly.

I jump from the loveseat on jittery legs.

She stands and squeezes the hand She's still holding. "You'll have to hurry."

"Where is he?"

"In the hospital."

The image from my head after the lighting—Luc in a hospital bed, wires and tubes everywhere—flashes in front of my eyes.

Time of death, six-thirteen.

I glance wildly at the clock over the kitchen table. 5:41.

"No!"

"He'll wait for you," She says. "And tell him there's a job for him if he's interested."

I swallow again. "But he would have to die . . . right?"

Her gaze is soft as She nods. "He has a choice to make."

"If he decides to live, will he stay human?"

She lifts an eyebrow. "Is that what you'd wish for him?"

"I want him to have a chance at a normal life."

"Even if it's without you?" She asks quietly, Her eyes trained on mine.

My heart contracts into a tiny, hard ball as I nod. "He deserves it. He's already more human than almost anyone else I know."

"Then I will make it so—if that's what he chooses."

"He will," I say, as I turn for the door.

She stops me with a gentle hand on my shoulder. "You're not using the door, dear girl."

"What do you mean?"

She reaches up and Her hand sweeps over my forehead. It's only then, as Her touch sends a rush of power through me, that I realize I'm not altogether solid.

"Oh my . . ." I whisper. "Did I die? Am I an angel?"

Her smile is soft as She shakes Her head. "No, Frannie. But you are unique in that you are born of three worlds. You are part Heaven, part Hell, and part Earth. And because of your ability, you are free to move among them."

I feel my insides churn again as something flares in my gut. The unease is almost unbearable, and I want to jump out of my skin. "I don't get it. What do you mean?"

"You know your purpose now, my child, and you know the scope of your power. This is what you chose in the Abyss. And to fulfill your purpose, you'll need to shift between planes."

"I thought my purpose was what I already did, with Lucifer."

"That was part of it, but there's still work to be done."

"So . . . I'm supposed to . . . ?"

"That's for you to discover." She levels Her gaze at me, and suddenly I feel the power of it. This definitely isn't my Grandma. It's God.

A sickening sense settles into the pit of my stomach. "I feel like . . . I don't know . . ." I lower my gaze, suddenly sure I'm not good enough to look at Her.

"What is it, child?"

"It's like a part of Him—Lucifer—is inside me. I feel all itchy and jittery."

She lifts my face so I'm looking at Her. "A piece of him does live within you, as does a part of me. It is your charge to find a balance within yourself, and within the universe, so the two sides can coexist."

I actually press my hand to my chest to make sure my heart didn't just stop. "He's inside me?"

"If it ever gets to be too much, Kate can help you."

"Kate?" The blurred memory of her grasping Lucifer's pendant during the battle flashes in my mind. It had burned Maggie, but when Kate grasped it, it went dead. "What can she do?"

"She dissipates both demonic and celestial energy. If either ever grows too strong inside you—out of balance with the other—she can help."

I stare at Her wide-eyed.

She smiles down at me. "You have support, Frannie. Your father, your sisters . . . and even your young man." She gives me a gentle shove. "Now, go! He needs you."

"Where?" I ask.

"Follow your heart."

"But—"

She lays a hand on my forehead and I close my eyes. Instantly, the sensation of floating makes me nauseous. "Luc," I whisper, and when I open my eyes, I'm standing in the corner of a hospital room, watching him sleep. As the nausea slowly passes, I realize I'm not alone. Luc is here, but so is someone else.

"Gabe?" I whisper. I sense him all around me. Then, like fog forming on a damp night, he's there, ethereal—just a whisper of himself.

"Gabe!" I say, louder.

"I'm here." He smiles but stands back from me.

I reach for him as both our forms become more solid. "Stop it!" I say, throwing my arms around him, my heart soaring. "I thought you were . . ." I can't finish. I pull away from him and look up into his eyes. "Are you all right?"

He's standing stiff, his arms at his sides. His gaze is soft as he looks down at me, but he won't meet my eyes. "I'm fine, Frannie."

I slip my hand into his and squeeze tightly, then turn to Luc. "Is he going to . . . ?"

"He's still deciding," he says, his eye shifting to the bed.

My eyes spring back to Gabe. "He's deciding? He gets to do that?"

Gabe nods. "He does."

My gaze gravitates back to Luc, and I can't take my eyes off his face. It's so pale—drawn and grim, like the weight of the world is pressing down on him, too heavy to bear. There are tubes coming out of his mouth and nose and wires everywhere, hooked up to beeping and clicking machines.

Just like the image after the lightning.

I step closer and slide my hand under his. He's so still—only the faintest movement as his chest rises and falls with the cadence of the loud ticking and puffing of a respirator at the side of his bed.

I look around at the antiseptic room: scuffed white walls; stiff white sheets; the smell of alcohol and death. And the noise from the machines. I want it to stop. I want a moment of peace with Luc to say good-bye.

But then I realize if the noise stops, it means Luc's dead.

I look back at Gabe. "Grandma said She had a job for him, if he wants it."

He glides up next to me. "So I've been told."

"Do you know what it is?"

"He's to be your liaison between Heaven and Hell."

My stomach kicks. "*My* liaison? Don't you mean Hers? God's?"

His eyes flit to mine and drop just as fast. "The Almighty is Heaven. *You* are charged with bridging the gap."

"Meaning?"

"You are the intermediary. It's left to you to negotiate the terms of the truce." A smile lifts the corners of his mouth. "You're getting what you've always wanted. You are the ultimate diplomat."

"Between Heaven and Hell," I say, knowing it's true.

Gabe nods.

My eyes turn to Luc, my heart bleeding. "But he'd have to die to take that job. I don't want him to die. She said She'd keep him mortal if he lives." I look back at Gabe as a tear slips over my lashes. "I want that for him."

"I can understand why you'd feel that way. He's sacrificed everything. But, ultimately, it's his decision."

I search his pale blue eyes for any sign of *my* Gabe, but he's keeping his distance. I reach up and lay my hand on his chest, but it's still. No heartbeat.

He doesn't back away from my touch. In fact, he doesn't move at all. He stands ramrod straight, his eyes fixed on a spot on the opposite wall.

"What happened to you?"

His gaze settles into mine, and, just for a second, I see him. I plead with my eyes, needing to know what he suffered 'cause of me.

He shakes his head, reading my mind. "Everything that happens is not your fault, Frannie. You need to stop shouldering the blame for all the evil that walks the Earth."

"Please," I beg.

He lowers his eyes again. "Lucifer sent Matt and Aaron for me." He finally says. "In my . . . weakened state, I couldn't defend myself against both of them. But when they dragged me to the Abyss and Aaron gave me to the Mages, Matt tried to stop him—which didn't go well for him."

"Matt tried to protect you?" I ask, remembering how he attacked Aaron during the battle.

He nods and peers at me from under long white lashes.

A wet lump starts to form in my throat. "You're . . . different now."

For the first time, he really holds my gaze. "The Hellfire burnt away my humanity, but it couldn't kill me."

My heart aches. "That's good."

"It is," he answers with a nod.

"Thank you," I whisper, my voice thick. "For everything."

A beeper goes off on one of the bazillion machines attached to Luc by the wires and tubes.

A nurse sweeps into the room to check the contraption and

I expect her to tell us to get out, but she only has eyes for Luc and the beeping machine he's attached to.

"Oh crap," she says, slapping a blue button in the wall at the head of Luc's bed. An automated message squawks from the intercom in the hall, announcing a "code blue, ICU four."

My heart stalls.

It's happening.

A storm of people charge through the door within seconds, pushing another machine in front of them. I start to move out of the way, but the staff circles Luc's bed, never giving me a second thought.

And it's only then that I realize they can't see me.

I climb onto the bed and wrap my essence around Luc, feeling the hands of the medical people pushing through me to pull Luc's gown open.

He feels so cold. I want to warm him. He needs to be warmer.

A pretty young doctor with too much makeup, red hair, and a white lab coat over her blue scrubs places cold metal paddles on Luc's chest and yells "Clear!" but I don't. I squeeze tighter around him, sending him all my strength, and whisper in his ear.

"Don't give up, Luc."

The electric shock jerks his body and I hold tight, feeling him grow colder under me as a little more of him slips away.

"*Live*," I whisper. "I need you to live."

I brush my white, opalescent fingers over his face—around the tubes protruding from his lips. Whatever I am, I'm sure I must still have a heart, because I feel it breaking.

As the second jolt shakes his body, I seep my essence through

Luc's lips. I wrap myself around his heart, willing it to beat—sending him every bit of love I have.

His heart sputters a moment, then picks up a weak rhythm. I feel something in him stir, like a wash of energy—his soul. I've felt it before, this intense rush of being closer than humanly possible. My soul soars as I feel his essence swirl into mine.

"We've got a rhythm," a voice calls, and I feel myself flood with relief.

"Luc?"

His dark energy wraps into mine like a building cyclone—a strengthening of his spirit. I listen for his thoughts, and at first I don't hear anything, but then his voice is as clear as if he were whispering in my ear. "Mmm . . . Frannie," he moans.

And in that instant, I feel it—that intense rush as he blends his essence with mine, making me forget everything but this moment—him.

I embrace him on the inside, touching every part of him as our souls merge, and I never want this feeling to end. Stars flash all around us as we dance, and I'm barely coherent, but I send him my message without words, begging him to live—to fight.

"For you," he says, "I'd do anything."

At his words, weak as they are, my heart explodes. "I need you to live. Please," I beg. In this form I can't cry, but it comes out as a sob anyway. "Don't die, Luc. Please fight."

I feel him grow stronger still. "I'll never leave you again."

The pang is fierce, causing me to ache all over, because that's what I need him to do—to live and let me go.

I don't really know what I am. Despite what Grandma said,

I'm not even sure if I'm alive or dead. But if I'm not dead already, it would kill me if Luc gave up.

I imagine wrapping my body around his—the feel of him against me, and my heart can't stay heavy. This feeling is euphoric. I wish with all my heart that this moment could last forever.

But just as I think that, his physical body stirs, then stiffens. I feel suddenly freezing as his essence pulls away from mine.

"Frannie. What . . . what's going on?"

I feel his confusion and I cut him off before he can get any farther down the tracks of this train of thought. "Don't worry about anything but getting better. I need you to get better, Luc."

He doesn't fall for the diversion. I feel his essence pull farther away from mine as he scans his surroundings.

"We're in me . . . my body. Tell me what's going on, Frannie. How are you in here?"

"Stop, Luc!" The thought erupts from my core more forcefully than I intend it to. I work to soften my tone—to keep the fear out of my thoughts so he can't feel it. "You need to focus all your energy on staying alive," I tell him. I swirl my essence closer, but he pulls away from me again.

"You're . . ." his thought trails off to an echo as he adds, "dead." Then I feel it—his despair, clamping down on his heart like a vice, causing it to sputter again.

I wrap myself around his heart, pouring my life force into him. "No! I'm not gonna let you give up, Luc. You can't die. Not 'cause of me. I couldn't take it." I hear the desperation in my thoughts and hope he doesn't.

Soft in my ear, I hear him, and I feel his energy build. "I'm not going to live without you, Frannie. There's no point. You're my life . . . my reason for . . . everything."

His soul blends with mine again and the sudden rush of love is so intense as we swirl together that I don't even notice we've left Luc's body.

"Clear!"

The shout from below pulls me from my reverie, and I'm suddenly aware of the room. We watch from above as the doctor places the paddles to Luc's chest again and my whole being contracts into a hard ball as I watch Luc's body convulse.

"It's all right, Frannie. I'm right here."

Luc's voice brings my attention back to him, his essence. Then we're floating, swirling together.

But the next instant, he's gone.

I look down at the form of his body on the bed, at the nurse still compressing his chest. I dive into that body, looking for his essence, willing him to live.

But he's nothing but an empty shell.

Luc's not here.

26

✢

Blinding Radiance

LUC

I stare in disbelief at the door in front of me—at the peeling sign.

Limbo.

One minute I'm blended with Frannie, and the next I'm standing here.

Talk about a rude awakening.

A shiver racks me, but it's only partly because of the sudden cold of being without Frannie. I draw a deep breath, even though I have no need of oxygen anymore, and push through the double doors.

Limbo hasn't changed. I glance around the endless room, the low ceiling lined with rows of humming fluorescent fixtures, casting an artificial glow over the multitude of souls milling around waiting for their fate to be decided. The same heavy wooden desk sits just inside the doors, with various magazines scattered over its dark, nicked surface. Someone has scribbled over the handwritten sign taped to the front of the desk:

Take a number and have a ~~seat.~~ nice eternity!

The hole in my chest where my heart used to be aches at the thought of not spending eternity with Frannie. I brace my hand on the desk and stifle a groan as the wave of despair washes over me. Because, reality is, I never belonged there with her. I was never truly good enough to belong in Heaven.

When the sensation passes I lift my head and pull the tab of green paper protruding from the dispenser:

64,893,394,563,194,666,666

I take that as a bad sign.

Glancing up at the lit monitor over the desk, I see, "Now serving number 64,893,394,563,194,109,516."

So, I'm in for a wait.

I tip my head back and blow out a sigh before dropping into one of the infinite black plastic chairs.

Next to me, a latte-colored soul with a moss-colored hue prattles on with her neighbor, a smoke gray soul with mustard streaks, about her plans to give her brother a piece of her mind when she gets to Heaven. I'm not going to burst her bubble by telling her the best she can hope for from Michael is Purgatory. There's a reason they don't post statistics. It would cause a riot.

I feel something whoosh past me, like an energetic whirl-wind. The magazines on the desk flutter and half of them fall to the floor. And then I catch the faintest wisp of currant and clove. The aching in my chest intensifies and all I can see is Frannie's face. I drop my head into my hand.

We were so close.

But it's done. I'm here.

I breathe a shaky sigh as an electronic bleeping sound from the monitor overhead signals that they're speeding right along to the next lucky customer. I glance up. "64,893,394,563,194,666,666," it reads. I look back at my number as I hear a few shouts and a not-so-pleasant stream of curses from the milling crowd. A mauvish soul with ochre streaks at the end of my row is charging the desk, spewing a string of expletives regarding ripping an unknown someone a new asshole.

I catch him as he storms past. "I'd like to point out that you're not helping your cause," I mutter under my breath.

"Go screw yourself! They just passed my number! I was next!"

You and about five hundred thousand other poor souls, I think to myself, looking back at my number as he pushes past and shoves the desk.

"Number 64,893,394,563,194,666,666, please report to door number one." The androgynous, monotone voice seems to come from everywhere.

When an intricately carved wooden door with a large, gold number 1 materializes near the desk, the pissed-off mauve and ochre soul shoves through it without hesitating, mumbling, "It's my goddamn turn."

I follow him through just as Michael stands from behind his immense mahogany desk. He raises one dark eyebrow and points to the soul. And poof. It's gone, leaving the faintest hint of sulfur in its place.

"I love it when they make my decision easy." A slow grin creeps across Michael's face as his startling blue eyes shift to me. "I have the oddest sense of déjà vu," he says, an amused smile twitching the corners of his mouth as he strokes his black goatee.

"Why am I here?" I ask wearily, bypassing the endless book-shelves and sliding into one of the beige leather chairs in front of his desk.

He sinks into the high-backed chair across the desk from me. "You have to ask?" His brow knits. "I've always questioned your intelligence."

I hold his sharp gaze. "I thought I was tagged for Heaven."

"You couldn't possibly believe that was going to stick." A cold grin slices across his face. "Quality control is very impor-tant. We can't let just *anyone* into Heaven."

I sigh, resigned. Turns out Heaven squirms out of contracts with the best of them. "Fine. Do what you have to."

His brow arches. "I'm not going to *do* anything." He looks at me, rummaging around in my head while I process that.

I get it. He's not going to do anything. He'll just let me rot in Limbo indefinitely. He can't send me to the Abyss, but he doesn't have to admit me to Heaven either, apparently.

He strokes his goatee, his dark face twisting into a smirk. "Maybe you're smarter than I give you credit for. I'm sure you know this is for the best, Lucifer. Search your soul . . ." his face pulls into a repulsed sneer, "if you truly have one, that is." He shifts in his seat, leaning toward me, elbows on the desk. "Did you really think you could ever belong to Heaven—to *her*? She has a purpose," his eyes flashed, hungry, "and you must see that you'd only be in the way—a distraction."

Fear flares in me. The look in his eye, filled with enough avarice to rival any of the greedy in Hell, makes me afraid for Frannie. "What are your plans for her?"

"The Almighty—"

I lean forward. "No. *You*. What are *your* plans for her?"

"That's not—"

He stops abruptly as a whirlwind sweeps past us. This time, the scent of currant and clove is unmistakable. I leap from the seat and spin toward the door, but the voice comes from the other side of the room, near the hearth of the blazing fireplace.

"This isn't right. You can't send him to Hell. He's tagged for Heaven."

I step away from the desk and wheel back toward Michael and *her* voice. A look of abject terror passes like a shadow over Michael's dark features briefly before he turns slowly to face Frannie. "I wasn't going to send him to Hell . . . yet. And you are in no position to tell me what happens in Limbo." He's trying to put up a bold front—to not let the terror show on his face or in his voice. But it's there.

Frannie shakes her head slowly. "See, that's where you're wrong. I'm in a position to do whatever's right. As a matter of fact, that *is* my position."

I'm gawking. I know I am, but I can't stop. She's incredible. She stands unflinchingly before Michael, her sandy waves shimmering in her subtle but undeniable Heavenly glow. What's also undeniably there is red Hellfire, crackling over her skin in her rage, the scent of ozone laced with a healthy dose of brimstone. But her beautiful sapphire eyes haven't changed: the windows to her soul. Both eyes and soul, still distinctly human.

A goddess of three realms.

Power radiates off her in waves, both celestial and infernal, pressing against me as though it has physical weight. I drop to my knee and bow my head. It just feels right that I should.

"What the hell are you doing?" she asks, exasperated.

I lift my eyes and can't stop the smile that breaks across my face at the scowl on that angelic face.

But when she shifts that scowl on Michael, I see him drop his eyes and stagger back from her in my peripheral vision.

"He's coming with me," she announces. "We have a job for him."

She pulls me to my feet impatiently. At her touch, electricity skitters through my essence, and I feel my power surge.

And once again I feel the urge to genuflect. I drop my eyes.

"Please, Luc, it's just me," she whispers. When I finally do look up, a single golden tear is coursing a crooked path down her cheek.

I gaze down into her eyes. Now that I'm looking into them, I can't seem to stop. Her soul swirls, opalescent white, and I lose myself in it. She leans in to kiss me. When our lips meet, the rush of her effervescent power surges through me, consumes me. Our souls blend until we're truly one.

FRANNIE

My power rushes through us both, and I feel the surge in Luc. Our souls blend, become one as we kiss, and when we finally separate, he's already making the change. White lightning crackles through him until he glows. The tattoo on his right arm isn't a serpent anymore; I watch as the black ink rearranges itself into a giant pair of wings that stretch over his shoulder and across his back.

"What is this job?" Michael interrupts.

I look into Luc's eyes a moment longer before turning to face Michael.

"Liaison to Hell. Appointed by the Almighty Herself."

Michael's eyebrows shoot up, and I'm not sure if it's the job title or the use of "Her" that got him. There's no way I'll ever be able to see God in any other form.

"How is that going to work?" Luc looks down at his white swirling essence. "Is He—" his eyes flick to mine and away, "—or, She—sending me back to Hell?"

I smile. "Actually, no. At least not how you mean it." I reach for his face and lift his chin, forcing him to look at me. I drop my voice. "But I want you to go back to your body."

"I can't. Not without you."

"I want you to live, Luc."

His face hardens and he finally meets my eyes. "Is this my choice?"

This time it's me who can't meet his gaze. "It is."

"Then the choice is already made." His jaw is tight and his expression set, but as he stares into my eyes, it softens. He lifts a hand to touch my cheek. "I promised I'd never leave you, so . . ."

Michael clears his throat, but I don't take my eyes off Luc's, so deep that I could crawl into them and live there. "This is really what you want?"

Half a smile curves his perfect lips.

I feel joy, the first I can remember in a long time, bubble up inside me. I turn to Michael. "Good-bye," I say, then press my lips to Luc's, close my eyes, and focus.

"Whoa!" I hear him say, and I giggle at the rush but then feel a little sick.

And the next instant, I'm wrapped around his body in the hospital bed. There are still tubes down his throat, but all the machines have been unhooked.

The pretty doctor looks mournfully at the clock on the ICU wall. "Time of death, six-thirteen," she says as the nurse starts to pull a sheet over Luc's face.

He gasps a loud, rasping breath.

The nurse screams and drops the sheet as the doctor rushes to the side of the bed. "Holy shit!"

Luc coughs and starts grabbing at the tube protruding from his mouth. The doctor unceremoniously rips the tape off his face and yanks it out with his next cough.

He opens his eyes. "Hi." The word is hardly anything, but it's loud enough that the doctor, who is leaning over him checking his pupils, hears it.

"Holy shit," she says again.

27

✟

Last Rite

FRANNIE

I've never once been inside a cemetery. I've driven by them and that's as close as I've ever gotten. After Matt died, I had vivid dreams of him crawling out from under a headstone and screaming for all the world to hear that I'd killed him. Mom knew I was traumatized and didn't make me go when we buried Grandma.

But I'm here now.

The simple gray headstone has an epitaph in smooth curved lines of clean letters that reads:

> I THINK OF YOU AS WATCHING FROM
> A TIME AND SPACE BEYOND THE SKY,
> A PLACE WHERE WE MIGHT SOMEDAY COME

On the left it gives, Vivian Elaine Shanahan and her dates. On the other side of the stone is the fresh inscription. Edwin Shanahan. Under his name there's his date of birth, followed by the date that everything changed forever.

Father Mahoney is saying something about Grandpa being a sheep in God's fold and preparing himself for an eternal life of glory, but I can't really listen. I keep trying to remember what happened.

It's all so foggy, coming only in shrouded images. Lucifer . . . angels.

I work on sucking air into my lungs and blowing it out as Father Mahoney finishes. My parents and sisters move forward as a group to put roses on Grandpa's box. I turn and walk the other way, to the small copse of trees near the road. Luc weaves his fingers into mine and keeps pace with me.

I lean on a rough oak for support and Luc folds me into his arms. He kisses the top of my head, but knows better than to say anything. The only thing getting me through this is that I truly believe Grandpa's in Heaven. And I also truly believe he's with Grandma—both the God one and the real one.

"You're right."

My heart skips at the musical silk of Gabe's voice. He steps out from behind the tree and there's no mistaking what he is. All in white, his platinum hair swirling around his face, he takes my breath away. "He's happy, Frannie."

I'd promised myself I wouldn't cry. Grandpa would hate it if I got all sappy. But at the sight of Gabe and his confirmation that Grandpa is okay, a tear slips over my lashes.

Luc squeezes my hand, dipping his head to catch my eye.

"I'll be with your family." He raises his eyebrows, waiting for my okay.

I nod and he backs away, still holding my gaze, before turning and striding back to Grandpa's gravesite.

Gabe steps up and wipes the tear away with cool fingers. "You have good people," he says, his eyes following Luc as he steps up next to Dad and rests a hand on his shoulder.

"Gabe, I'm so—"

He stops me with a finger to my lips, then leans forward, smothering me in the scent of clean winter sunshine. "Everything is as it should be," he says, low in my ear. "I—" I wait through the catch in his voice, fighting tears. "I just wanted a chance to say good-bye."

My voice is thick with the lump in my throat. "Will I see you again?"

He pulls away then and looks down at me with sad eyes. "No. But I will always serve you."

My tears spill over as he kisses my cheek, and then he's gone.

28

Deal with the Devil

FRANNIE

Riley sits cross-legged on the bed behind me, braiding my hair. "You should take classes at Community," she says. "Just to start."

"I think I'm just going to take the year off," I say, feeling a stone sink in my gut. "UCLA deferred my admission, so . . ." So I just need to figure out what comes next—what I'm supposed to do and if I can ever get my life back.

I hear her sigh. "Don't give up on college, Fee. You were meant for bigger things."

If only you knew.

"I won't." *I hope.* "So . . . how's Trevor?" My heart squeezes tight as I ask. In the few weeks I've been home, I haven't been able to bring myself to go over there—to see Taylor's family.

"Okay. Started school a few weeks ago."

"Senior year," I say, remembering how everything changed for me when Luc walked through the door of Mr. Snyder's English class.

"Yep." She crawls around in front of me and plunks herself down. "Do you miss it? High school?"

I think about Taylor, how she, Riley, and I were attached at the hip. Everything was so simple then. "Yeah."

There's a knock on the open door and I look up to see Luc standing there. "Hello, Riley," he says.

She slides off the bed. "Hey, Luc."

"Don't go," I say to her as she bends to grab her bag off the floor.

She hikes her bag onto her shoulder. "Sorry, Fee. Told Trevor I'd be over." She shoots me a Taylor-esque smile. "And besides, you're in good hands."

I haul myself up from the bed and hug her. "Talk tomorrow?" I say. It feels a little desperate coming out of my mouth, but there's a deep piece of me that *is* desperate to hold on to this small bit of my old life.

She smiles and squeezes me a little harder. "I'll text you when I get home. I need some stuff for school. Maybe we can go shopping."

"'Kay." I usually hate to shop, but there's something comforting in the thought of hanging out at the mall with Riley. A step toward normalcy.

Riley sweeps past Luc on her way to the door. "Treat her right," she says.

"Always," he answers with a smile.

When she's gone, I close the door and saunter over to Luc,

pushing him onto the bed. He flops on his back, and I climb on top of him. "You heard her. Treat me right."

The spark in his eye makes my belly flutter. "Your wish, my command."

His hands smooth cautiously over the curve of my waist as I lean forward to kiss him. I pull back and look into his liquid obsidian eyes. "You really think I can do this?"

My fluttering belly is joined by my sputtering heart at his roguish smile. "I'm sure of it."

I sit up and stare at him, my insides tightening. "They're not gonna listen to me, and even if they did, I have no idea what to say."

"You'll know the right thing when the time comes."

Panic crawls through my chest. I think he has way too much faith in me.

The door swings open and I spring off Luc. Dad stands in the doorway sporting his best scowl. "Things haven't changed so much around here that you can start breaking the rules, young lady." He fixes me in a hard stare and taps on the door with a knuckle. "Door open."

Luc pushes to his feet, and I thread my fingers through his, my face burning. "I'm eighteen, Dad. Plus, I'm in charge of, like . . . stuff."

As hard as he tries, Dad can't hold the scowl, and he cracks a dubious smile as he leans into the doorframe. He flashes his wings and gives them a quick ruffle, to remind us of his new responsibilities as my guardian angel. "That may well be true, but you're still my daughter." He sends a look of paternal consternation at Luc. "Hands off, demon boy."

I grin at Dad. "He's not 'demon boy.' He's my Left Hand." I press into Luc's side. "You can't argue with God."

Dad raises an eyebrow at me. "Fine, as long as he keeps *his* hands to himself."

I let go of Luc and sink onto the bed. "So, I'm still not sure I'm really getting what I'm supposed to do."

"Well, the way I see it, someone needs to pick up the pieces and figure out how things are going to work."

I feel my face scrunch and Dad laughs. "It's not funny! I don't even know what I'm supposed to do, but whatever it is, you know I'm gonna screw it up."

Luc's arms pull me tighter. "You have lots of support, Frannie. We'll figure it out as we go," he says.

As if on cue, Maggie walks past my door and peers in. Dad grabs her and tucks her under his arm. She squirms for a second but then settles into his side and looks at me expectantly.

I heave a sigh. "But . . ."

"You've already accomplished so much, Frannie," Luc says, brushing his fingertips over my cheek. "You just need to tap into your power and—"

"Spread the love," Grace interrupts.

I look up to find her tucked under Dad's other arm. The way she looks at me still creeps me out a little, but at least I understand it now.

"Spread the love," I repeat skeptically. "How is that gonna bridge the gap between Heaven and Hell?"

"Have faith, Frannie," Grace says, and I can't help thinking of Faith. Lead rolls through my stomach at the thought of everyone I've already lost. Faith, Taylor, Grandpa . . . and Matt.

"Matt . . ." I look at Dad. "Is he gonna be okay?"

"He's safe. Once he's atoned, the Almighty has agreed to allow him to join the Grigori. He may be of some help to you, but his powers will be limited."

Out of nowhere, I feel the pull. It's becoming more familiar now. The first time I felt the faint tickle in my chest, I thought I had indigestion. But now I know what it is. And I know what I have to do.

"Speaking of Her . . ." I jump into Luc's unsuspecting arms and he fumbles for me, almost dropping me. "Bye, Dad!" I say as I close my eyes. I think of where we need to go and instantly I have that sickening sense of floating again. I hear Luc groan.

"This is so different from phasing. I keep thinking I'll get over the motion sickness," he says through clenched teeth.

The rush stops and I open my eyes. I grab Luc and pull him tighter when I feel him let go of me, suddenly afraid of losing him too.

He reaches up and trails a finger along my cheekbone, and I can see my glow reflected on his hand. "This . . ." he says, ". . . is going to take some getting used to."

I weave my fingers through his. "It's just me, Luc."

His eyes slide to mine and his expression is reverent. "I always knew you were too good for me."

I shove him hard. "Stop looking at me like I'm some sorta god!"

"But you are."

"I am not!"

"Well, you're certainly *something*," he answers, waving his hand in a circle at me.

I pull him close, rubbing strategic parts of myself into strategic parts of him, wanting him to look at me the way he used to—with reckless abandon. I close my eyes and spin us in a circle.

When I open my eyes again, Luc is gazing into them, a wicked smile on those angelic lips. "Well, this opens a whole new world of possibilities," he says with a spark in his eyes, his voice thick.

I press my lips to his and his electric kiss causes my heart to skip. "So, you're getting over that 'too good for me' crap?" I say when our lips part.

"Working on it," he whispers into my ear, then his lips glide across my cheek and find mine again.

I jump at the sound of a throat being cleared. When I turn and look around the Collective, Grandma is sitting in a white wingback armchair.

Luc is immediately on his knee.

"The meeting is set," She says into the silence. "Are you ready?"

I feel myself starting to shake, but then Luc's fingers thread into mine from where he kneels next to me. "As ready as I'll ever be."

She gains Her feet and the chair instantly vanishes. "Good."

"I still don't really understand this," I say. "Am I still mortal? And why did Luc go back to his body?"

"Both of you need to be able to travel through planes into all three realms. That's easier if you have a corporeal form to return to on Earth, but neither of you is mortal."

I feel dizzy as I try to process that. "We're immortal."

She nods, moving closer.

I buzz all over and realize I'm glowing. "So . . . are we angels?"

She laughs. "No. You are . . . *unique*."

I'm not sure if I like the sound of that. "Unique," I repeat warily.

"Both of you are one of a kind. You, my dear, are borne of three worlds, and Luc . . ." She touches Luc's shoulder, beckoning him to stand, ". . . is borne of Hell but belongs to Heaven."

Luc stands and we share an uncertain glance.

"So, that makes us . . . ?" I press.

Her iridescent smile broadens. "Unique." Her expression turns sympathetic when She sees the apprehension break across my face. She loops an arm around each of us. "I know this is a little overwhelming. We're charting new territory. But things will unfold from here and we will all learn. You will figure out the rules as you go."

Panic flutters through me, making me feel queasy. "I'm gonna screw this up."

"You will be fine, my dear girl, as long as you follow your heart."

"My heart . . ."

She gives my shoulders a squeeze. "You should always keep Grace close when you're on the mortal coil, but there's no point bringing her where you're going now. Maggie and Kate, on the other hand . . ." She contemplates this, tapping a finger on Her chin. "I don't think so. I don't expect any trouble this trip, so we should show good faith."

"Maggie's been a total pest. It will be good to give her something to do," I coax.

"Next time." Grandma grasps Luc's hand. "Are you ready for your first day on the job?"

He drops to his knee again, keeping his head bowed. "Yes, your Grace."

"Very good."

"Will Michael be there?" I ask.

Grandma's smile is warm. "It will go better if you meet with them individually to start. You'll know when it's time to bring them together."

She winks and cold mist swirls around us, like being sucked inside a cloud, and then She's gone.

Luc stands from his kneel and I weave my fingers into his hair. "So, where were we?"

His laugh is indignant. "You're joking, right?"

I press harder into him. "Not really."

"The Almighty just sent us on a diplomatic mission, and you're going to blow it off . . ." he says in a clear attempt to scare me into submission. What he fails to realize is that the defiant set to his face just makes him that much hotter.

"I wasn't gonna blow it off. Just delay it for a few minutes," I say with a shrug.

His strong arm around my waist crushes me to him. "We'll have time for that later," he whispers in my ear.

I love how his body is saying one thing and his lips are saying another. My hands slide up his chest. "You're sure you want to wait," I tease.

With his smile, warmth spreads through me like a wildfire.

"You're stalling," he says. "The sooner we get this over with, the sooner I can get you alone."

An involuntary grin pulls at my lips. "Now we're talking."

He kisses me as I close my eyes, and we swirl through time and space.

We're still kissing when I feel the crush of lava rock under our feet and the stench of brimstone stings my nose. A trickle of sweat rolls between my shoulder blades and I squirm in Luc's arms.

"*Damn*, it's hot," I say when he pulls away.

He closes his eyes, his face pinched in a grimace, his whole body tensing.

I reach up and trace my index finger over the piercings in his eyebrow and down his cheekbone. "Is it hard being back here?"

He heaves a sign and nods. His eyes open and he peers over my shoulder at the source of the flickering vermilion light. All his defenses bristle. "It's too quiet," he says warily. "No screaming."

The strong sulfur of brimstone makes my eyes water as I glance around and take in my surroundings. High stone walls rise in front of us, scarred by heat and eons of abuse. Over the top of them, ruby waves illuminate the surrounding gray, like light reflecting off a pool. The blistered iron Gates are ominous, black and bulky, and a sense of hopelessness creeps into my heart just looking at them. Through them I see the flicker of a huge white flame in the distance, and past that, roiling violet and gold lava. As I stare, the Gates swing wide, and Rhenorian saunters through in his ginormous human form. In his hands is a heavy wooden sign. It's roughly carved, and from this angle I can't read what it says.

"Are you going to stand there like a couple of Ozone Heads," he calls, with a red-hot glare in our direction, "or are you going to help me with this?"

Luc grasps my hand and we move to where he stands, our heels crunching loudly over the coarse lava rock. Rhen props the large chunk of wood against the Wall and unhooks the old, charred sign hanging next to the Gates from the rusty chains. He hands it to Luc.

"'Abandon hope all ye who enter here,'" I read and grin at Luc. "Your boy Dante?"

He nods without taking his wary eye off Rhen.

"You've always been so melodramatic," Rhen says with a scowl as he hooks the new sign up. "I've never liked that. So cliché."

Luc glares and I'm starting to think bringing Maggie might have been a good idea.

"Hey, bitch. You dead too?"

My breath catches at the sound of Taylor's voice.

I spin and find her propped on the Wall just inside the Gates. She looks catlike, in sleek black, with her pink and yellow spiky hair.

For a second, I can't even move except to shake my head.

She pushes away from the Wall and starts to walk through the Gates, but Rhenorian holds up a hand and growls. She stops and shrugs with a doleful smile. "If you're not dead, what are you doing here?"

I glance at Luc, who inclines his head toward Taylor, indicating that it's okay for me to go to her. "I'm . . . um . . ." I stumble, unable to think. "Is that really you?" I say, moving slowly toward her, feeling a little numb.

"The one and only," she says with a sideways smile.

I can see her essence, pale gray with specks of green, gold, and brown. "Oh my God," I breath.

When I reach her, she pulls me into a hug, even though that was never really our thing, then shoves me away and smirks. "Yeah . . . about that. Think you could put in a good word for me? This heat is killing my complexion."

Rhen leers at Taylor and growls, but she doesn't back off. Instead, she gives him her signature lascivious smile. "Don't be that way, big boy. You knew it was too good to last."

I find myself smiling so hard I'm convinced my face is gonna crack. "Careful, Tay. I'm not sure you're helping your cause," I say in warning.

Her eyebrows shoot up in surprise. "There's a cause to be helped?"

"That's what I'm here to figure out . . . how to make that work."

Her face goes slack. "Seriously?

"The Almighty never planned for Hell to be like this," I say with a wave of my hand toward the Gates.

Her eyes pull wide. "And you know this because . . . ?"

I cringe a little against Taylor's reaction. "Because She told me."

"*She* told you," she says, incredulous.

I nod as Luc steps up beside me and lays his hand on my shoulder. "She did," he confirms.

"Guess there was more to that holier-than-thou thing you had going on than I gave you credit for."

I glance down at myself and still can't get over the glow. "I guess so." I step back to get a better look at the new sign hanging over Rhen's head:

UNDER NEW MANAGEMENT

I meet his gaze. "Let's talk, Rhen."

ACKNOWLEDGMENTS

There's something bittersweet about wrapping up a trilogy. My characters are so real to me that it feels sort of like saying good-bye to a close friend. I hope you've all enjoyed Frannie, Luc, and Gabe's journey. I want to thank you from the bottom of my heart for coming along for the ride.

I also want to thank all the people who have been so patient in their guidance and support of this trilogy. They deserve more credit than I do for getting these books into so many hands. First, thanks to my truly fabulous agent, Suzie Townsend, for her love of Luc, Frannie, and Gabe and for all her tireless work on my behalf. She's a sparkly rock star. My seriously cool editor, Melissa Frain, has once again helped me make this book into the book I thought I wrote. I'm forever indebted to her for her faith and trust in me as a writer. Thanks to the Tor Teen team, including but not limited to Aisha Cloud and Seth Lerner, for all their support behind the scenes.

I learned early on that the most valuable tool to my writing is a critique partner who will be honest and supportive with her feedback. Andrea Cremer has been a godsend. Not only did she help make this book what it is, but she named it too! Thanks also to Kody Keplinger, sounding board extraordinaire, who, on several occasions, has dropped everything at a moment's notice to read for me.

There aren't words to properly thank my family, who has been uber-understanding about all the time I've spent with my imaginary friends. I couldn't have asked for a more incredible group of people in my corner.

And because, yes, my muse is still a wannabe rock star, I want to send a special thanks to the amazing artists who shaped the characters and the story. Ben Burnley and Breaking Benjamin were a huge influence to the overall story. Breaking Benjamin's "Give Me a Sign" is the song that embodies Frannie's journey; "Dear Agony" is the musical embodiment of my most conflicted character, Gabe. A huge thanks to Rob Beckley and Pillar for "Rewind," the song that shaped Luc. Thanks also to David Draiman and Disturbed for the dark and haunting song "The Night," which shaped this novel as a whole.